C000318933

CHOSEN?

MEL MENZIES

malcolm down
PUBLISHING

21 20 19 18 17 16   7 6 5 4 3 2 1

First published 2016 by Malcolm Down Publishing Ltd.
www.malcolmdown.co.uk

British Library Cataloguing in Publication Data
A catalogue record for this book is available from the British Library.

ISBN 978-1-910786-32-1

Cover design by Esther Kotecha
Photography by Peter Butler and Paul Williams

Printed in the UK

Acknowledgements

As always, I'd like to express my thanks to my writing buddy, author and psychologist, Angela Hobday, who checks the integrity of my manuscripts and makes suggestions.

Thank you to my friends Wendy John, Anne Haines Nutt, David Scott and David Coffey, who have encouraged me so much along the way, and Rachel (Tidball) Martin on the front cover.

My grateful thanks, also, to my publisher, Malcolm Down, without whose expertise and input Evie Adams might never have been breathed into life. My thanks, also, to Torbay Photographic Society, who provided images for the front cover, and to Esther Kotecha who designed it so beautifully.

It goes without saying that the support and inspiration of my husband, Paul, and daughters, Susie and Amanda, are paramount to the success of all I do.

Chapter One

Evie and Phoebe:
Where There's A Will...

THEY SAY THERE are only six degrees of separation between you and anyone else on the planet: someone, who knows someone, who knows someone you know. So what, I wonder, is the chance of two complete strangers walking into your counselling rooms – into your life! – less than a week apart and discovering, ultimately, that they share the same story? Not only that, but, through them, you learn that you're not who you had thought you were for the past thirty-something years?

'It's enough to make a girl shiver in her Jimmy Choos,' I tell my colleague, Guy Sampson, knowing full well he won't have a clue I'm referring to designer-wear shoes. 'Always assuming she'd be rich enough and shallow enough to own a pair!' I finish.

Oh, would you Adam and Eve it! Guy looks at me beneath his bushy eyebrows in such a way as to remind me that statements like that could be viewed as judgemental and, therefore, professionally unethical. At the same time, he grins and shakes his head as if despairing of me.

'Oh, Evie Adams! Will we ever get those dainty feet of yours toeing the line?' He makes a show of tutting, then turns towards the door to make his way back across the landing to his own room.

Duly chastised, albeit kindly, I bid him goodbye, and glance out of the first-floor window of my place of work as a reminder of my good fortune. Exeter's Cathedral Green, The Close and The Yard are spread before me, a mishmash of history and architecture,

5

comprising the site of Roman baths and basilica, Saxon burial grounds, a 6th Century church, and an 18th Century hotel – allegedly the first ever in Britain. In their midst, in all its splendour, stands the 12th Century St Peter's Cathedral, its Purbeck marble structure, bell towers, and flying buttresses a monument of Gothic beauty.

How can I fail to be impressed? Who needs fashionable, but disposable, footwear with such enduring and majestic structures at their feet? Returning to my desk, I mull over the story I've recounted to Guy, reliving the event as if it were only now unfolding.

The first of the duo to arrive for an appointment on a sunless Monday morning in August is a Mrs Phoebe Hamilton. A small but feisty lady, she is probably only in her sixties, but has an air about her of someone much older and, judging by the smell of mothballs that precedes her, is of a make-do-and-mend mentality. I check my diary and see I've written a note to myself stating that it was Mrs Hamilton's youngest daughter, Sophie, who booked the appointment a fortnight ago. And the eldest, Liz – of whom there is no sign – who has brought her in.

'Please take a seat.' I indicate the easy chair reserved for clients, and Mrs Hamilton seats herself. Facing one of the windows on either side of the fireplace, this ensures that her face is illuminated and I may observe her. Immediately, she leaves me in no doubt that she has no wish to be here.

'I want you to know, Mrs Adams,' she says sweetly, in the precise Received Pronunciation that marks her out as a lady of status and privilege, 'that I've only come because Sophie insisted. I really don't believe in all this nonsense, washing your dirty linen in public.'

I smile, in what I hope is an empathetic fashion, and say, 'It's Evie, Mrs Hamilton. No need for formality.'

Professional integrity to the fore, I remind her that she concurred with her daughter making the appointment and that, anyway, this is only a preliminary meeting to see if she is comfortable with the idea of proceeding. She jerks her head upwards with what I take to be reluctant acquiescence.

Phoebe Hamilton is impeccably dressed in twin set and pearls, and has about her the air of a debutante who has lost her way in modernity. She places her leather handbag at her feet and folds her hands in her lap. Vestiges of bygone prettiness are still apparent in her now fleshy face and, as I study her for a moment, she seems startlingly familiar.

'Have we met before?' I ask, aware that it's unlikely as she lives in Kingswear, overlooking the River Dart, and I in a downmarket area of Exeter.

'I hardly think so,' Mrs Hamilton replies in what can only be construed as a rap-on-the-wrist tone of voice.

Forty minutes later we have made little progress in the purpose of her visit. Mrs Hamilton has proved a master – or should that be mistress – of prevarication. All I have established is that her eldest daughter Liz, who it seems is browsing the swanky fashion boutiques in Cathedral Yard as we speak, has been instructed by the youngest daughter, Sophie, who is otherwise engaged, that if 'things' continue as they are, their mother might well have a stroke. Or a heart attack. Or both.

'So what brought this on – your daughters' concerns?' I ask.

Phoebe shrugs. 'My husband rang Liz. He's a GP. Retired. But once a doctor, always a doctor.'

'And – was that a problem?'

'There was no need! Sophie was with us. She'd just brought us home after our weekly shopping trip a fortnight ago. She's perfectly capable, as Phil knows. But he seems to have developed a mind of his own.'

To hide the smile this image of bravado conjures up, I brush an imaginary speck from my black work trousers.

'Phoebe –' I look my client in the eye and tilt my head on one side '– are you happy for me to call you Phoebe?' She nods stiffly and, I suspect, reluctantly, and I continue. 'I'm trying to ascertain why your husband and daughters are concerned for you. When Sophie rang to make the appointment, she said you were in a state of some distress. Can you tell me what had upset you?'

'The phone call, of course!' Phoebe explodes, her pale complexion suddenly flushed. 'This man. This complete stranger. An American. He rings me up. Out of the blue. I mean – wouldn't you be concerned?'

To buy time I glance around my counselling room, at the uneven plaster on the walls, the Tudor beams and stone-mullioned windows, the floor that sags in one corner and rises like the bow of a ship in the other. Catching sight of myself in the mirror over the empty fireplace, I realise how untidy I look. My hair, dark and curly, has frizzled in the damp atmosphere as I cycled into the city to work that morning and, though I'm not unduly obsessed with appearance, I attempt, unsuccessfully, to smooth it down with my hand.

'You mean you thought he was a con man?' I prompt.

Phoebe's face is filled with withering rebuke. It tells me, in no uncertain terms, that I have entirely confirmed her original opinion about the efficacy of this visit. Recognising my unprofessionalism in supplying answers instead of asking open questions, I try a different tack.

'So what did he say? This man?'

'He said,' Phoebe pulls herself up to what I suppose would be a full five foot two and a half were she standing, 'he said he was my nephew. Or great-nephew. And that he'd traced me through my father's will. My father's. Not his. Now what, I ask you, would he be doing with my father's will?'

For the briefest of moments, I fancy I see a chink of vulnerability in Phoebe's feisty façade. Then the reason for her daughters' anxiety becomes apparent. Blanched and breathless, my client is clearly in distress. Leaping into action, I realise that I may, otherwise, be called upon to administer more than a command for deep breaths, followed by the dispensing of a glass of water. Where, oh where, I ask myself, is the absentee daughter?

It's evident that, for now, continued discussion is pointless and will only cause further upset. Fortunately, by the time I've brought Phoebe Hamilton's panic attack under control, her daughter, Liz, has prised herself out of the shops and arrived to collect her. It's only when they've left that I realise I am, myself, in a state of agitation.

My hands are shaking, and there's a sinking feeling swilling in the pit of my stomach. The tension in the back of my neck is taut as the flag staff on the cathedral turret. And I have another client due in less than fifteen minutes.

I pinch and massage the rigid tendons and muscles with my fingers. I know exactly what has triggered this attack. It's the mention of a will. And you'd be quite justified in telling me, sternly, that this is a case of 'physician heal thyself'. A familiar sense of self-contempt rises in my throat. Shall I never be free of the bitterness that engulfs me, I ask myself?

My workload proceeds in predictable fashion with my next three clients, one an alcoholic who has yet to admit to a drink problem being the root of his marriage difficulties, the second a young woman with recurrent symptoms of depression who is proceeding well on a mindfulness-based therapy, and the third, a myopic, bespectacled boy who, it appears, is being bullied at school and dreads the start of the new term in two or three weeks' time. A shared sandwich lunch with my colleague, Guy, gives some respite, and by the end of my working day, I've almost forgotten the incident with Phoebe Hamilton and the negative emotions it induced in me.

Almost. But not quite. So I'm pleased when my significant other, Scott Bingham, Skypes me to tell me that visiting family in America is not all it's cut out to be in my absence, and that he's missing me. A lecturer at a theological college in London, his face fills the computer screen, his clear blue eyes full of sincerity, his square jaw the epitome of American Bible-belt honesty. Abandoning the task of filing the contents of my out tray and tidying my desk, I reflect that it's good to know somebody cares.

'I had a new client today,' I tell him when he's shared his news. 'From a village over the river from Dartmouth. I must take you down there, sometime. Dartmouth, I mean. Such a quaint place. It's been a naval port since the time of the Crusades.'

Knowing Scott's penchant for all things ancient, me included, I'm confident that this will be of interest to him.

'Sounds great. I'll get my suit of armour polished up and join Richard the Lionheart any day.'

'You'd love The Shambles,' I tell him, knowing he'll have his camera out and will be clicking away, American-style.

'The Shambles?' he laughs. 'Sounds a bit chaotic!'

'It's medieval. A merchant's house. Well, it's a café now. So you can actually go inside and see it.'

'Can't wait,' says Scott. 'Will you be going down to see your client sometime soon?'

'I wouldn't think so. Don't think she'll be coming to see me again, either.'

'You mean there's someone who doesn't find you as irresistible as I do?' Scott teases.

'Yeah, yeah! Overwhelmingly *not* as far as this lady's concerned. Rather stiff and starchy, methinks. Not sure she wanted to pour herself out to anyone, let alone a peasant like me.'

A discordant trumpet blast from down below on the Cathedral Green makes me jump. Someone messing about? I rise from my seat, and still in view of my computer screen, lean on the windowsill and look out to see what's going on. A large coach has drawn up at the west door of the cathedral, and appears to be disgorging an entire orchestra. Men in dinner jackets and bow ties, and women in evening dress assemble on the forecourt, beneath which, probably unknown to them, are the remains of the Roman baths.

Of course, I remember now. There's a concert tonight in aid of charity. I watch as the coach's hold is emptied of violins, cellos, drum kits and other musical paraphernalia, with which the musicians disappear inside the cathedral, cradling their instruments.

'Bit toffee-nosed, was she?' Scott asks, continuing our conversation.

I turn to face him again, and seat myself back at my desk.

'Actually, she wasn't that bad. Though when I asked if we'd met, and I'm sure we have, somewhere, she made it quite clear what she thought of that idea! Not that I'm going to let a bit of snobbery get to me.'

'So what's the problem?' Scott's voice softens, his facial expression one of discernment and diplomacy despite the fact that I've said nothing revealing.

'Oh – I don't know!' I feel full of impatience with myself and my re-awoken attitude of self-pity. 'It's just that my client's problems raked up a whole lot of garbage from my past. Made me think of my mother's death. I'll get over it!'

'Come on, Honey. It's still early days. Don't be hard on yourself.'

'I s'pose!' I feel myself glow. It's the first time Scott has used a term of endearment when addressing me.

'Nothing wrong in feeling sad,' he continues. 'You need time to grieve.'

Having advised dozens of clients on the grief process, I'm hardly in need of tuition, as Scott well knows, but I'm immensely grateful for his compassion and understanding. Even so, I feel it inappropriate to allow myself to wallow and deftly change direction.

'How's your mum`?' I ask, and get a blow-by-blow description of Mrs Bingham's baking skills, and the family barbecue scheduled for that evening.

Nearly an hour later we've talked ourselves out and I dash over to the cathedral bookshop to collect an order I put in a week or so ago. Rain is in the air when I emerge once more and cross The Green. A gossamer film floating down from a pearly sky, it carries the promise of cleansing and refreshment. I lift my face and embrace its restorative powers.

With my book in my backpack, I retrieve my bicycle from its storage place beneath the glass-roofed passage alongside my place of work, and tilt my head. From the cathedral, carried clearly on the still air, I can hear the orchestra warming up for the evening's entertainment. I hope they raise plenty of money for the charity, I muse. By heck, they ought to! The tickets cost the earth.

At home that evening, in my modest terraced house on the outskirts of the city centre, I open a tin of cat food for Pumpkin, who rubs herself affectionately against my legs, and shove a carbonara ready-meal into the microwave for myself. I've been living alone since my husband's departure for more clement climes in the form of Bosomy Barbara from the Post Office. It has its compensations, I reflect, and not having to produce a meat and two veg meal every day is one of them. Pouring myself a glass of Merlot and tidying away the remnants of that morning's breakfast, I ponder the day's events.

The Code of Ethics to which all accredited counsellors are required to adhere stipulates, among other things, that a counsellor *must, at all times, honour the subjectivity of the counselling experience, and be able to undertake a rigorous self-examination of their work and practice.* I'm acutely aware that I have failed on the first count and am in the process of failing the second. No one tells you, when you begin training to be a counsellor, quite how hard you'll still be finding that code of ethics years later. Well, perhaps they do. But you forget.

Abandoning the carbonara, I walk through to my tiny front room. Net-curtained, to obscure the curious gaze of passers-by on the pavement only a few short steps from the window, its womb-like warmth wraps itself around me. Throwing myself onto the sofa, I ring my supervisor and then, on impulse, my counsellor-cum-mentor.

'Grace, it's me. Evie. Have you got a moment?'

'What's up, m'dear?' she asks.

Clutching the phone, I find tears swilling my eyes. Tears of self-pity. Angrily, I dash them away.

'Oh, nothing much,' I say, lightly.

Grace, dear Grace, is familiar with my background. Only child. Mother a not-so-secret drinker, recently deceased. Father a self-sufficient Yorkshireman, having risen from working class obscurity to the status of chairman of the city council. And, as he would often remind us, from impoverishment to relative affluence. A distant figure with not an inkling of affection about him, little, if any, rapport ever existed between him and me. Or, indeed, he and my mother.

'Just a difficult client this morning,' I continue. 'And – oh, hell! – she was talking about a will. I never actually got to the bottom of it. I know! It's ridiculous but everything flared up again inside me. If my poor mother had been properly provided for, life would have been a heck of a lot easier for her.'

'And for you, of course.'

'And for me,' I agree. 'In more ways than one.'

Thinking about it now, I realise anew that nothing had prepared me for the hurt I'd felt on seeing my mother alone and barely able to fend for herself on my father's death. Nor had I anticipated the fact that my name would be omitted entirely from the will in favour of some distant cousin. Despite the decades of silent hostility that had existed between my parents, I'd been oblivious to the possibility of further rejection. Barren and empty, the years yawned around us like a frozen glacier, conversation reduced to a slow drip as from an icicle. We'd made no provision, Mum and I, practically, mentally or emotionally.

Is it any wonder, I ask myself now, that I'd reacted so negatively to Phoebe Hamilton's visit? Yet I know the importance of maintaining an emotional distance from such thoughts. My grip on the telephone tightens.

'I suppose –' I venture, anticipating Grace's expectations of me, '–perhaps Dad felt he'd already given me my share in his estate.'

'How do you mean?' Grace asks.

I stand and walk to the window, looking out at the tiny patch of garden between my front room and the pavement. Little more than a cabbage patch, a dump, littered with defunct electrical goods and cast-offs when it became mine, it is now rich in colour and form, a plethora of plants and shrubs.

'Well as far as I'm aware, my dad paid the deposit on the house, if not the whole amount, when Pete and I married.'

'Really? You've never mentioned that before.'

'Sorry. But I'm pretty sure Pete had no claim on the property when we divorced!'

I'm aware that I sound defensive, and it's no surprise when, after a slight pause, Grace follows through.

'We ought to meet to talk about the repercussions,' she says. 'I can't do anything until the beginning of next week, I'm afraid. What about Monday?'

Seating myself once more, I scoop Pumpkin up onto my lap and give myself a moment to think. What's the point of meeting with Grace? I've talked through the issues surrounding my father's will time and again. The fact is that I'm a hypocrite. I think nothing of helping my clients to see for themselves the value of practising forgiveness. But it's obvious that I am constitutionally unable to do so myself. I fondle Pumpkin's ruff and she responds by kneading my thighs with her razor-sharp claws. It's clear that she understands exactly how I feel.

'Monday's no good for me,' I reply to Grace. 'I've got rather a full day. Look, I've no further appointments arranged with this client. It was only a prelim. I'm sure it's going to be okay.'

In the silence that follows, Grace's reluctance to leave it at that is palpable. I owe her so much. The counselling rooms in Cathedral Yard are a combined initiative of the local doctors and the city's clergy. Despite the fact that I rarely cross the threshold of a church other than on high days and holidays, Grace was highly influential in securing a place there for me.

'I won't do anything foolish,' I assure her. The sigh of relief I imagine I hear is only to be expected.

'Well, make sure you get back to me if your client follows through.'

'I will, Grace. Promise.'

My thoughts return to Scott's call earlier that evening. If only he were still in London instead of visiting family back home! Sensitive and caring, he'd have restored my equilibrium in no time.

I put Pumpkin down on the floor, replace the phone on the sideboard and make my way back to the kitchen to investigate the state of my pasta meal. Taking it from the microwave, I can't help thinking that its congealed state rather resembles the puzzle before me.

What lies hidden behind Phoebe Hamilton's visit, I wonder? It's not often I have to admit defeat in the counselling room, but I confess I have not learned much more than I already knew from Sophie when she made the appointment for her mother.

How does it all fit together? All I can recall is that it had kicked off following their usual weekly shopping trip. Taking a lap tray into the front room, I cast my mind back to our telephone conversation, and the story Sophie told me.

Chapter Two

Sophie and Phoebe:
Dutiful Daughter

IN HER TERRACED cottage on one of the cobbled lanes in Dartmouth, Sophie thought back over recent events, in particular those of nearly a fortnight earlier. She had, she realised, come to think of Thursdays as food-land days. A challenge! Something to rise to. An obstacle to be overcome. With the August Bank Holiday looming at the end of the month, she fed herself the clichés as one would a remedial herbal infusion. Cheerfully. Expectantly.

Negotiating the supermarket car park on a weekly basis with two parental back seat drivers, she'd decided long ago that you had to take whatever part life doled out to you. Rising and overcoming was all about hamming it up – playing to your audience for all you were worth on stage, and waiting patiently in the wings when not.

Being blonde, long-legged and nubile, for instance, was no guarantee of coming across a disabled parking spot near the supermarket entrance (for Daddy's sake) which wasn't already occupied by the vehicle of an able-bodied shopper. Nor were trolleys without wonky wheels and minds of their own a given. But playing dumb had its merits when having to endure the embarrassment of dealing with the endless vouchers Mummy collected. An enticement to spend more than you intended, they were almost invariably out of date by the time they surfaced from the nether regions of the maternal handbag at the check-out till.

In such circumstances, Sophie felt she was well-practised in the art of looking artless. She found it met with people's expectations of blondeness and, having been proved right, other customers looked more kindly on her. With the embarrassment of an elderly parent holding up the queue, she felt she needed all the kindnesses on offer. The routine, on arrival at the supermarket, was that Mummy went off alone – 'I can't concentrate on shopping with your father in tow' – leaving Sophie to make her own purchases with Daddy's 'help'. He leaned on the trolley while she was the gofer.

'See you in half an hour, Mummy,' she said, with the same teacherly emphasis she employed at school, knowing full well she would be ignored. Half an hour would become fifty minutes, twenty of them spent searching the aisles for her errant parent. Turning to her father with an affectionate look of exasperation on her face, she rolled her eyes and shook her head.

'Come on Daddy. Let's get going.'

She began with the five-a-day portions of broccoli and two-for-the-price-of-one nets of Clementines demanded by the political correctness of the times, and considered the phenomenon that had crept up on her. The weekly shopping trip with her parents seemed to have become a fixture. Entailing a journey on the ferry across the River Dart to her parents' home in Kingswear, it was a big commitment.

Though she would never admit it aloud, and hardly dared do so in the privacy of her thoughts, there were times when she found it something of an intrusion in the easy-going disorder of the life she lived. Never mind eldest child syndrome! There was no doubting the fact that the youngest had just as demanding an obligation in order to live up to parental expectation.

To begin with it had been an occasional outing following Daddy's recovery from what had turned out to be the first of a series of mini-strokes. Though more-or-less physically unscathed, his sight had been affected, plus his short term memory. Unable to be left alone, his disability had impacted on her mother's life, whose love of pounding the streets looking for bargains had, over the decades, been thwarted by the universal demise of the town centre, but could, generally speaking, be appeased by its modern-day equivalent, the out-of-town superstore.

The occasional shopping trip had thus been intended as a treat for her. Personally, Sophie would have preferred to order her meat and veg from the organic farm at the top of the hill and to shop, daily, for bread from the local baker. But being the youngest of three sisters, unmarried, childless and currently unattached, it was only natural that the role of dutiful daughter should fall to her. She could see that.   She really could. Fiona, fourteen years her senior, lived north of Birmingham – too far for more than the occasional visit when work permitted. And Liz, the eldest and named after their maternal grandmother, was, like her namesake, formidably, and sometimes enviably, assertive.

Sophie gazed, unseeingly, at the array of supermarket shelves before her and made an effort to address herself to the business of shopping. Such treacherous thoughts about her family induced a sense of guilt which she found uncomfortable. Under Daddy's watchful and gleeful gaze, she dropped a single, large bar of chocolate into her trolley. Then, after a moment's wrestling with her conscience, added the discounted second bar that made better value of the first, but a mockery of the five-a-day fruit and veg.

Half an hour later with the trolley laden, and knowing there was no question of Mummy ever looking for anyone, Sophie set off to search for her. Tracking her down eventually, she marvelled at her mother's stamina.

'What do you think?' asked Phoebe. In one hand she held a large tub of double cream, discounted because it was almost on date, and in the other a smaller tub which, at full price, was a few pence more.

Sophie looked at her mother. People sometimes asked what it was like to have been a late addition to the family, too polite to comment outright on the fact that Mummy must have been getting on a bit when she gave birth to her. But surveying her now, so smartly dressed and with her pale yellow hair newly coiffed and coloured, Sophie felt a surge of pride and affection. How many of her friends had mothers who managed to look so glamorous?

'When's it for?' she asked, taking the larger tub of cream and examining the sell-by date.

'The Mullers are coming for dinner on Saturday,' Phoebe

explained, 'I want to make a Pavlova.'

Sophie shook her head, in teacher mode once more.

'Mummy! You can't give them this. It'll be two days out of date by then. I keep trying to tell you how risky it is –' she nearly said *at your age* but stopped herself in time. 'Besides, why do you need this quantity? You know it's not good for Daddy's cholesterol.'

Phoebe sighed noisily and replaced the larger tub in favour of the smaller. It was a game which was regularly played out between them. A game which, Sophie knew, gave her mother immense satisfaction, as if she relished the opportunity – though only when it suited – for a bit of role reversal, whereby she became the child and Sophie the mother.

Sophie patted her arm and they made their way towards the checkout. When the three of them had settled up, with the inevitable unloading and reloading of trolleys this entailed, they set off home in Sophie's battered Peugeot hatchback.

Home, or at least the imposing Victorian pile in which Phil and Phoebe Hamilton lived, was just outside Kingswear, on the River Dart. Newly converted into three flats, with the Hamiltons occupying the ground floor, the mansion was set in two or three acres of gently sloping lawns which looked across the water to Dartmouth, and down towards the open sea. The family had moved here from London shortly after Sophie was born, occupying the entire property until the recent decision to remodel the building and downsize. She'd thus enjoyed an idyllic childhood, riding, sailing, and, in due course, flirting at a distance with the cadets from Britannia Royal Naval College.

Sophie helped unload the shopping before taking the car to her parents' designated parking spot. By the time she returned to the house, Daddy had transported most of the bags inside to the kitchen, and the kettle was on for tea.

'I can't stay too long,' Sophie warned. 'I'm meeting Hannah at the club.'

Sophie taught English and Maths four days of the week at Ladybower Primary School in Dartmouth, and augmented her salary with extra-curricular work whenever she could get it, along with tennis coaching in the evenings and holiday time.

'Who's Hannah?' asked Phil.

Phoebe ignored him and began to butter a couple of toasted teacakes.

'Your granddaughter,' Sophie replied, well used to having to act as go-between.

'Liz's girl, you mean?'

'No, Daddy. Liz doesn't have any children. Hannah is Fiona's eldest. She's staying at Liz and Gordon's for a few weeks.'

Liz, Sophie felt like adding, was wedded in equal measure to Gordon, and to his income as a hospital consultant. Spending it as extravagantly as possible was her mission in life. She had no room in her busy schedule for a daughter. Childlessness was a choice which, though she rarely spoke of it, could be taken as a given.

'Why is she staying there?' asked Phil.

The reason was that Fiona was in hospital having minor surgery but, knowing how he'd fret, Sophie wasn't about to enlighten him.

'You've got time for a quick cuppa, surely?' her mother asked, pressing Sophie into service as a waitress by indicating the tea tray. Without waiting for an answer, she sailed off towards the French doors which opened onto the terrace, the plate of buttered teacakes in her hand.

Obediently, Sophie picked up the tray, followed her father outside, and put it on the table at which her mother was seating herself. She remained standing to pour the tea – a half-cup for Daddy because his hand shook so badly since his last stroke, a milky one for her mother, and a stronger one for herself. She passed them round, ensuring that her father's was close enough to him to be easily reached, with the handle to the right.

Down below, a flotilla of Laser dinghies sailed serenely between larger visiting vessels moored on the river. Among them was HMS Argyll, the Type 23 Naval Frigate which, so the local paper said, would shortly be setting sail for the Far East.

'Oh, look! It's the Regatta,' Phil said excitedly.

'Not yet, Daddy. Not until the end of the month. I just hope the weather will hold for the August Bank Holiday.'

Phoebe looked annoyed. 'Damn. I meant to take my gabardine to be re-proofed.'

Sophie laughed at her mother's assumption that Bank Holiday equated to rain. 'Do they still do proofing?' she asked. 'I'd have thought it went out with the Ark.'

Inside, the telephone began to ring.

'I'll get it,' she said. 'It might be Hannah to say she'll be late.'

In the kitchen, Sophie picked up the handset and said hello. There was a slight pause, then an unknown male voice said, 'Is that Mrs Hamilton? Phoebe Hamilton?'

Instantly alert to the possibility that this could be a double-glazing salesman, Sophie said, in clipped tones, 'Who's speaking, please?'

'Look, er, you don't know me, but I'm Elizabeth's son. Elizabeth Rae.'

Sophie relaxed. It was obviously a wrong number. 'Elizabeth Rae? There's no one here by that name. I'm afraid I can't help you.' She began to take the handset from her ear ready to replace it on the cradle but at the other end of the line the deep tones of the unknown caller took on a new urgency.

'Elizabeth Gore, as was,' he said. 'Or perhaps you knew her better as Elizabeth Myers. Don't hang up. Please. I believe I may be your nephew. It is Mrs Hamilton I'm speaking to, isn't it? Phoebe Hamilton?'

Sophie went to find her mother in the garden and handed her the phone. It was evident, almost immediately, that Mummy was ill at ease. Sophie's curiosity, already aroused by the caller's introduction, rose to new heights. She'd told her mother he was some long lost relative, with what she thought was a slight American accent, but it was clear that Phoebe had not registered any of it.

Once the first flurry of confused introductions had taken place, the conversation appeared to be entirely on the caller's side and Sophie was, frustratingly, excluded.

Out of sight, beyond the trees, the Dartmouth ferry sounded its klaxon. A flurry of seagulls shrilly repeated the warning, and in the trees lining the bank at the bottom of the garden, a pair of magpies added their contribution.

Clearly agitated, Phoebe clamped her hand to her free ear, then rose from the table and moved away to take the remainder of the call indoors. She was only gone a few minutes, during which time Phil asked endlessly where she was and how long she would be.

'Are you all right?' Sophie asked when her mother emerged from the house, still absent-mindedly clutching the phone. Phoebe sat down at the garden table. 'Of course!'

'He was – *bona fide* – wasn't he?' Sophie asked.

Phoebe shrugged. 'As far as I could tell.'

'Libby's son? The illegitimate one?'

Phil looked from one to the other of them. 'Who's Libby?'

No one answered him.

'Yes,' said Phoebe. 'The illegitimate one.'

'Who's –' Phil began again.

'Libby,' Phoebe answered, impatiently. 'My niece.'

'Libby is Mummy's sister's daughter,' Sophie explained, pre-empting the next question. 'We think that might have been her son on the phone. The one who was adopted.'

She turned back to her mother. 'You look as if you've seen a ghost. Are you sure he was who he said he was? How did he know about you?'

Phoebe's hand shook as she smoothed a stray lock of her newly-coloured hair. 'Well that's just it! He says he's started researching the family tree.'

Sophie relaxed. 'Of course! It makes sense now. I suppose he wants to trace his birth mother. With the records available online, these days, it's so easy.'

Phoebe reached for the teapot. 'Any more left? I'm parched.'

Sophie got to her feet. 'It'll be cold. I'll make a fresh pot.'

Phoebe grabbed her wrist. 'He's got a copy of *my* father's will,' she hissed. '*My* father's! Not his. Not that he would be able to trace his father. But what business is it of his, I want to know, to be looking at my father's will?'

Sophie took in her mother's heightened colour, the tremor in her hand. 'I suppose a will could be part of the research,' she said slowly, soothingly.

Phoebe snatched her hands from the table and clutched them in her lap. 'He's just snooping!'

'You don't know that, Mummy. He sounded genuine. Very nice, in fact.'

'Libby!' said Phil, nodding agreement as recognition dawned. 'Your niece. Lovely girl. Very genuine. Very nice, in fact.'

Exasperated, Phoebe stood up, so abruptly that her chair toppled back against the dining room window. She righted it and began to stack cups and saucers on the tray.

'He wants to come down to see me,' she said in curt tones. 'At the end of the month. Bank Holiday weekend.'

'And have you agreed?'

'I've had to, haven't I? You'll have to come over, Sophie. To help me out.'

Sophie tried to make light of it. 'How exciting. A long lost relative. What intrigue! I must say he had a lovely accent. Too soft a burr to be –'

'Don't be silly, Sophie. Don't you understand? We'll obviously have to give the appearance of welcoming him to the family. But the reality is, he'll have to be kept at arm's length.'

Sophie stared at her mother in amazement.

'Whatever for?'

'Don't you understand?' Phoebe said again. 'He's obviously going to contest the will.'

She seized the tea things and began to march towards the kitchen. Before she reached the step into the house, one of the cups wobbled off the tray and smashed on the terrace. Phoebe let out a little cry and sank to the ground, shaking uncontrollably. Sophie rushed to her side, while her father, momentarily shocked out of his forgetfulness, took one look, picked up the phone from the garden table, rang Liz's number, and summoned her to their aid.

For some reason, I've found that the story Sophie told me, when she booked her mother in for therapy, keeps playing on my mind. Keen to restore my equilibrium, I seek therapy in spending time with my godchild. Having miscarried, myself, when I was married to Pete, and with no hope of further pregnancies, Lily-Rose-Marie is the closest I am going to get to motherhood. I'm blessed in that she is the child of my next-door neighbours, and doubly blessed in that they welcome my input as a babysitter. Oh, okay! Perhaps they did have an ulterior motive in asking me to take on the role of 'godmum', but I prefer to view it as an honour bestowed upon me.

With the help of Lily's brother, seven-year-old Jason, I get to bath her and feed her on a fairly regular basis, while her parents, Ben and Sharon, go pubbing. We've done what's required of us one evening and, with Lily-Rose-Marie burped and deposited her in her cot, I'm reading *Stig of the Dump* to Jason. Suddenly, he asks me a telling question.

'Is it naughty to tell a secret, Auntie Evie?'

I pause to consider the matter. The adventure story I'm reading to Jason is of a young boy, named Barney, who, while staying with his grandparents on the South Down, falls into a chalk pit and forms a friendship with a caveman, named Stig. The trigger for Jason's question, I'm guessing, is that because no one believes in the existence of cavemen, Barney's new friendship is kept a secret. However, trained to pick up on any suggestion of sexual grooming or exploitation, I'm immediately alert. Is Jason, prompted by the story, trying to tell me something significant?

For the next forty minutes, or so, we probe the question of secrets, the merit of trust, the quandary of recognising abuse. It's a delicate matter, and one I know I shall have to convey to Ben and Sharon on their return. In the end, though, Jason appears to resolve the matter. 'If I tell you, Auntie Evie, will you promise to keep it secret?'

I can't promise, of course, in case that makes me complicit in something underhand. Clearly Jason has had enough, however, and, in hushed and serious tones, he decides to convey the secret to me anyway.

'Zac told me his mummy's 'specting a new baby –' he says, his angelic little face full of earnest appeal.

'Oh, that's nice,' I reply, before realising I've interrupted something further.

' – an' it was David's daddy wot put it in her tummy,' he finishes.

Despite the gravity of the news, my relief is so great it's all I can do not to laugh out loud. Shaking with the effort of keeping my emotions under control, I look Jason in the face.

'So why can't you keep the secret?' I ask.

Jason looks indignant.

'Zac sez his mummy sez no one must know. But David's my friend, too. An' if I was David, I'd want to know if I was havin' a new baby bruvver or sister.'

I'm not sure whether to laugh or cry. If what Jason has been told has any truth in it, then clearly the potential is set for disaster. Using all my powers of persuasion, I eventually convince Jason that some secrets are better kept. I hope!

Jason's secret is safe with me, at least as far as Ben and Sharon are concerned, though I can't resist having a chuckle about it with my work colleague, Guy.

'Out of the mouths of babes and sucklings,' he retorts, his grey beard shaking with laughter when I tell him the story. We part company, each with our morning client list, aware that the reality of the situation will not be quite so humorous if it comes to light.

I'm still at work when Sophie telephones me late afternoon, the day after Phoebe's appointment.

'Sorry I couldn't ring earlier,' she begins, somewhat breathlessly. 'I've been trying to sort things out with Mummy.'

I leave the files I've been reading on my desk, stand up, and turn to the window where I can see out onto the Cathedral Green.

'Not at all,' I respond, arching my back to iron out the kinks that come from too much sitting. 'I've been busy with clients most of the day, anyway.'

'I gather Mummy wasn't very forthcoming, yesterday?' Sophie continues.

'She was – well let's say she wasn't altogether comfortable with the idea of talking therapy,' I reply, aware of my need to keep client confidentiality, while at the same time seeking to reassure an anxious family member. 'I'm just sorry I wasn't able to be more helpful.'

Through the latticed window I can see the St George's flag on the north tower of the cathedral lying lifelessly against the mast, while down below shoppers and holidaymakers bask in the vapid warmth of the August sunshine.

'Well that's just it,' Sophie says. 'The last fortnight, since the phone call, has been a bit of a nightmare. I wondered – would it be too much to ask you to see Mummy here, at home? This whole business seems to be causing her no end of stress. And it would be good to know there was someone – a professional – who could deal with her anxiety.'

I turn away from the distractions of the summer scene, and frown.

'I do undertake home visits, but I'm not a medic, Sophie. Or a psychologist. Perhaps your mother needs rather more than I could offer?'

'How do you mean?' Sophie's intake of breath rasps down the phone line.

Clearly, there's something odd going on in this family. Some sort of secret which, perhaps, threatens to be revealed by the arrival of this American on the scene? Whatever it is, it certainly seems to be causing a good deal of distress all round. Instinctively, I find myself seeking to calm Sophie while, at the same time, encouraging her to consider alternatives.

'I'm not saying I wouldn't be willing to see your mother again – if she agreed. I'm just asking if a visit to her GP might be a better option?'

'Oh!' The relief in Sophie's voice is palpable. 'I thought you were saying she'd been so difficult you wouldn't consider –'

'Not at all.' I bring to mind some of the clients I've had over the years, by comparison with whom, Phoebe Hamilton is a pushover.

'Well, what I was wondering – and I realise it may be a bit of a cheek to ask – well this American is coming to see Mummy at the end of the month, Bank Holiday and – I'll be there, of course – but I wondered if you would be willing to be present at the same time so you could make an assessment of his credibility. Either to put Mummy's fears at rest. Or to forewarn her of trouble.'

Whether it's the breathless speed of Sophie's delivery and the anxiety in her voice, or whether it's sheer curiosity and, therefore, lack of professionalism on my part I don't know. But before I can think it through, I find myself engaging in a conversation I probably shouldn't be having.

'Has he said why he wants to see your mother?' I ask.

'I don't know any more than I've already told you. He says he thinks he's Mummy's nephew, or something. He seems to have traced her through a will.'

I pull Phoebe Hamilton's file from the filing cabinet and seat myself at my desk once more. Opening up my notes, I see Sophie appears to know no more than her mother divulged to me when she came for counselling.

'Your mother's not said anything further, then?' I venture to ask.

'I can't get anywhere with her.' There's a tremor in Sophie's voice that speaks volumes. 'Nor with my sisters. It's all very well them clamming up like this, but I'm the one left holding it all together if Mummy has another panic attack. Please come, Evie. Please.'

I rub my hand over my chin, and finding myself unable to ignore her obvious distress, I reluctantly agree to her request.

'You must clear it with her, though Sophie. I could be in trouble if I just turned up.'

'Of course, I completely understand,' Sophie assures me. 'But Mummy's fine about it. Really.' She bids me goodbye. Replacing the telephone receiver on the charger, I stand and return to the window, gazing down at the revellers below. In scattered groups, they are all taking advantage of the enchanting elements of hot summer sun, wide open spaces, and thousands of years of history spread before them. Some are strumming uninhibitedly on musical instruments, some dancing in a world of their own, while others are simply watching while imbibing refreshments at the various tearooms around the Cathedral Green.

What, I wonder, returning to my desk, have I let myself in for? And just how ethical is it to be making an assessment of a complete stranger without his knowledge? Could it be deemed to be in the same category as telephone tapping? Or am I merely going to be taking on the role of peacemaker in what could become a bit of an affray, if I'm right about the revealing of secrets? Who would have thought that one old lady could be the source of such consternation for her family? And for me? But at this point, of course, I have no idea what is yet to come.

Chapter Three

Evie and Matt:
Who Did You Say You Were?

THE SECOND PART of the puzzle, though I have yet to recognise it as such, occurs five days after Phoebe Hamilton's visit. It comes in the form of a male visitor to my counselling rooms. To say he is dishy would be an understatement. Add blue tights and a red cape to the shock of black hair and flashing white teeth and you'd have Superman. Were it not for my attachment to Scott, I might have been drooling. As it is, I feel faintly irritated.

Exeter, or *Isca Dumnoniorum*, was once a Roman garrison, chosen for its favourable location on a ridge of high land. Okay for strapping young soldiers to march up the incline, I suppose – less so for an unfit female like myself, on a bike. Although it's little more than a mile from my home to the city centre, I arrive at work hot and sweaty. Consequently, the proximity of a man with box office appeal not only fails to ignite my enthusiasm, but fills me with embarrassment.

'Evie Adams?' he asks, proffering a hand the moment I appear at the top of the stairs.

Does he think he has an appointment with me? Do I have *any* appointments this morning? None that I can recall. Having had to change my non-contact day from Thursday to Friday this week, my plan is to catch up on paperwork.

'Forgive me,' he says, obviously sensing my reluctance to engage. 'Your boss said you'd be along soon.'

I frown, perplexed.

'Guy Sampson?' He jerks his head in the direction of one of the doors on the other side of the landing.

My irritation increases.

'He's not my boss. Just a colleague. We share consulting rooms.'

The man's hand drops to his side, though his voice remains eager.

'But you are Evie Adams? Allow me to explain –'

My brain is whirring. Several factors have dropped into my consciousness. This man is dressed like a tourist in T-shirt and jeans. Designer jeans, if I'm not mistaken. In addition, reeking of New World money, he has an American accent. I think, immediately, of Phoebe Hamilton and the telephone call she received.

'Forgive me,' he says, again. 'I shoulda telephoned ahead.'

We are still facing one another on the landing.

'Are you wanting to make an appointment?' I ask, curious in spite of myself.

'Gee, you look so like her,' he says, seemingly oblivious to my question. 'Or at least, like the photograph I've seen.'

I haven't the foggiest who he's referring to, so ignore his remark. Turning away towards my counselling room, I insert the key into the lock.

'Look, I don't know what this is all about or who you are,' I say over my shoulder, 'but I suppose I'd better give you a chance to explain. Let me have a moment to freshen up, and I'll be with you.'

As the door swings open and throws light on this stranger's face, for the second time that week I am filled with a sense of *déjà vu*.

Ten minutes later, having made the necessary adjustments to my face and hygiene, I join my American visitor in the lounge of the Royal Clarence Hotel where we've arranged to meet, on the edge of the Cathedral Green, not far from my counselling rooms.

'Matt McEwan,' he says, leaping to his feet and offering his hand for a second time.

At this stage the name means nothing to me, but I see from the flicker of surprise on Mr McEwan's bronzed features that it should. When we are seated, and the waiter has brought a large latte for me and an Americano, what else, for Mr McEwan, I take a second look. There is definitely something familiar about the full mouth and peaty brown eyes. However, as I am being subjected to the same scrutiny, I find I can't hold my gaze.

'So – what can I do for you?' I ask, reaching forward to lift my cup to my lips.

He leans back on the sofa in that expansive way that only Americans manage successfully, both arms draped along the buttoned back and side, one trainer – sorry, sneaker-clad – foot resting on the other knee.

'Gee. Where to begin? Suddenly, I'm lost for words. Not a good place to be for a writer.'

The penny drops, and my latte almost goes the same way.

'You're Matt McEwan –'

'That's me.'

'The author. Novelist –'

I feel such a fool! So stupid. Around me, I'm aware that others in the lounge are fully cognisant. Matt McEwan, author of a couple of dozen espionage style thrillers, is the subject of more than a few curious stares.

'I thought your face looked familiar! Now I know why. You must think me such an idiot.'

I'm gabbling. Matt shrugs, and grins.

'Not at all. Makes a change. Great not to be fawned over.'

'Go on!' I say in jocular fashion. 'Don't tell me you get tired of the adulation.'

Matt's eyes are full of humour. 'Put it this way, it's a necessary obstacle.'

I don't believe him, of course. Who in their right mind would turn up their nose at such success? Certainly not me, I think, humorously. Could do with a little adulation myself, especially since my mother's recent death. Recognising the onset of self-pity, I chide myself and revert to professionalism.

'So what can I do for you?' I ask again.

'Well, it's a long story,' he replies, leaning forward and becoming serious. 'I've imagined this meeting and rehearsed it a thousand times, but the reality is quite different. Hard to know where to begin.'

An inexplicable sense of empathy all but engulfs me. Again, I pull myself together.

'Look, I don't mean to be rude,' I say, gently, 'but I shall have to do some work this morning.'

Matt straightens up.

'Yeah! Of course. I'm sorry. It all started last summer when I was visiting my mother in Boston. She'd had a letter. From my daughter.'

'You're married?'

I blurt the question out without stopping to think how it must sound.

'Not any more. My wife – my ex – is Australian. She moved herself and our daughter back to Sydney four years ago. I rarely hear from them. Which is why what my daughter had to say to her grandmamma made me realise I had to do something.'

He tugs at his hair, then looks down at his hands. I'm reminded of clients I've seen over the years; people confronted with issues they'd rather not face; men and women who need the trust and assurance that they will not be alone in taking the next step.

'Do something?' I prompt him, gently.

He lifts his head, looks me straight in the eye.

'Yeah,' he says. 'It's something I'd been putting off. But last summer, I knew I had to set about tracing my biological family.'

Matt leaned back on the sofa and began his story, recalling the events vividly in his mind, recounting them to Evie in detail. He'd been undertaking a book launch at the behest of his US publishers, he began, when he'd visited his mother in Boston, Massachusetts the previous summer. She'd greeted him at the door with great affection plus, he fancied, a little sadness, the reason for which soon became clear.

Well powdered and rouged, she had retained the soft, peachy skin of her youth, and he reflected that only those in the know would have discerned the slight thickening of her corseted hourglass figure as she clasped him to her. Behind her, on the sofa in the living room, lay a white leather photograph album, open at the pages showing him as an infant. She had, it seemed, been indulging in a little nostalgia prior to his arrival. Picking up the album, she led him out through the patio doors into the back yard.

With a novelist's eye, he looked about him, taking in the story behind the substance of what could be seen. The large white clapper board house in the prosperous suburbs of the city, spoke of gentility, restraint; the neatly cut green lawns at the front of conformity, neighbourliness. And there, in the back yard where tea was laid, English style, with bone china cups and saucers on a wrought-iron table beside a profusion of clematis and roses clambering over trellises and arbours, there was an overwhelming sense of another life, a past life, a happier life.

He felt a warm infusion of affection run through him. Whatever he was, whatever success he'd achieved, it had its roots in this woman, his mother.

'Just look at you here, Matt,' she said, when she'd made the tea and they'd seated themselves in the leafy arbour, shaded from the glare of the sun.

The photograph she indicated showed Matt as a skinny little kid grinning from ear to ear and riding high on his dad's shoulders. Alastair, a Scot, and a captain in the British Royal Navy, was in uniform but someone, possibly Bonnie, who must have taken the photograph, had removed his cap and placed it, askew, on Matt's shock of dark curly hair.

'People used to say you looked the image of your dad,' Bonnie said, now, her voice soft and full of longing.

'We sure look as if we're sporting the same black busby hair style,' Matt said, recognising her need and humouring her.

He flicked through the album she'd handed him. Stuffed full of pictures of himself throughout his childhood, each was inscribed in Bonnie's hand: *Matt – eight months*; *Matt's wee sporran*; *Matt meets his American cousins*. And then, one of the three of them: mother, father, and son – only he wasn't, was he?

It was true, people who weren't in the know used to say how alike they were, father and son. But his parents had never kept Matt in the dark about his adoption. On the contrary. Sketchily, he called to mind the family history which, in the way of these things, had percolated down to him through the years.

Bonnie Belvedere was the daughter of a wealthy business tycoon who had made his money in steel in WW2. Dad – then Lieutenant Alastair McEwan – had been on secondment to the White House when they'd met at a ball. The courtship that followed was formal but purposeful, with a society wedding always the ultimate aim; a comfortable settlement from Bonnie's father an unintentional bonus.

By the time they'd returned as a married couple to the sprawling conurbation that was Portsmouth, the Royal Naval base on the South Coast of England, it was clear to both that Bonnie was having difficulty in conceiving. Harley Street physicians were consulted. But it was not until a decade later, by which time the McEwans were living in London, that she became pregnant with what would have been their first child. The miscarriage, and the knowledge that she would never again be able to conceive, had led, soon afterwards, to Matt's adoption.

'Chosen' was the way Bonnie had described the transaction in what, as a five-year-old, Matt had thought of as something special, extraordinary. Age and cynicism had since revealed the notion to be no more than a syrupy, hackneyed, phrase used by many adoptive parents, and designed to induce just the sort of gratitude it had achieved in his young mind.

The success of this ploy was patently obvious.

'I never entirely lost my sense of having been special to my parents,' he'd once told his badminton partner in a rare moment of confession, aware, as he did so, that it left an unspoken *but* hanging in the air.

Falling silent as he re-examined the sentiment of that statement, he cast his mind back to his early childhood. A happy though solitary affair, he realised he'd since grown into an understanding of the way things really were. Inadvertently conveyed by his adoring parents, was the notion that the responsibility for their happiness lay on his shoulders. Somehow, instinctively, he'd come to know that the loss of their earlier child, and the ache he imagined he saw in their eyes, had never completely been assuaged by his occupation of the blue, beribboned nursery in Boston.

When the Earl Grey and jam and cream filled Victoria sponge had been dispensed with, Bonnie wiped her fingers on a delicately embroidered napkin, and produced from her leather handbag a vellum envelope on which his name was penned.

'Ah guess this is something you might be needing in the near future,' she said with the nasal drawl of a true Bostonian. It was a statement, not a question.

Mystified, he took the envelope, opened it, and unfolded his original birth certificate, adoption papers, a letter and some other odds and ends. In possession of copies only, to date, he found himself moved. For implicit in her gift was the invitation to break free of all previous expectation.

He'd always told himself he would make no attempt to trace his birth mother while either of his parents lived, if at all. Alastair's death, many years earlier, had confirmed him in this decision. Now, he found himself overcome with a mixture of surprise and relief, liberally laced with guilt.

'The letter is from Samantha,' Bonnie said, by way of explanation. His head jerked up.

'Sam?'

'Yes Matt. Surprising as it may seem, your daughter still keeps in touch with me. From time to time.'

'She's not left Australia?'

Bonnie arched a heavily pencilled eyebrow and gave him a withering look. 'You think that mother of hers would allow it?'

'She has no legal hold. Not for much longer.'

'Emotional bonds can tie you in stronger knots than the law. You, of all people, know that, Matt. Even with her fourteenth birthday behind her, it's her mom she's gonna feel for. Until she knows better.'

'You know I would have done anything for her. It was never my choice -'

'I know.'

Matt tapped the envelope Bonnie had given him on his thumb nail. 'She didn't ask about -?'

'About you? How could she? Her mom wants you out of their

lives. Sam knows nothing about your background. But I guessed from what she *has* said that you'll want to tell her. Sometime soon.'

It wasn't until Matt had bid Bonnie goodbye and returned to the Sheraton Hotel where his book launch was to take place the following day, that he opened the letter Sam had written to Bonnie.

Dear Grannie, he read. She had gone on to describe her life and school achievements in Sydney, and then finished the letter with a silent and moving plea.

I had a nasty turn in class last month. It was scary. One minute I was ok. The next I was on the floor writhing around like a demented banshee. Some of the other kids at school started calling me names.

The Head had to call Mom and an ambulance. I had to have loads of tests at the hospital. Then they said I had epellepsy (spelling?) and Mom says it sure as hell isn't from her side of the family. So where did it come from? I'm gonna have to take pills and injections from now on. For ever!!! What do you think of that, Grannie? A real druggie for a granddaughter? I hate it. I shall end up like a zombie. Or a drop-out. Or probly both –

Epilepsy. Seizures. Drugs and bullying. His daughter – his precious little Sam.

Alone in the hotel bedroom, Matt wiped his eyes. He read the letter again. Then for a third time. What had he done? If Sam's mom was right and there was no evidence of the condition on her side of the family, that could mean only one thing.   Not only was his daughter growing up fatherless, in a one-parent family, but somehow, he must be responsible for her current misery.

He sat on into the evening, trying to fathom out what he should do. Then, heedless of the need for sobriety under the glare of the press interviews and book signings that lay before him next day, he went downstairs to the bar. Seating himself alone, in the corner of the room, he ordered a large Scotch. Closely followed by another.

I'm intrigued! The lounge of The Royal Clarence has emptied, somewhat, since Matt began his story, its occupants no doubt bound for business appointments, sightseeing trips or shopping. But I've scarcely noticed my surroundings, so enrapt have I been

– not only with the frankness and detail of Matt's account, but with the facial expressions and body language I've observed in him since he began. A famous author he might be, but his demeanour when he mentions his daughter is more that of a failed father.

'It took me till Christmas to make any headway with my research,' he says, his shoulders tense as he leans forward, forearms on knees, hands clenched together. 'It was so frustrating! So slow. Months of juggling time. Hours spent pouring over birth, marriage and death records. And all the while having to promote the last book while writing the next.'

'But you got there in the end?' I smile in an attempt to loosen him up, help him relax.

'Sometimes I'd follow up on a lead. A name. An address.' He shrugs and grins. 'And sometimes it'd just peter out.'

'So what gave you the breakthrough?' I ask.

'My mom died. In the Fall, last year.'

'Oh, I'm sorry.' More sorry than he knows, I reflect, given the recent loss of my own mother!

He acknowledges my sympathy.

'It was pretty devastating. Especially as my dad went some years ago, so I'd no further point of reference. But when I was goin' through my mom's papers I came across an address. A London address. And with a bit more digging, it led me here, to Devon.'

'Excellent!' I exclaim.

Matt nods. 'Seems there's a woman livin' in these parts who's my aunt. A great aunt. Or a second cousin or something. Haven't quite worked it out yet. I'm hopin' she'll be able to tell me where I can find my biological mother.'

'So have you made contact with her?'

'Yeah! She's a Mrs Phoebe Hamilton. And she lives near Dartmouth.'

No! I slump back in my seat, my heart racing. The mention of Phoebe Hamilton has floored me. The coincidence is incredible. Astonishing.

'Do you know her?' Matt asks, evidently registering my reaction.

'So let me get this straight,' I begin, recapping his narrative to give myself time to process this extraordinary fluke, while ignoring his question. 'You're divorced, your daughter, Sam, lives in Australia with her mother, and it was a letter she wrote to her grandmother – your adoptive mother, Bonnie – that kicked off your search for your biological family?'

Matt's face lights up, and again I'm struck by its familiarity. Just shows how good a job his publishers and PR people have done!

'I'm impressed,' he says, grinning. 'I realise how garbled my account of events must have sounded. But you seem to have sifted through it and come up with a coherent story.'

'Goes with the job,' I respond, drily. 'You wouldn't credit how tongue-tied and muddled people become when trying to tell me what's brought them to see me.'

'Oh, I would! I have the same problem when I'm interviewing people for research. They're much more responsive over a pint in the pub.'

'So what about this letter from Sam?' I ask. 'The epilepsy. Did you get anywhere with that?'

Matt tugs at his hair. I've noticed him doing so from time to time as he's recounted his story. A habit from childhood, perhaps?

'Would you like another coffee before I get on to that?' he asks.

'How about we walk around the Cathedral Green instead?' I make the suggestion more as a statement than a question. This is not, after all, a formal counselling session. Only me satisfying my curiosity about an interesting man who's sought me out.

Matt summons the waiter, pays the bill and we leave the hotel. Outside, the air is warm, and vibrant with the sound of people's voices. The grassy spaces surrounding the great cathedral are a natural gathering place. It's as if the building and statue of Richard Hooker – co-founder with Thomas Cranmer of Anglicanism, following the Reformation – contains some other-worldly magnetism that draws people to it. Even I, with hardly a religious bone in my body, feel the energy of this place each morning when I arrive for work. There is something about it that is empowering.

Matt lifts his head and breathes in the atmosphere.

'Great architecture,' he says, looking up at the flying buttresses.

'What is it? 12th, 13th century? We have nothing of this age in the States.'

We begin a circular tour, away from the coffee houses, restaurants and boutiques of Cathedral Yard, and down past the half-timbered houses of The Close, towards the Bishop's Palace and Roman city wall.

'I reckon Sam's letter to her grandmamma was, actually, intended for me to see,' he says, pensively. 'I think she just didn't want her mom to know she was writing to her dad.'

I nod, but keep looking down at the cobbled road beneath my feet. Often, I find, a lack of eye contact makes it easier for people to unburden themselves.

'And what, exactly, do you think your daughter was trying to convey?'

Matt flings his head back, and I sense the depth and gravity of his emotions.

'It seems there's no evidence of epilepsy in my ex-wife's family. And there was certainly no sign of Sam having seizures in infancy.

'Of course, that doesn't mean a thing. I don't know what type of epilepsy Sam has. But from what I understand from my own research, there's a syndrome that can be inherited, even though it may not appear until later in childhood. Sam, apparently, had her first seizure on her fourteenth birthday.'

He shoves his hands in his trouser pockets.

'I'm convinced she wanted to know if the cause of her seizures could possibly be laid at my door. I suspect, with good reason, that her mom is trying to convince her that this is Bad Dad Syndrome, yet again. Which, of course, it might be.'

Matt's voice breaks and, despite my professional training and the fact that he is a stranger, I find the urge to squeeze his arm in a gesture of comfort almost overwhelming.

'And you think this Phoebe Hamilton may be your mother's sister?' I ask.

We've reached the end of The Close and turn right, back towards the West Door of the cathedral. A burst of organ music assails our ears, a Rachmaninov concerto I recognise but can't name.

'I expect they're rehearsing for a concert,' I explain to Matt. When he fails to respond, I glance towards him. His head is down and he looks as if he's fighting with something inside himself.

'I've since uncovered evidence that leads me to believe my birth mother was Phoebe Hamilton's niece,' he says, at last.

Of course, there is no way I can disclose that Mrs Hamilton is a client of mine, but I'm curious to know how his search has led him to me. Has she told him something about our preliminary counselling session? I rack my brains, failing to see what this could be.

'Matt, I can see how painful this is for you and I want to help, I really do. But I can't quite understand where I fit into this story? What are you expecting from me? What brought you to me in the first place?'

We've reached the front of the cathedral again, the West Door, and Matt stops beneath the gargoyles. He eyes me, quizzically.

'My mother was Elizabeth Rae.'

He waits for my response.

'So?' I shrug my shoulders. The name means nothing to me.

'Elizabeth Myers, as was. Or more recently, Elizabeth Gore.'

I feel myself sway. The trees, the crowd, the buildings on the periphery of The Green – everything swirls before me. Matt takes my arm to steady me. The music inside the cathedral swells to a crescendo.

'Libby Myers? She was your mother?'

Matt's eyes are locked on mine. 'Yes.'

'That was her maiden name?'

He nods.

'And her married name was?'

'Rae. My name, apparently, before my adoption.'

His eyes remain fixed on mine. I stare back at him.

'And then Gore? But that was – that was –' I'm trying to say that was my maiden name. My parents' surname. But the words elude me.

'Yes,' he says again, and I can see, before I look away, that he's willing me to jump to the only possible conclusion.

My mind is reeling. Steadying myself against the cathedral wall,

I grapple with the ramifications. If Libby Myers became Libby Rae – and Libby Rae was Matthew McEwan's mother – and Libby Rae became Libby Gore – and Libby Gore was my mother. Does that mean that this man – this Matt McEwan – is my brother? Or at least, my half-brother?

His grip on my arm tightens. I glance up at him. Is it possible? I can't believe it! But there's no getting away from it. I can see it now. No wonder his face looks so familiar. Apart from the hair colouring, and the fact that it's a male version, the image of the Matt that swims before me is – well, it could be – it's almost the same as the one I see of myself in the mirror each morning.

Chapter Four

Evie and Matt:
Deposed and Dispossessed?

PATIENCE, KINDNESS AND clemency were what Sophie considered to be her lifestyle choices. When she failed to practise these attributes, self-condemnation followed swiftly in the form of impatience, irritability and shame. The sequence, she thought, was as inevitable to her as were cats and sneezes.

Poised on the baseline of the tennis court, she bent forward, racket in hand, and swayed from side to side. Today's lesson with her niece, Fiona's daughter, Hannah, was not going well and Sophie knew she had only herself to blame. Her mind was too fragmented to concentrate on the game. She felt impatient with the situation, and irritable with herself for her impatience.

It must be a fortnight or more, she thought, since the American claiming to be Libby's illegitimate son had rung, and several days since the abortive attempt at sorting her mother out with the counselling service in Exeter. She'd phoned Evie Adams the next day and they'd agreed Evie would be present at her parents' home in Kingswear when Matt McEwan visited at the end of the month, so she could act as mediator, if necessary.

Uncomfortable with her thoughts, Sophie missed Hannah's serve. Evie had insisted Mummy be party to this arrangement for Matt's visit. Without Mummy's acquiescence, Evie had implied that her job could be in jeopardy. In good faith, aware of her mother's need of Evie's presence, Sophie had told a little white lie. She fully intended to tell Mummy that Evie would be there. Really, she did. But just not yet.

43

Her mother had commandeered her to help with the practicalities – refreshments and so on – but it was the emotional consequences that most concerned Sophie. If she told Mummy too soon about Evie coming, she felt sure there would be repercussions. Despite her best efforts to understand the antipathy this event seemed to have conjured in the family, there appeared to be no more answers than there had ever been. Full of anxiety, she tried to put it out of her mind and concentrate on the tennis lesson. But to no avail.

Her mood hadn't been helped by the fact that Hannah was late. Exceedingly late. Sophie had made herself practise patience and calm for half an hour before her student turned up. But faced with a sullen fourteen-year-old, she'd found kindness and clemency a step too far. Things had gone downhill from there on. Hannah was moving about the court with all the vim and vigour of a J-cloth in the hand of a waitress cleaning the tables at a motorway service station.

'Run, Hannah!' Sophie yelled. 'For goodness sake! The ball isn't going to come to you. That's the point. Your opponent will be aiming for the spaces. You need to occupy them.'

Half an hour into the lesson, Hannah was in tears. It was so unlike her! Sophie felt terrible. When, with a bit of coaxing, her niece disclosed she had started her first period, she felt worse still. Kindness was required in large dollops. Especially as Hannah was away from home staying with Auntie Liz while her mother, Fiona, was in hospital for a minor operation.

'I'm so sorry, love,' she said, an arm around the shoulders of her niece. 'What a monster you must think me.' And then, gently, 'You should have told me. We could have cancelled your lesson.'

Hannah showed her forgiveness with a small, chastened smile – which, by Sophie's reckoning, was completely the wrong way round, and not at all how she'd imagined things when first presented with an adorable baby niece. Determined to make amends, she took her bag from the locker in the changing rooms.

'Now, we can't have you waiting for the bus,' she said, 'I'll run you home and explain to Auntie Liz.'

Negotiating the narrow country lanes between banks of vibrant rose herb willow and undulating meadows beyond, Sophie realised it actually suited her to have a reason to take Hannah home, because she very much wanted to quiz Liz about this business between their mother and the American. She had the feeling that the family, all of them, were closing ranks, and that she, alone, was excluded from whatever mystery surrounded Matt McEwan and the will he was supposed to be contesting.

Since the phone call, her mind had been teeming with questions. Where, for instance, had this cousin been all these years? Why had he left it until now to make contact? And why on earth should her mother think he would be out to dispute a will which had been made and executed well over half a century earlier?

Something, Sophie felt, just didn't add up. And despite the questions she'd put to her mother, it was obvious Phoebe was not going to do the calculations for her. Not yet, at any rate.

There was no sign of Liz when Sophie parked her old Peugeot alongside the smart silver convertible with the personalised number plate, which Gordon had bought for her sister's fortieth birthday a couple of years ago. Hannah, after a muttered thanks, disappeared into the house leaving Sophie to scrunch her way up the drive and through the side gate to the back garden. She found Liz, book in her lap, half asleep on a reclining chair under the shade of a spreading Cedar on the far side of the lawn. It was clear from the way she jumped guiltily to her feet that she had not expected Hannah's arrival so soon, nor, indeed, Sophie's, at all.

'To what do I owe this pleasure?' Liz asked, her neatly coiffed hair brushing Sophie's cheek as she leant towards her to peck the air.

Sophie suffered the chic greeting with the same easy-going tolerance with which she viewed Liz's entire lifestyle. Liz and Gordon's house, a five-bedroomed, Victorian, limestone villa, was out of town at the luxury end of the market. Surrounded by open countryside, it commanded stunning views of the River Dart, a grey-blue ribbon winding down to the broad reaches of the sea beyond. Upstream, the densely wooded foreshore climbed steeply in billowing folds to a gently swelling canopy of wide open green spaces and red Devon soil. In addition to the large landscaped garden surrounding the house, there was a paddock attached, in which Liz kept ponies.

That's what you get, thought Sophie, for marrying a surgeon who's prepared to commute. There was no sense of envy in the thought. As far as Sophie was concerned, Liz, neat and petite, was the ideal surgeon's wife in a way she would never be, nor would ever want to be. Liz shopped in Kensington, wore Manolo shoes, attended fund-raising lunches at the County Hospital where Gordon worked, opened bazaars at Dartmouth Parish Church, and was invited to dinners at Britannia Royal Naval College.

Sophie, when she could be bothered, browsed through charity shops, went barefoot whenever possible, and might, at best, be asked to organise a tombola stand at the school fete. And then, of course, self-discipline was required of Liz in a way Sophie knew she would find restrictive and controlling. Being a Nicky No Name – as the kids at school had it – was, in her view, infinitely more attractive than being a Mrs Somebody. In fact there were times when, without a hint of irony, Sophie caught herself feeling ever so slightly sorry for Liz.

She flopped down, uninvited, onto the second garden lounger opposite the one Liz had vacated and explained, between sips of water from the bottle she'd taken from her kit bag, that Hannah had the Curse, and this was why she had brought her home.

'Poor kid. I'm afraid I gave her a bit of a rough time before she let on. She was obviously embarrassed about telling me,' she finished.

Liz had remained standing, her slight weight and one sparkly flip-flop clad, toenail polished foot already inclined towards the house.

'Oh, my goodness! What on earth do you say to a teenager in a situation like this? I hope she hasn't wrecked my new bed linen. Oh, that sounds awful. But you know what I mean. I suppose I'd better go and look.'

'I'll hang on until you come down again,' said Sophie, tipping her head back and half-shutting her eyes.

'I might be a while,' Liz warned, in what was all too obviously a bid to secure the departure of an unwelcome visitor.

Sophie didn't bat an eyelid.

'Not to worry. I'll just enjoy the sunshine until you get back. I want to know what you can tell me about Libby's son. The illegitimate one. I expect Mummy told you he's come to light. Turned up. Out of the blue. Well, at the end of a phone line.'

As expected, Liz stopped in her tracks.

'Really, Sophie! Does one talk about people being illegitimate these days?'

'Born out of wedlock, then, if you prefer. The point is he's coming to see Mummy tomorrow. And she's getting herself into a terrible a state.'

Liz shook her head. 'I can imagine!'

Now why would that be? Sophie squinted upwards, surveying her sister, certain she must know more than she was letting on.

'Mummy's convinced this man is going to contest our grandfather's will,' she said, giving Liz the benefit of doubt. 'What's it all about?'

'Nothing!'

The denial was too abrupt. Sophie raised an eyebrow.

'No. Really!' Liz was clearly seeking to remedy the impression she'd given. 'I don't know what you're talking about. But I suggest you leave well alone. Now I must go and see to – things.'

Liz scurried off, ostensibly to see Hannah. Staring after her, Sophie was far from persuaded.

Returning home after her visit to Liz, Sophie realised she had learned precisely nothing! On the grounds of conveying Hannah's initiation into womanhood, and knowing Fiona was now home from hospital, she put in a call to her middle sister the moment she got in.

'Poor kid,' she began, once she'd asked after Fiona's health. 'I did give her rather a hard time.'

Fiona was every bit the concerned mother. When the topic was, eventually, exhausted, Sophie brought up the matter of Matt McEwan's impending visit.

'It was odd, the way Mummy reacted,' she said, making a deliberate assumption that Fiona would have heard about the telephone call.

'In what way odd?' Fiona asked.

'Well you'd think, when a long lost member of your family turns up out of the blue, you'd be pleased, wouldn't you? I mean there's this poor man. It's not his fault he was born out of wedlock at a time when it was considered a mortal sin. If, indeed, it was.

'Then he's had to endure all these years living as an adoptee, or whatever the word is. And now he wants to trace his family. I just think he should be made to feel a bit more welcome.'

'Well Mother's invited him to visit, as you know!' Fiona retorted.

'I think he invited himself and she agreed. But not very enthusiastically.'

Sophie gazed out of her cottage window at the steep cobbled steps leading down to the quay and the River Dart. At the other end of the phone line she could hear Fiona's husband calling, then a door slammed. She imagined her brother-in-law off out somewhere, leaving a pile of washing up for Fiona to deal with. He was spoiled rotten, in Sophie's view, and despite the fact she didn't always understand Fiona or agree with her way of doing things, that didn't stop her feeling sorry for her sister.

'I think you have to accept Mother's reaction as normal for someone her age,' Fiona said, in what sounded to Sophie to be a careful weighing of her words. 'Her generation adopted a policy of *least said, soonest mended*. And I have to say I agree with it to some extent. There's too much emphasis on openness these days. And it's not always helpful in my view.'

Sophie turned away from the window.

'Helpful to whom?' she asked. 'Are you saying this poor man, our cousin, Matt, is supposed to go quietly to his grave without ever making any attempt to trace his family?'

'People do. Or rather they did. It's only recently this sort of intrusiveness has been encouraged – this looking into the past trying to catch out your ancestors, wanting to judge people, condemn them.'

'Okay, okay! You've made your point. Anyone would think you had something to hide. And I'm not sure I agree with you. I think it's perfectly natural to want to know where you've come from. It's human nature.'

'I thought it was the business over the will you rang to ask about,' Fiona interrupted.

Sophie stopped. 'Oh, you know about that? Has Mummy been in touch?'

Fiona cleared her throat

'She wrote to me when I was in hospital. But not about that. At least, not specifically.'

'So what did she say? She wouldn't tell me anything last week. Just said not to be naïve. I asked Liz what was going on, but she didn't seem to know anything. Or wouldn't say.'

'It's nothing to worry about,' said Fiona. 'As I say, it's probably just an age-thing. People in Mother's day were very secretive about their affairs. I expect she feels her privacy has been invaded by this man.'

'I suppose you're right,' Sophie conceded, wondering what there was to be secretive about. 'Though I think Mummy's over-reacting. After all, he could be famous. He could be that American crime-writer. He has the sexiest voice. Like brown treacle, or deep water running through a gorge.'

'Sophie! He's supposed to be a cousin.'

'Well he has. It's a cross between North American and Scottish. Or Irish. It's certainly not the voice of a con man.'

Fiona gave a dry laugh. 'There speaks the voice of experience.'

Crossing the room and seating herself on the sofa, Sophie shook her head.

'We shall see. You and Mummy may think what you like about Matt McEwan. I think he's genuine. And I, for one, will be making him welcome when he visits.'

I'm sprawled on the sofa, following my evening meal, pondering the events of Matt's visit that day. And what a day! With no clients, it being my non-contact day, I'd given up on the idea of office work following the mind-blowing news I'd received from Matt. After clearing it with my colleague, Guy Sampson, I'd then taken the rest of the morning off.

At my suggestion, Matt and I had walked away from the cathedral and city centre, and spent our time together in the relative peace of Northernhay Gardens. Sitting on a bench in sight of the Roman wall, Matt went through what little evidence he had to support the fact that my mother was also his. Then I gave him details of her death.

'Yeah, that was hard, knowing she'd passed on only months before I began my investigation and I'd never get to meet her,' he said. 'The death certificate cited liver failure?'

Recognising the ploy to get me to open up, I'd deliberately by-passed her drink problem and focused only on the hard life she'd led.

'You're the spittin' image,' Matt said, reiterating his earlier statement when we first met, as he produced what he told me was the only photograph he had of her.

It was not one I had ever seen before. She looked young. Too young to have been married. Too young to have had a child.

'How did you get this?' I asked, aware of a feeling of betrayal that my mother should have had a life unknown to me. The thought was swiftly followed by a sense of guilt and absurdity. Why should I expect to have a monopoly on my mother's life – especially before my birth?

'Bonnie. My adoptive mom. Apparently, Elizabeth – Libby, as you call her – left it at the orphanage and asked for it be passed on if and when I was adopted.'

There was a poignancy in his 'if and when' that spoke volumes, I thought. The counsellor in me tried to empathise with Matt's feelings. The 'little girl' in me cried out. And inside my head, she was the louder of the two. Was Matt trying to make out that in putting him up for adoption my mother was being heartless? What was behind it? Given my state of confusion at the time, I hadn't taken it any further, and had eventually returned to the office none the wiser. Instead of catching up on filing, I'd spent the afternoon drawing up a family tree.

Trying to make sense of the relationships, I'm poring over it now, here, at home.

The phone rings, pulling me from my reverie.

'Evie? Matt here.'

He has, he tells me, spent the afternoon researching local newspaper cuttings in the library for his next book and, following my having turned down his invitation for dinner, has dined alone at his Exeter hotel. His purpose now, he says, is to persuade me to accompany him to see Phoebe Hamilton.

'Gee, Evie, she's your aunt every bit as much as she is mine,' he says gently. 'You've as much right to meet her as I have.'

My brain is teeming with questions, but before I can make any enquiry Matt asks me, again, 'So will you come with me to the Hamiltons' tomorrow?'

Setting aside my personal feelings, I attempt to address my work ethics. I have no idea what, if anything, Matt knows of my counselling session with Phoebe. Nor, within the boundaries of professional confidentiality, am I at liberty to make even the smallest of hints in that respect. I certainly can't tell him I've already agreed to go down to Kingswear, at Sophie's request.

What are his expectations from this visit to the Hamilton home, I wonder? Is he aware of the hostility his proposed visit has evoked in Phoebe Hamilton? Does he know the family is anticipating a feud over the will he is purported to have in his possession? A will made by Phoebe Hamilton's father.

These were not the sort of questions that could easily be raised, or answered, over the telephone. And certainly not by me!

Our encounter, earlier in the day, had left me with a wild sense of unfinished business. My mind is still reeling. I can make no sense of what has been revealed to me. If Matt McEwan is my half-brother, as he claims to be – No! It's impossible. My mother was still in her teens when she had me. She'd have been barely out of school if she'd fallen pregnant with Matt prior to that.

'You're, what, a year or two older than me?' I'd asked him, as we walked back to the Cathedral Green. 'So who was your father?'

Matt was unable to give a satisfactory answer. Adopted at eight months of age, he had been known as Dean Rae in the orphanage. However, there was no name on his birth certificate, he said, simply *Father Unknown*. His hope was that Phoebe Hamilton, the only other surviving relative of that generation known to him, would be able to shed further light on the matter.

We don't share a father, then, I'd thought, relief flooding through me as we'd bade one another an awkward farewell and I'd made my way upstairs to my counselling room. So at least Dad was exonerated in that respect. His persistent indifference to me was not the result of guilt because he'd made my mother give up her first-born for adoption.

Thinking about it now, at home in my own front room, a further thought strikes me. If Dad did not father Matt, did he even know of his existence? What, if anything, did he know of Mum's past life? Had she taken her secrets to the grave? A stab of pain twists my guts. To think of the lies she must have been compelled to weave into the warp and weft of her life. No wonder she'd drunk herself to death. Throughout her life I'd defended her. Assuming her to be guiltless, I'd always thought her badly done by. Was I wrong? Was she, in fact, the author of her own misery?

What, for years, has been pity for her begins, now, to manifest itself as shame. Shame and disappointment. Picking up a biro, I let it drop, repeatedly, through my fingers, the point stabbing the newspaper on my lap.

Deliberately, I turn my thoughts to a higher plane. Alongside my raw emotion stands the professional practitioner in me. Unconditional positive regard of self and others is a core requirement in therapy training and practice. Complex, and difficult to implement, it entails constant reappraisal if a counsellor is to achieve any degree of non-judgemental acceptance. In true talking therapy fashion, I conduct a debate within myself.

I have no right to judge. I know little or nothing of my mother's circumstances. I've always thought her badly treated, cast aside by her family. At no time, however, has there been any concrete evidence. What Matt McEwan is offering is an opportunity to rectify that. Could the will Phoebe Hamilton fears might be contested be the very one from which my grandmother, and thence my mother, was erased? I twist the telephone flex in my hand, unintentionally recreating the twists and turns of my mind .

'Okay. I'll come,' I tell Matt, impulsively.

Jumping to my feet, I can hear the pleasure in his voice as he affirms my decision. My stomach lurches.

'But I need to go on my own terms,' I add. 'I want to remain neutral. I'll travel down with you, but I don't want you to disclose anything about your relationship to me. You can introduce me as someone who's helped you in your research if you like. Okay?'

Having secured Matt's agreement, I end the call and cross the room to stare out of the window at the deepening shadows on the street. I have no idea how my accompanying Matt will go down with the Hamilton family. Nor any confidence about the professional ethics of what I'm about to embark upon. But what the heck. This is my life we're talking about. If I mess up I mess up. At least Grace can put me right at a later date. But in the meantime, I need to warn Sophie that, for reasons I cannot divulge due to 'client confidentiality,' I shall be travelling down with Matt. Does she even know we've met, I wonder? Unsure, I dial the number she has given me and leave a message.

'Whatever it looks like,' I add, with a confidence I don't possess, 'I can assure you I shall remain neutral throughout.'

Naturally, I email Scott at my earliest opportunity, to impart the fact that I have news. He rings me at home later that night.

'So what's happened?' he asks, without a pause for the usual pleasantries.

I've come to bed early, indulging myself with a mug of tea and a novel written by one of my favourite authors – a charity shop purchase. Setting both down on the bedside table, I pull myself upright against the pillows.

'Ah, well! I hope you're sitting comfortably,' I begin, building the drama.

'You've won the Lottery,' says Scott, responding in kind.

'Mmm. Could be.' Pulling my knees up to my chin, I question whether being the impoverished sister of a famous, and no doubt wealthy, American author is in the same league as winning the Lottery.

'You're gonna be a dame, and you're lettin' me down gently cos you're takin' someone else with you when Her Majesty taps you on the shoulder.'

'Close.'

'Or worse still, you're ringing to tell me it's all over between us,' Scott continues.

'Yep. That's it. There's a new man in my life. Another American.'

'The butcher? The baker?'

'The candlestick maker, actually.'

With the banter over, I proceed to fill Scott in on the day's events.

'Gee, Evie!' The fact that he's lost for words tells me he's in tune with my own feelings.

'I still can't quite believe it, myself,' I tell him.

'But you're okay about it?'

For the briefest of moments, I hesitate. I pick up my mug from the bedside table, take the last sip and replace it.

'I guess. Lot of mixed feelings swirling around about my mother concealing it from me all these years. And knowing it's now too late ever to hear her version of events.'

'That's hard,' Scott concurs. 'And what about your dad? What did he know, if anything?'

'Exactly! I'll never know now, will I?'

I thrust my legs out straight in front of me. I can't bring myself to admit to it, out loud, but I have grievous misgivings in respect of my dad. Things that have been pounding in my head all evening.

Could it be, I ask myself, that he'd found out at some point about my mother's previous pregnancy? And that the fear of having another man's child share in his estate was the reason for his having omitted the two of us from his will? For having named some distant relative as his beneficiary, instead of my mum?

I rather think it is a possibility. So not only have I been deposed by an older sibling, I've also been disinherited as a result. The thought leaves a sour taste in my mouth as Scott bids me goodbye with a promise to pray for me.

Chapter Five

What's in a Wedding?

∽◉

UNDER NORMAL CIRCUMSTANCES, I would, at some point, be evaluating and summarising a client's situation prior to formulating a means of dealing with it. Nothing, however, is normal about the situation in which I now find myself. My ex-client, Phoebe Hamilton, has been revealed as my aunt; my potential client, Matt McEwan, as my brother. Understandably, I tell myself throughout a long and sleepless night, my brain is a fog of confusion and doubt.

Despite my phone call off-loading some of my news to Scott the previous evening, I know I have crossed a line in agreeing to Matt's request to accompany him to the Hamilton's, when, without his knowledge, I've already agreed to Sophie's invitation. Not a lot I can do about it now without breaking the rules of confidentiality to which I'm bound. Besides, I might never again have the opportunity to meet what appears to be my new-found family. The internal argument is interminable and compelling.

My immediate reaction, once I'm showered and dressed, is to dive into the cupboard under the stairs to retrieve the photographs, papers and memorabilia which I acquired following my mother's death. Fifteen minutes later, I've found nothing to further my quest. I turn to the second box. This appears more hopeful. On top lies a bundle of dog-eared black and white photographs. True, most of the subjects are unrecognisable to me, though the locations look vaguely familiar.

And then – bingo! – I come across something more promising: a black and white wedding photo, mounted inside a flimsy white cover portraying the photographer's name and a London address. Opening it on my lap, I stare down at it. Instantly, despite the difference in hair colouring, I can see the familial features I recognised as my mother's in both Phoebe and Matt. No wonder I thought I knew them both! No wonder Matt had seen it in me, too.

'Oh, Mum!'

I stroke my thumb over the image, trying to capture the emotions behind the face looking back at me. It's a pretty face, no doubt about that. But despite the smile, surely summoned into being by the photographer, I discern a sadness. A forlorn look of appeal in the eyes. A vacant expression of – hopelessness?

'So not what you'd expect from a bride,' I say aloud to the empty room. On the hearth rug, Pumpkin yawns, stretches out her paw, and returns to sleep.

I turn my attention to the bridegroom at my mother's side, my dad. He bears little resemblance to the man I knew for thirty years or more. A man of political persuasion. A man of power. A man of self-importance.

The photographic image before me portrays none of that. I frown, lean forward, scrutinise my dad's expression, attempt to analyse the body language, to read into what is merely visual. Straightening up, I hold the photograph at arm's length. It can't be. But it is. There's no doubt about it. What I can only interpret as another forced smile, barely conceals the look of grim resignation on his face.

What on earth was going on, I ask myself? Aren't wedding photos meant to be a record of a happy occasion? Something to celebrate? Something worthy of being displayed for all to see? Why, then, have I never seen the reality behind this photograph before? Why has it been hidden from me all these years?

Jason comes suddenly to mind. The little boy next door with the terrible secret. What was it he'd said when I was babysitting? That Zac's mummy was expecting a new baby. That it was David's daddy who had put it in her tummy. And almost certainly that Zac's daddy knew nothing about it.

Could something similar be true of my parents? But if so, what? Did my father know all along about Matt? Did he find out only after they married? Or had he known nothing at all throughout their marriage? Will I ever find the answer? With renewed concern, I search for clues behind the grim reality of the wedding photo in my hand. Then I jump to my feet.

A whole box of photographs and papers stands on the carpet before me. Plus a further two behind that. They will have to wait. I can't take any more for now. Besides which, I'm going to have to get ready to cycle into town. For some reason, reluctant to give Matt my home address, I've told him I'll meet him near my place of work so we can then go on to the Hamiltons' for lunch.

Is there a sense of shame in this decision, I wonder now? An unwillingness in me to reveal my straitened circumstances to someone of Matt's obvious fame and wealth? A feeling of inferiority? Or inverted snobbery?

Looking about my humble abode as I scoop Pumpkin up ready to put her outside, I can only conclude there is. Does this make me a hypocrite? Or am I merely intent on making it easier for him? Physically, because he won't have to find his way across town to pick me up? And mentally, because he'll have no reason to make comparison between my circumstances and his. And, therefore, no reason to feel guilt?

Aware of the Hamilton family's wealth and status, I dress for the occasion, donning my favourite swirly cotton skirt, with an embroidered T-shirt in a paler shade of lilac, topped with a deep purple linen jacket. All charity shop purchases, but very respectable. Even so, I feel quite apprehensive as I park and immobilise my bike in the lean-to behind my counselling room, and proceed to walk down The Close, past the 16th century black and white timbered façade of Mol's Coffee House, said to have been a meeting place for Sir Francis Drake and Sir Walter Raleigh, and already teeming with tourists. In contrast, the area between the cathedral and the red sandstone Roman wall, where Matt and I have arranged to meet, is devoid of people and noise.

Dressed in stone-coloured chinos, an open-necked shirt and linen jacket, Matt is standing beneath the arch, awaiting my arrival.

'Hi! Good to see you.'

Greeting me with a peck on the cheek, he tells me he has parked only a short distance away in Southernhay. He then escorts me past the terrace of grand Georgian buildings that line the avenue, opens the passenger door of a silver sports car and invites me to seat myself.

I know little or nothing about the brand, performance or prestige attached to such vehicles, and am adamant in telling myself I couldn't care less. How wrong can you be? The roof is down and, despite my avowed distrust of all things concerned with wealth and ostentation, I find myself glowing with a sense of excitement and privilege.

'I've never been in anything quite so posh before,' I say, suddenly shy as I realise, anew, that we are related.

'Well, Sis, we shall have to rectify that,' Matt drawls, his eyes alight with humour as he holds open the door for me to clamber in. And mingled with the shyness, I feel overwhelmed with sadness and loss for what might have been had we grown up together.

Seating himself behind the wheel, Matt puts the car into gear and sets off downhill away from the city centre, *en route* for the River Exe and the end of the M5 motorway.

'The Hamiltons live in Kingswear, opposite Dartmouth,' he says, unaware he is telling me what I already know. 'Shouldn't take us too long to get there by my reckoning. I texted the daughter, Sophie, to let her know I wouldn't be alone, and she said we were expected for lunch.'

A squall of terror overcomes me. What are they going to think when they discover who I am? I glance sideways at Matt, taking in, again, his firm jaw and full mouth, his likeness to me.

'She sounds okay, Sophie,' Matt continues. 'Not so sure about the old lady. Bit frosty, unnerving. Almost felt she resented my ringing her when I got in touch at the beginning of the month.'

'I suppose she might have good reason,' I offer, still grappling with what, if anything, I should tell Matt.

'Yeah, I guess so.'

Leaving the city behind, Matt negotiates his way onto the road that will eventually take us up over Haldon Hill towards Torbay and from there across to the Kingswear side of the River Dart.

'She doesn't know me from Adam,' he continues. 'As my badminton pal, Tom, reminded me, I could be anyone. He's a financial advisor and he spends his life cautioning elderly clients not to be taken in by strangers on the phone.'

'But surely the fact that you could give them enough detail about your mother – our mother – convinced them you were genuine?'

'So I thought, initially. Trouble is, they *might* know me from Adam. Chances are they're more *au fait* with my failings than I am myself.'

'How do you mean?'

'Gee, I might have come from criminal stock for all I know. Or been the product of a layabout and a benefits fraudster.'

I feel myself flush with anger.

'Your mother – *our* mother – was neither a layabout nor a benefits cheat.'

Matt glances sideways. 'No! Forgive me. I'm relying on you to fill me in in that regard. But I didn't mean her. What about my dad?'

I shrug to indicate my ignorance and attempt to adopt a more caring and professional attitude.

'It's me who should be apologising. What do you actually know about my mother?'

'Very little,' Matt says, and behind the affluent, self-confident exterior, I glimpse a hint of vulnerability.

'But didn't your adoptive mother give you any information?' I ask, gently, recalling the unopened boxes of memorabilia I have at home and determining to explore them further before I tell Matt of their existence.

'Bonnie, my mom, waited years to get pregnant, and then lost her only hope of having a child when she miscarried,' Matt replies. 'She adopted me soon after. I don't suppose she was in a fit state to register much about where I came from.'

'But there must have been screening, to ascertain the suitability of your adoptive parents?'

'Sure! I may be getting on, at forty-plus, but I'm not so old it could all be done clandestinely. We had laws in place in the U.S of A long before you had 'em here in Great Britain. Of course, my parents were living in England at the time. Dad was British, a Scot. He was in the Royal Navy. But Bonnie, as an American citizen wouldn't have had any expectation of the sort of private arrangement with the unmarried girl in the next bed on the hospital ward that used to go on over here.'

However unintentional, Matt's dialogue comes across to me with the sting of rebuke. I turn away and stare out of the window, my gaze penetrating the dark, un-walked-in glades deep in the forested roadside of Haldon Hill.

'Better watch out, there are deer in these woods,' I warn him. 'Not that I've ever seen any around here.'

Matt shifts down a gear and reduces his speed.

'Yeah, I saw the signs.'

We lapse into silence.

'So what *do* you know?' I ask at last.

'Not a lot. Only that I was eight months old when I was adopted –'

'Mother kept you all that time and then let you go?'

Matt shrugs. 'I don't think she was married, was she! I don't suppose she had much choice. As Tom pointed out to me, even in those days, Unmarried Mom equalled Loose Woman.'

'This is my mother we're talking about,' I rebuke him.

'And mine! I'm not being critical. Simply acknowledging that the social mores in those days were harsh.'

'She must have been very young when she had you.'

'Exactly! Taken advantage of by an older man, perhaps? I've no idea what the circumstances were. I mean, I suppose I could be the result of a rape.'

I'm stunned. Struck dumb with a mixture of horror and pity. A sickening, plummeting, sensation takes place in my innards. Then a deer bounds out of the woods right in front of us.

Matt gripped the steering wheel and slammed on the brakes.

'Whoah!' he said, feigning a coolness he didn't possess. 'That was a near miss.'

Steadying the car as the deer leapt from sight on the other side of the road, he winged a silent prayer of thankfulness heavenwards. Fortunately, there was little traffic about. Had the road been busy – gee, who knows what might have happened?

Habitually drawing parallels as a writer, he was struck, suddenly, by the treacherous nature of the emotional journey that lay ahead. Jolted from any sense of complacency, he considered his position.

From the open, sunny meadows of his childhood, the shadowy woodlands of his origins had appeared distant and insubstantial. But now – now he was venturing into the deep, dark depths of the unknown, who could tell what lay ahead? What skeletons he might stumble upon? What swamps of emotion? Tangled undergrowth? Dead-ends?

He'd assumed, at the outset, that he would retain his present position. Or that he'd occupy a temporary location like a high turret or an aerial vantage point, from which an overview would miraculously disclose itself. At very least he'd thought that if he had to hack his way through buried emotions there would be a retreat open to him, a way back. Bruised and battered he might be, but he'd expected, fundamentally, to remain the person he had always been.

Now it appeared that, despite the distancing features of time, that expectation was flawed. What had been achieved through archives, searches and the census was limited. His journey would not, could not, be simply a research into dead, historical facts. He was now embroiled in other people's lives. Living people. People whose lived-out lives touched those of others.

People like his biological mother, for instance, who, for reasons perhaps known only to her, had made decisions and then had to live with them. Whatever the guilt! Whatever the shame! He knew little about her, other than that she had died shortly before he'd begun his search for her. The poignancy of the timing hit him anew.

And what of those who had been close to her? Those, like Evie, his sister, or Phoebe Hamilton – either of whom had perhaps been hurt by his mother's predicament? What of the others, who might have seen him at his birth, touched him, pronounced upon his future, convinced themselves, and others, that adoption would be for the best and who might, even now, have regrets? There was no escaping the impact his appearance would have on these people. The knock-on effect it might have on their families. Nor was there any means of avoiding the way their lives would impinge upon his.

The brief telephone conversation with Phoebe Hamilton had shaken him. He wished, fervently, he'd written rather than rung. That, after all, was his metier. He knew there were those who would disagree, but in his view there was something more measured about the written word. In its execution and interpretation it had the potential for calm, unhurried deliberation. And having none of the immediacy of the spoken word, it was less threatening.

It was not, he reasoned, that he shrank from further verbal contact with Phoebe because he was vocally or socially inept. Far from it! Whatever his genes might have dictated, his upbringing had offered little option for introversion. Though Dad's side of the family had been numerically small and quietly academic, Bonnie's was extensive and hospitable in the way that only Americans can be. Their home, Matt recalled, had been filled with people, politics, laughter and fun.

He turned to Evie, the small but determined woman who, it appeared, was his sister, and felt a sudden, unfamiliar, sense of protection towards her following the episode with the deer.

'You okay?' he asked, taking his hand from the wheel and laying it briefly over hers.

She nodded, turned to him and smiled, uncertainly.

'Well, that was a first.'

'Sorry. Shoulda heeded your warning. Guess I'm a bit preoccupied about what's coming up. Or not! There's no guarantee the information I'm hoping for will be forthcoming.'

He thought, again, about his daughter's condition. Epilepsy! He'd known almost nothing about the disease other than the stigma attached to it. But still more shocking was the thought that, at this moment, he had no way of ascertaining whether it had a familial link through him.

He brought to mind the letter Sam had written to her grandmother – two pages of round, looped script, more reminiscent of a child, he thought, than a teenager. Sam had little to say about the affliction, other than that she had suffered, to date, only two *petit mal*. Only two, thought Matt, with a shudder. It was two too many in his view. And didn't *petit mal* mean there could, also, be *grand mal* to follow? Proper seizures? Convulsions?

Was that what the future would hold for Sam? Was this the legacy he might have passed on to the daughter he'd last seen on her twelfth birthday? The daughter he'd tried to blot from his mind because remembering was too painful. Well, he could blot her out no more.

'You may want to investigate,' Bonnie had said to him. 'To reassure her. Her mom has told her, categorically, that it's nothing to do with her side of the family. According to Sam, she's adamant that it's on our side. But of course, the poor girl doesn't know there's no genetic link with me, her nana.'

And here he was! In less than thirty minutes he would meet Phoebe Hamilton face to face. You'd think all this – his mind made an expansive sweep of his achievements – would give him the confidence to face up to her. To probe from her the secrets of the past. But even as he psyched himself up, the conviction felt hollow. He was depressingly aware that the results would be out of his hands.

Given Phoebe Hamilton's response on the telephone, would he have continued with this search if it were not for Samantha's needs? Epilepsy was not the sort of infirmity anyone would readily admit to. Was he going to draw a blank?

Emerging from the woods, he began the descent down towards Newton Abbot and Torbay, and then the ring road that would take him to his geographical destination. But would it take him, also, he wondered, to the end of his quest for information? That, he thought, remained to be seen.

Glancing at Matt, I realise he's been deep in thought for some time. I, meanwhile, have been rehearsing various questions in my mind, questions I now feel I must ask before we arrive at the Hamiltons'.

'You said our mother, Libby, wasn't married when she had you. So how come her surname – and yours – was Rae?'

My hair is streaming behind me as we hurtle down the hill past

Newton Abbot race course, it's cooling effect a welcome relief from the relentless heat of the August sun.

'Gee! Well that's the bummer.' Matt glances towards me. 'Some of the research I've done has been via the internet, but I've also been to Somerset House to look at records. So far, I haven't yet managed to locate a marriage certificate for Elizabeth – Libby. I'm rather hoping Aunt Phoebe will be able to shed some light on the matter.'

We both fall silent as we soar across the new bridge at Penn Inn and take the by-pass around Torbay. At the top of the hill, at Gallows Gate, the tors of Dartmoor are clearly visible, a stark silhouette against a cloudless blue sky.

'Wow!' says Mark, taking it all in. 'If only life were so clear cut.'

'That's Haytor you can see over there,' I tell him.

'Haytor? Isn't that where Sir Arthur Conan Doyle is thought to have set his thriller, the *Hound of the Baskervilles*?'

I shrug. 'It's supposed to be somewhere on Dartmoor,' I concur. 'But I don't think anyone knows exactly where.'

We lapse into silence again as Matt negotiates the increasing traffic on the road to Brixham. Once we're clear of the worst of it, I turn again to the matter of my mother's past.

'Are you telling me you've not found any evidence of my parents' marriage either?' I ask.

'No, I'm not saying that at all,' Matt replies. 'Your parents were married in a registry office in London, right? Midsummer's Day '75?'

It takes me a moment to register that Midsummer's Day is the 21st June.

'You're correct in saying it was London. And it was definitely 1975. But you're wrong in thinking it was June. It was, actually, February. February 1st I think, 1975.   And I was born nine months later. 5th November. A Guy Fawkes' bonfire baby.'

Matt keeps his eyes on the road and it strikes me that there's something ominous in his silence and lack of eye contact. Counting, surreptitiously, on my fingers, I do some calculations and realise, suddenly, that the maths doesn't stack up right.

'So when were you born?' I ask, as we approach the traffic lights just before Churston Common and the turning that will take us down to Kingswear.

'Wow!' says Matt again, glancing over his shoulder as he negotiates the junction and a glimpse of the whole of Torbay opens up before us. 'Great view.'

It's true, and it's too good to miss. I turn my head to look.

'The Bay's like a C,' I explain, lifting my hand to indicate the letter of the alphabet. 'You have Torquay at the top, looking South – favourite palm-tree watering hole for the Victorians. And Brixham and Berry Head, with one of the largest fishing fleets in the country, at the bottom, looking due North. They launched some of the ships for the WW2 D-Day landings from there. I believe there's a museum somewhere near Battery Park. Not that I've ever visited.'

Matt nods. 'Sounds interesting. In fact I think I've heard that some of my countrymen were involved in the D-Day launches in these parts.'

The built-in SatNav in the dashboard of Matt's car interrupts with a vocal indication of the route ahead, and pausing at the junction to allow for oncoming traffic, Matt takes the road away from the coast to begin the descent down to the River Dart.

'So?' I return to our earlier topic, 'When is your date of birth?'

'Me? Oh, I'm a harvest baby. No fireworks to announce my coming into the world. Only hard graft to get the crop in before the winter rains.'

I fall silent. There's something telling about Matt's analogy. Something quite negative in his manner of speech. And something significant in what he's not saying.

Have I been in denial, I ask myself? Or is it he who is? I don't want to have to admit it. But if my mother was speaking the truth and she was seventeen when she had me, then she could only have been sixteen, or younger, when she had Matt. Hardly time to fit in two marriages with a divorce between them. Especially as Matt's already got it wrong with the date of my parents' wedding.

Hasn't he?

Chapter Six

Teeth of the Tiger

A YOUNG WOMAN opens the door when Matt and I arrive at the Hamiltons'. Given her petite, blonde, English-rose likeness to Liz, whom I met when she brought Phoebe Hamilton to my counselling rooms, I take this to be her youngest sister, Sophie, the one who booked Phoebe's appointment by phone in the first place. The one who begged me to come down today. Mentally, I rehearse my spiel. My reason for having arrived with Matt. My insistence on staying neutral. My underlying wish to get to know what I'm told is my mother's family. My family!

My concern is lifted, momentarily, by the comical scene unfolding before me.

'Goodness me! You *are* the American crime-writer,' Sophie gushes in girlish tones. 'I've been kidding everyone you might be, ever since you rang.'

Matt switches into teeth-whitened, Florida-tanned, all-American livin-and-lovin-the-dream boy as he offers Sophie his hand.

'And you must be Cousin Sophie?' he says, his Boston accent ever more pronounced as he steps over the threshold.

His eyes widen as he continues to grasp the hand of this attractive young woman, and it's certainly not a cousinly interest taking place before me. Her lowered eyelashes and blushing cheeks say it all. Disney style! Behind them, I'm convinced cupid awaits, arrow at the ready.

Touched, but surplus to requirement, I gaze beyond Sophie at the large, oak-panelled baronial-style hall. The walls are littered with oil paintings in ornate gold frames, and I wonder, for a moment, if I've stepped back in time. Or at least into the wrong film set.

If this is, indeed, my family, as Matt appears to believe, then there's a huge gulf in wealth and social standing between what I experienced as a child and what I see before me. My mother rarely spoke of her past. What I'd learned had come from the mouth of my father. Bitter and condemning, he'd led me to understand there had been some sort of a rift; that my grandmother had been cast adrift, virtually penniless; and that my mother had suffered a pretty miserable childhood, as a consequence.

Was my mother's loss Phoebe Hamilton's gain? I haven't quite worked out the relationship between them, but one thing is clear. Despite my geographical proximity to the Hamiltons, our social standing is poles apart. No wonder we've never met.

'Mummy will be down in a moment,' Sophie says at last, dragging her eyes and hand from Matt's. 'Come on in.'

For the first time, she notices my presence.

'Evie,' I say, aware that although we've spoken on the telephone, we've never actually met. 'Evie Adams.'

Sophie pays no heed to the hand I extend in greeting and appears momentarily confused. Hardly surprising, despite my telephone message warning that I'd be arriving with Matt, when the arrangement I'd made with her originally was that I'd be there, in the background, as mediator if required. My hand shakes as I withdraw it, and my mouth is dry.

'All will be revealed in due course,' says Matt, and instantly Sophie's attention is diverted.

She ushers us into the sitting room, a vast space furnished with plush rugs and carpet, button backed leather sofas, yet more paintings and *objets d'art* and, in one corner, a grand piano. Floor-to-ceiling bay windows reveal sloping lawns leading down to the river, beyond which, on the far side, lies the town of Dartmouth, and Britannia Royal Naval College. Almost before I can take it all in, Sophie introduces us to her father, Phil. Robust in physique, he is clearly frail of mind.

'Libby,' he says, grasping hold of me in a huge bear hug. 'Lovely girl. Phoebe will be so pleased to see you. Thank you for coming.'

He thinks I'm my mother! The realisation takes me by surprise. I suppose, like Matt, he must fancy some resemblance between us though, personally, I've never thought I looked the least bit like either of my parents. 'Milkman's daughter,' my dad would say of me disparagingly whenever we fell out, which we did, frequently. And I'd be left feeling even more insecure.

My childhood frailties are not the fault of this poor man, however. Phil Hamilton smells of mothballs, reminiscent of his wife's aroma when she visited my consulting rooms. Reminding myself of my mission, I prise myself gently from Sophie's father's embrace. When, at last, I break free, he continues to envelop my hand in both of his. Sophie comes to my rescue.

'Now Daddy! Let go of Mrs Adam's hand.'

Turning to me she explains, as if explanation were necessary, that her father's confusion is the result of a stroke. Vascular dementia.

A familiar voice behind me alerts me to Phoebe's arrival. My heart and stomach somersault in an attempt to change places with one another, and I wonder if my brain has deserted me in the process. What on earth was I thinking about? Agreeing to accompany Matt to the home of a client whom he believes to be related to me, and whose own expectations are purely of a professional nature, must rank as one of the most stupid things I have ever done. Apart from marrying Pete, of course! And by contravening the ethical framework for good practice, by which I'm bound, my behaviour will almost certainly lead to the loss of the job I love. I cringe to think what my supervisor will have to say.

Matt and Sophie turn in the direction of the door. I continue walking towards the window, ostensibly to admire the view, in fact to take in an oblique overview of what's going on to one side of me.

'Mummy, you'll never guess what. It *is* Matt McEwan, the crime writer. I told you so.'

'Mrs Hamilton, ma'am.'

I have to hand it to Matt. He could charm the fish out of the sea. Or tame a tiger. Phoebe melts into a pool of virtual ghee.

'An author in the family,' she coos. 'Wasn't your last book made into a film?'

'It was indeed!'

'And didn't I read in the newspaper that your mother had –'

'What a charming place you have here, Aunt Phoebe,' Matt cuts in, before whatever made his mother newsworthy can be revealed. 'Now let me introduce you to –'

The moment has come. I turn – too quickly – and knock a large, blue, Chinese urn from its wooden stand on one side of the bay window. Miraculously, the ornately decorated porcelain piece bounces on the carpet, while the lid rolls across the floor and comes to rest at Phoebe's feet. Her face is inscrutable.

Cheeks aflame, I press my hand to my mouth. Now I'm for it. Not only have I broken trust with my client, I'm within a whisker of breaking up her home and possessions. I hardly dare think of the outcome.

Matt leapt into action. Retrieving both lid and urn, he reassembled them on the stand, his antennae bristling. He could see, instantly, that a situation had arisen. Was he the cause? On one side, scarlet faced, stood Evie; on the other, her cheeks white as chalk, was Aunt Phoebe.

'Aren't you –?' she stuttered, steadying herself on the back of the sofa. 'I don't understand. Did Elizabeth ask you to come? It is Mrs Adams, isn't it?'

Matt looked from one to the other. 'Oh! You two know one another?'

Aunt Phoebe sank down on the sofa.

'No,' said Evie, firmly. 'Not really. We've met. That's all.'

Matt stood stock still. He observed the glance that flashed between the two women. Of complicity? Confrontation? Confusion?

'But *you* two obviously know one another,' Aunt Phoebe said, her tone accusing.

Something was definitely going on. He'd have to sort it. In the meantime –

'Forgive me, Aunt Phoebe. I shoulda warned you I was bringing someone else.'

He seated himself on the sofa beside Aunt Phoebe, half-turned towards her, and flashed the smile he reserved for his most ardent fans.

'I can explain. I asked this lady, Evie Adams, to accompany me. And for very good reason.'

He felt a pang of guilt. Had Sophie not conveyed the message to her mother, when he'd spoken to her on the phone? Should he not have brought Evie? Had he been insensitive? He tried to transport himself into the minds of this family. Did he represent a threat to them in some way? Was the mere concept of a stranger turning up in your midst claiming to be kith and kin upsetting? And turning up with yet another stranger, Evie –

'You're not an item, are you?' asked Sophie, clasping her hands together and sinking down onto a velveteen chair to one side of the marble fireplace.

Matt looked at her. Her face was pale, her eyes troubled. He thought her quite the most beautiful woman he had ever seen, and he'd seen a few. Wearing a cotton sundress in a striking shade of *eau-de-Nil*, her shoulders and legs were bare, revealing her smooth, creamy, skin. Still smiling, and trying to make light of the situation, he shook his head.

'Not exactly –'

A grandfather clock in the corner of the room began a mellifluous chime sequence announcing it was about to strike the midday hour, while on the marble mantelpiece a gilt and ormolu clock chimed a strident and unsynchronised twelve dongs.

'It's Libby!' Sophie's father exclaimed, full of excitement. 'She's come to see us. After all this time. Lovely girl.'

Everyone turned in unison, first to Phil, who had remained, forgotten, by the door, then to Evie, still transfixed in the window.

'Don't be silly, Phil,' said Phoebe but, Matt noticed, without any real conviction.

'He's nearly right.' Matt began, shifting awkwardly on the sofa, aware of his promise to Evie to conceal her identity.

The last chime rang out from the grandfather clock in the corner of the room, fading, gradually, to nothing. For a moment, Matt thought it was going to fall to him to have to break the news. Then

Evie spoke.

'I'm Libby's daughter,' she said, her cheeks flushed, her voice breathy.

'And my sister. Or half-sister,' Matt finished.

A stunned silence ensued. Then Aunt Phoebe said, 'Of course,' as if it were the most natural thing in the world.

Sophie spent the next hour making small talk, and generally attempting to fill and smooth the crack that had appeared between her mother and their guests. By the time she opened the double glass doors leading from the lounge, and showed their guests outside, she was more than ready to sit and relax. The sun was shining and a gentle breeze stirred the foliage, with a rippling effect on the eucalyptus tree halfway down the lawn. On the patio stood the glass-topped garden table, laid, ready for lunch.

'Now, Evie, you sit here. And Matt – no, that's Daddy's place if you don't mind –'

Ushering everyone to their seats, she remained standing. Before them, covered to keep the flies off, stood a simple meal of cold meats and salads which she'd helped her mother select on their last shopping trip. Removing the cloths and cling film, she began passing the dishes around. Finally, seating herself, she unfolded her paper napkin and placed it on her lap.

There were just the five of them, her parents, Matt and Evie and she, herself. Her eldest sister, Liz, had declined lunch but had agreed to join them afterwards 'if she had time'. Somehow, Sophie rather doubted this would be the case.

It was weird, she thought, the way her sisters had reacted to Matt's emergence from the past. Liz, the eldest, was well-known to be taciturn. Awkward, one might say. You never knew what was going on in her head. It was as if she were from a different planet, as the kids at school would say.

But Fiona? No! She was usually much more forthcoming. So why was she so reticent? True, she lived in Birmingham and was newly out of hospital, but she planned to make the journey down to Liz's the following week with her husband, to convalesce, and to collect

Hannah. A few days earlier would have made little difference, one would have thought, given that she could then have been here for Matt's visit.

Thinking now, about their reaction to the news that Matt was coming for lunch, you might almost believe it was down to some guilty secret in the past. But what had they got to hide? Still, looking at her mother's animated features, Sophie comforted herself that at least Mummy appeared to have come round.

'Would you mind passing the mayonnaise to Daddy, please,' she asked Evie, busily handing food around the table and ensuring everyone was comfortable with what was on offer.

Outwardly composed, her brain was actually in over-drive. It was hard to make sense of what she'd learned so far. If she and Libby were cousins – which they must have been if Libby was her mother's niece – and if Evie and Matt were Libby's offspring – then what relation were they to her?

She glanced across the table, then down at her plate. Matt and Evie, she thought, must be – what? – twelve, fourteen years older than her? So they'd be late thirties, early forties? In which case, they surely couldn't be second cousins? Because although only twenty-six, herself, she was a generation above them. So did that make them cousins once-removed? It was all so confusing.

Her eyes flickered again down the length of the table, where Matt and Evie sat opposite one another. They did look like brother and sister, she thought, though Evie was nothing special to write home about, whereas Matt… She shivered. She actually shivered! And was immediately ashamed.

'Would you like any more salad?' she asked of no one in particular. 'Or some more cold meat?'

There were no takers, but the request served the purpose of taking her mind off Matt.

She watched Evie, surreptitiously. Her face was crumpled, and she looked as if she was in pain. It must be awful, Sophie thought, to discover that your mother had borne another child, presumably when unmarried, without your knowing anything about it. Difficult as it must be to acknowledge your parent's failings, Matt's existence

73

would, effectively, have deposed her. Evie would no longer be her mother's eldest. She couldn't begin to imagine how that must feel.

Still, if she and Evie really were cousins, she was glad. She really was. There was something about her, something – wistful? a melancholy? perhaps a yearning for something that eluded her? She couldn't quite put her finger on it, but she found herself feeling ever so slightly sorry for her. At the same time, she was oh, so pleased, that Evie and Matt were not an item.

She caught his eye across the table as she seated herself, and her heart missed a beat. He really was stunning. So handsome!

Concentrate, Sophie, she admonished herself, passing a dish of prawns to Evie and inviting her to help herself. She glanced, again, around the table. With all the evidence of past hostility from her mother and sisters towards these new cousins, it was down to her to make them welcome, she thought. And not just Matt. Evie too.

Matt shifted his weight on the cushion pad of the garden chair and looked down at his plate. Conversation, so far, had skirted around the subject of his mother's circumstances and centred on the means of his search for his biological family. Unacquainted with modern technology, Aunt Phoebe had expressed amazement at what could be achieved on the internet by way of research. It was, she seemed to imply, almost an intrusion of privacy. As if pen and paper records were any different, he thought!

He understood the curiosity surrounding the means of his quest, but suspected it might, also, indicate a reluctance to engage in the real issue. Sooner or later he was going to have to turn the discussion around in order to furnish himself with the answers he required. With another book launch due any day, and the proofs of its sequel to return to his New York publishers, vacations in Devon, however appealing, would be limited.

He raised his head. Phil being too frail, Aunt Phoebe was indicating that Sophie should pour the wine.

'What made you start looking into your background so late in life?' Aunt Phoebe asked. 'Not that I'm implying you're any great age.' She smiled, politely.

Matt grinned. Gee, she wasn't so bad, after all. A queen bee she might be as far as her husband and daughter were concerned, but the formidable telephone voice he'd encountered had been replaced with something altogether more sociable.

'Old enough!' he said.

'But you must have been curious years ago, surely?' Sophie asked. 'Unless, of course, you didn't know until recently that you were adopted?'

Matt shook his head.

'It was never a secret. My parents were always open about it. I guess it was simply that I didn't wanna upset my mom by asking too many questions, or chasing off looking for my birth mother.'

'So what changed?' Aunt Phoebe asked.

Matt raised his glass to his lips and drank briefly. He was used to being scrutinised in his line of work, but this felt different. Uncomfortable.

'My dad died some years ago.' He set his glass down and began spreading butter liberally onto a piece of French bread. 'But although I'd sorta made up my mind I wouldn't do anything while Mom was still around, it was, actually, she who urged me to make a start.'

'Oh?' Sophie paused, in the middle of helping herself to salad. 'Why was that?'

'And how long did it take you to make any headway?' Phoebe asked, simultaneously.

Unwilling to answer Sophie's question at this point, in case the matter of his daughter's epilepsy should prove controversial at best, offensive at worst, Matt turned to Phoebe.

'I live in London at least half the year,' he explained. 'And I'm used to conducting research for my books. So knowing where to find the appropriate records wasn't a problem. But even so, it wasn't that easy to trace Elizabeth – Libby, as you call her.'

'It never is,' said Evie. 'I remember my mother having problems when my birth certificate went missing. I was about to start university, and she couldn't find it anywhere. In the end, she had to get me a new one.'

Sophie stared, open mouthed as Matt looked on. 'How strange,' she said. 'Something similar happened to me when –'

A glass of water shot across the table, soaking the cloth and landing the last dregs in her lap. She gasped as the cold liquid penetrated her thin clothing.

'Phil!' Phoebe exclaimed. 'Do be careful.'

Sophie grabbed her napkin and began dabbing at herself, while her mother did likewise with the table.

'I'll have to go and change,' said Sophie. 'I'm soaked to the skin.'

Matt rose to his feet and pulled Sophie's chair out for her. Was it his imagination, or was what he'd witnessed been contrived? He could have sworn Phil was nowhere near the water that had been spilled. He shook his head. Get over yourself, he thought. He was becoming paranoid, envisaging secrecy and stealth at every turn. He seated himself once more.

When Phoebe and Evie had finished moving the dishes around and drying the top of the glass table, conversation turned to other things. Matt admired the house, the garden, the view.

'Stunning,' he exclaimed. 'And so peaceful. You must have found it very different from when you were living in London.'

By the time Sophie returned, order had been restored, the trifle was being served, and Matt launched forth on the next part of his story.

'I thought I was onto something just before Christmas,' he continued in answer to Sophie's queries. 'The records showed Libby had been living in Scotland, as a child.'

'How exciting,' said Sophie, seating herself again.

'Not really,' Matt said. 'I drove all the way up to Glasgow and went to the address but no one seemed to have heard of her. Or at least, if they had they weren't for saying.'

'I suppose people close ranks if a stranger appears to be prying into someone's private life,' said Aunt Phoebe.

Matt looked at Sophie. An odd expression passed across her face. Was this how she and Aunt Phoebe had reacted when he'd telephoned in the first place? Had mother and daughter 'closed ranks' on him?

'You may be right,' he said. 'Even the local newsagent was cagey.'

'And what about your father?' Sophie asked, belatedly finishing her first course and helping herself to trifle. 'Have you been able to trace him?'

Matt shrugged. 'I don't know who he was. *Father unknown* it says on my birth certificate. I sure am hoping I can get some answers here.'

Phil began to say something, but choked on his words. Immediately, Phoebe began to thump him on the back, remonstrating with him about speaking with his mouth full.

'How awful,' Sophie sighed when the moment passed, and Matt felt moved to see her casting an affectionate glance in the direction of her father.

'What I don't understand,' said Evie, clearly addressing him but looking down at the table, 'is that you used three surnames for my mother when you came to see me.'

Matt felt everyone's eyes upon him.

'Myers, Rae and Gore.' He looked at each of them in turn. 'Libby Rae seems to have been the name held by the orphanage from which I was adopted. And it's the name on my adoption papers.'

Evie turned to Phoebe. 'So isn't it possible that Rae was the surname of Matt's father?' she asked. 'And if so, why did the birth certificate state him as *unknown*?'

Matt nodded, grateful for Evie's intervention. 'That's exactly what I've been wondering,' he admitted.

Phoebe raised her wine glass to her lips and took a sip before replying.

'Libby was a very mixed up young woman,' she said. 'She'd had an unhappy childhood.'

Seeing Evie frown, and feeling himself responsible for her distress, Matt tried to catch her eye, and failed. She remained looking directly at Phoebe.

'But you must have known my mother?' she said, her tone cool and professional. 'Known who she was seeing?'

'Oh yes!' Fully recovered from his fit of choking, Phil spoke up from the end of the table. 'She saw a lot of us. Lived with us on and off.'

'Phil!' A frown passed across Phoebe's face, quite startling in its ferocity. Again, Matt sensed this air of secrecy. Did Phil know more than he was saying? Was Aunt Phoebe intent upon silencing him? If so, what was there to hide?

'So you knew her well?' he asked, setting down his knife and fork.

'We were very close as children,' Phoebe admitted.

'There wasn't much difference in age between you, as I recall,' said Matt.

'Five? Six years?' said Phoebe. 'I was the youngest of a big family, so my eldest sister was grown-up when I was born. When Libby came along I thought of her as my baby sister. I suppose it was only natural.'

'But didn't she live in Glasgow, as Matt suggested earlier?' asked Sophie. Phoebe nodded. 'Her father was a Scot.'

'So he would have been my maternal grandfather,' said Evie, setting aside her napkin, her meal finished. 'And yours, of course, Matt.' She turned towards him and Matt sat back in his chair. 'I guess so,' he said.

'I don't think I ever met him,' Evie continued. 'In fact I'm pretty sure I've only seen one photograph of him when my mother was young. There's no sign of him in my parents' wedding photo.'

Matt whirled in his chair, towards Evie.

'You have photos of our mother? Of course you must have! I'd love to see them.'

'I have some, too,' said Phoebe, setting her napkin aside. 'In fact, I have a wedding photo. Look, why don't you two walk down to the river while Sophie and I clear up. And then we'll go through to the sitting room and I'll see if I can find them.'

'Good idea!' Sophie began clearing the table. Aunt Phoebe rose to her feet to help.

Matt turned to Evie to see if she was happy to comply with Aunt Phoebe's suggestion. She looked bewildered. Which was exactly how he felt. At least if they went for a walk together, he thought, they could summarise all that had passed.

Chapter Seven

Spilling the Beans

THE AUGUST SUN is relentless as Matt and I set off for our walk down to the river; as relentless as the shock I've been experiencing since our arrival at the Hamiltons'. My brain is teeming, but professional and social etiquette prohibit my conveying these fears aloud. Together we make our way in silence down the grassy slopes and wooded hillside of the Hamiltons' garden, until the rocky foreshore of the estuary is in sight and we can go no further.

To our left, on the seaward side, lies the town of Kingswear, a plethora of tall, pastel-coloured terraced houses, while upstream, the hills and valleys, through which the River Dart has carved its path, gently enfold us. Side by side, we watch myriad bobbing boats in the marina, until Matt turns to face me, a frown scoring lines on his brow.

'Is it just me?' he asks, hesitant yet clearly in need of answers. 'I mean, I know I tend to see everything through the eyes of a crime writer, but did you find anything odd about what was going on over lunch?'

I'm glad he's raised the matter. His eyes are inscrutable behind dark glasses, but the way in which his mouth is set indicates beyond doubt the extent of his bafflement. And it's a feeling I share.

'Very odd!' I respond. 'I kept wondering if it was just me. Thought I must be reading too much into the situation. It's not just writers who over-analyse you know.'

Matt looks relieved. He nods, and tugs at his hair.

'No. There's definitely something going on. All that business with Phil. He obviously thought you were Libby. And he obviously remembers her well! But every time he brought something up about her – about the past – Aunt Phoebe shut him up. Why? What's she hiding?'

Upstream, the higher ferry, also known as the floating bridge, begins its journey across the river from Dartmouth. We watch for a moment as the sailing dinghies in its path give way, going about to avoid collision where necessary, their booms swinging, their sails luffing in the breeze.

'And then there was the matter of Sophie's lost birth certificate,' I say, recalling the look on her face when I'd recounted the story of my parents' trip to London to furnish me with the necessary documentation when I went to uni.

Matt turns to me, a frown on his face.

'Yeah! What was that all about? And what happened with the glass of water? Did you see who knocked it over? It sure as hell wasn't Phil. But he got the blame.'

'No, I didn't see who did it, I have to admit. But I know for a fact it wasn't Phil. He was drinking from his own glass at the time.'

'Well I'd swear it was Aunt Phoebe,' says Matt. 'But it all happened so fast it's difficult to be sure.'

I push my hair from my face as the breeze increases, and try to recall the scene.

'You're right,' I tell Matt, unable to keep the excitement from my voice. 'And her immediate reaction was to blame Phil. Do you think she *is* trying to cover something up?'

Matt has removed his jacket and left it up at the house, as I have mine. He shoves his hands in his trouser pockets, and I'm aware, as he does so, of the effect of the air rippling through the black hair on his arms. I'm filled with a sudden yearning for Scott.

'I'm quite sure Aunt Phoebe has something to hide!' Matt is emphatic. 'Didn't you notice, she interrupted Phil again when I asked about my father? Phil may be a bit gaga about what's goin' on now, but I'm pretty damn sure he remembers the events of that time. Don't they say it's only short-term memory that's affected for people with his condition?'

Matt's right. Thinking about it, I can see the pattern.

'So you think that every time Phil threatens to spill the beans, Phoebe shuts him up?'

'Absolutely.'

We fall silent again, the only sound the water lapping against the hulls of the yachts and power boats berthed in the marina. Then I raise the question that's uppermost in my mind.

'She said she had a wedding photo. Phoebe. Is that of my parents or yours? It can't be mine, because they were married in a registry office and the only people there were the two witnesses. And it can't be your parents, because if they were married, your father would have been named on your birth certificate.'

A look of perplexity passes across Matt's face. He shakes his head.

'No idea! I haven't located a marriage certificate for Libby at all, yet. But how else can you explain the two surnames, Rae and Gore?'

'Unless, of course, she wasn't married to my dad, either. That's what you're thinking, isn't it?'

'Of course not! I may not have a copy of the wedding certificate, but I've seen the records of your parents' marriage. Besides, you wouldn't have a wedding photo if they weren't married.'

Feeling somewhat foolish, I turn away from the trees on the river bank, and Matt takes my hand to help me down from a rocky ledge onto the foreshore.

'If you don't mind my sayin' Sis, you seem a bit – agitated, hostile toward me. I realise this is all comin' newer to you than to me, but, hey! I'm on your side.'

He continues to hold my hand, and I feel, quite suddenly, overcome. This guy, unlike some in my life, is genuine in his attitude to me. More than that, he cares! Tears well in my eyes. And to my shame, I realise that despite counselling others to *face their fears*, rather than *take flight* or *fight* them, I've failed to do so myself. I've been in denial. I've buried the hurts I've experienced at the hands of my dad and my husband, Pete. Pretended to Grace, and to myself, that those wounds never existed. Or at least, if they did, that I've dealt with them. And now? Now this new brother has disarmed me. Found me out. Revealed my vulnerability.

'Hey,' he says, seeing my tears and putting an arm around my shoulders. 'Hey! We're in this together. We may not have grown up together but the fact is you're my little sis, and I'm the big bro. If you want one of course?'

Do I? Of course I do!

He produces a clean handkerchief from his pocket.

'Look at it this way,' he says, releasing me so I can blow my nose and wipe my eyes, 'you got the older, improved model without havin' to endure the obnoxious pigtail-pullin', lad about town of yesteryear.'

I laugh out loud, and a startled rook flaps overhead, cawing in protest.

'That's better,' says Matt. 'Now take in this view, cos we're bound to be asked to report to Aunt Phoebe. Then we'd better head back before they send out a search party.'

I feel so much better as we walk back to the house and go inside, where an elegant tea trolley bearing coffee and chocolate mints awaits us in the lounge. Phoebe has several photograph albums piled on the table, plus a few old cardboard boxes of loose, grainy images, and Sophie is sitting cross legged on the floor looking through them.

'Oh there you are,' says Phoebe, adding, as Matt predicted, 'I thought you must have got lost.'

'Beautiful view. Lovely location,' says Matt, equally predictably switching into – No, Evie! Cynicism. Don't go there.

'It is, isn't it?' Phoebe settles back on the sofa, clearly well pleased with Matt's response. 'We moved here from London shortly before Sophie was born. Twenty-five years ago.'

'Twenty six!' Sophie corrects her. 'In fact, nearer twenty-seven. And it was *after* I was born.'

She sounds like a little girl – *I'm nine years, eleven months and twenty-six days old* – trying to establish her maturity in the face of opposition. Actually, now I think about it, ever since we met she's struck me as quite juvenile, more adolescent than a woman in her mid to late twenties. I glance across the room, first in Sophie's direction, then Phoebe's, shaking my head, metaphorically. Nope! I would never have put Sophie as a twenty-six-year old. Not that she could be any less given Phoebe's age

'Yes, well,' Phoebe concedes, not without some irritation, I notice. 'The previous owner of this place was the son of an earl. Sadly, he drowned in a boating accident. Elizabeth and Fiona were still living at home then so we needed the space. It's only recently we split it into apartments.'

I endeavour to hide the smile that threatens to reveal my view of Phoebe. Clearly, she feels the need to boast a little in the presence of an eminent author.

'Now, Evie,' she turns to me, 'how do you like your coffee?'

'Oh, as it comes,' I reply, with the utmost diplomacy.

'Sophie, will you pour, and I can then show our guests the photographs we have of Libby.'

Obediently, Sophie leaps to her feet.

With coffee served, we seat ourselves on the sofa, Matt and I, with Phoebe in the middle. She opens the first album, and together we peruse the black and white images. First up are those of a chubby baby Libby, followed by colour photos of her as a sad-looking little girl, and then as a flighty-looking adolescent. Finally, as Phoebe turns to the last page, we see a wedding photo, but with my mum as the bridesmaid and, unless I'm very much mistaken, Phoebe and Phil Hamilton as bride and groom.

'I thought it was my parents' wedding you were going to show us?' I blurt out before I can stop myself.

Phoebe rises from the sofa, crosses the room and seats herself in an easy chair, opposite Phil, leaving the album with me.

'I'm sorry,' she says, and for the first time I detect a grain of sympathy in her towards me.

Why I should have expected Phoebe to have a photograph of my parents' wedding I don't know. There's no evidence, in the photographs in my possession at home, of the Hamiltons having attended the event. I turn back to the photograph on my lap and stare at the young woman I know to be my mother. She's dressed in a long bridesmaid's gown, her dark, shoulder-length hair ripples about her face, and her floral headdress is slightly askew.

'She looks,' I hesitate, unwilling to imply that she might be inebriated. 'She's obviously enjoying herself.'

Phoebe smiles. 'That's Phil's brother she's hanging onto. His best man. They both enjoyed the same sense of humour. And your mother was a pretty girl. Quite a head-turner. She enjoyed the attention.'

'But I thought you said she'd had an unhappy childhood?'

Phoebe nods. 'Indeed! As Phil indicated earlier, Libby and her mother, my sister Beatrice, spent a lot of time with my mother. Bea's marriage wasn't good. Her husband would pack her off with Libby on protracted visits until things calmed down between them. Or, more likely, until my father packed them off back home to Glasgow.'

'Glasgow?' Matt exclaims. 'So how come I couldn't trace her when I went there?'

Phoebe shrugs and shakes her head.

'I've no idea.'

Sophie, I notice, is sitting enrapt.

'Please go on,' I entreat our hostess.

Phoebe puts her chin in her hand and gazes back into the past.

'The frequent visits to my mother meant Libby and I spent a lot of time together as children. We grew up like sisters. She was the baby sister I never had. Which was lovely as we got older, because my sisters married and left home, and my brothers were – well, they were insufferable!'

Matt gives me a not-so-secret grin at the mention of insufferable brothers. Phil speaks up, addressing Phoebe.

'Jack was a sponger,' he says. 'Never worked a day in his life. Took your mother for a ride.'

'Yes, well, they don't want to hear about Jack,' says Phoebe. She turns to Matt. 'My mother, your great-grandmother, was widowed when she was quite young. She and my father ran a series of hotels in London during their marriage. Mother continued to do so after my father's death.'

'You were saying how much you enjoyed having my mother to stay,' I remind Phoebe.

'We had a wonderful time together as teenagers,' she says, the glazed look of recall in her eyes. 'Of course, I was that much older so I was working some of the time. And she didn't live with us full time. Her mother needed her at home. Or rather, her father did when her mother became too difficult to manage.'

'Oh?' Matt pricks up his ears at the mention of Beatrice being 'difficult to manage', and I imagine he must be wondering whether this is a euphemism for something more sinister. If so, Phoebe is not for saying.

'Let's just leave it at that.' She sets her coffee cup back on the table. 'She – wasn't well. She could be – difficult at times.'

Phil begins to speak, but is silenced by Phoebe. Matt appears to accept the deviation graciously, but I can see the spark of interest that remains in his eyes.

'So what happened about Libby?' he asks.

Phoebe visibly relaxes. 'It was sad. Naturally, when Phil and I married, she and I spent less time together. Well, you can understand. I had a home to create, and a husband to look after. Libby, so I understand, went a bit – wild, I suppose you'd say. When she found out I was expecting a baby – I don't know. There was nothing I could do about it.'

Phoebe gets to her feet, begins to clear away the photograph albums and indicates that Sophie should do likewise with the trolley. It's clear that, however frustrating, we've got as far as she's willing to go. At least for now.

'Aunt Phoebe,' Matt gets to his feet. 'You've bin great. So generous with the hospitality and information you've shared with us. I couldn't have asked for more. I hope we can keep in touch.

'In fact, I know! Do you ever come to London? That book of mine you mentioned, the one that was made into a film? Well, the sequel's about to launch with a reading and signing. Let me treat you. All of you. How about it?'

Sophie, who has been quietly, and adoringly taking in all Matt has to say, clasps her hands together like a small girl, her eyes alight with excitement.

'Oh, Mummy, do let's. How thrilling. And we could show Matt – and Evie, too, of course – around Grandma's properties. They could see where you and Libby grew up and went to school.'

'Why thank you,' Matt says, effusively, obviously missing the fact that in Sophie's eyes I am merely an add-on. 'That would be great.'

By the time we've waved goodbye and are in Matt's car speeding back up the hill from Kingswear to Torbay and then Exeter, it's a *fait accompli*.

Matt drove up the hill away from the Hamiltons' home in silence. Traffic was heavy on the main road between Brixham and Torquay, a consequence of the Bank Holiday, he guessed. Given the alluring qualities of the translucent aquamarine waters of the Bay before him, it was no surprise that holidaymakers flocked to the location. What was a surprise was the way in which the day had panned out. Mentally, in author mode once more, he summed up the stories behind each of the characters he'd met that day.

Sophie he'd thought stunningly beautiful, her delicate features like that of a china doll, her figure lean and lithe. Yet there was something odd about her demeanour – an immaturity he couldn't quite fathom, a childishness that didn't sit well with her. Had it been there when she'd greeted them at the door? He thought not, but couldn't be sure. Without doubt, though, it had become increasingly apparent when in the presence of her parents. Or rather, her mother.

And what of Phil and Aunt Phoebe? Phil, dependent upon his wife and others because of his dementia, was difficult to assess. He would, Matt guessed, have had autonomy during his working life, when operating as a general practitioner of medicine. But would that have been true, also, of his domestic arrangements? Somehow, Matt doubted it. Phoebe, for all her graciousness and hospitality throughout the day, was quite obviously the matriarch, the one to whom all other members of the family were expected to defer.

His mind returned to the issues he and Evie had raised during their walk down to the river. Gee, he could barely believe what they'd witnessed over lunch. The silencing of Phil. The not-so-accidental spilling of the glass of water!

What was more disturbing, by half though, was the way Evie had reacted to him. Why so defensive? Why so hostile to him? Wasn't it her parents' marriage certificate they'd been discussing? And – yeah

– hadn't they had a similar disparity about dates on the way down in the car? The date of her parents' marriage? His birth date? And hers. What was that all about?

Matt glanced out of the car window to one side, marvelling again at the dark silhouette of Dartmoor's crags and tors in stark contrast to the clear blue sky above. If only life were so simple! So easily defined.

He looked sideways at Evie. They'd been travelling for a good thirty minutes since leaving the Hamiltons', both lost in their own thoughts, and would soon be approaching the Penn Inn flyover. Matt changed down a gear ready to filter into the single lane. As he did so, Evie turned to him.

'I know it's none of my business,' she said, 'but I just wondered why you didn't tell Phoebe about your daughter's illness? Or at least enquire if there was anyone else in the family with epilepsy?'

Matt dragged his mind back to the matter Evie had raised – the very reason for his visit in the first place.

'I guess I didn't think it appropriate when we were all together,' he replied.

Out of the corner of his eye, he saw Evie nod her head in affirmation.

'I suppose not. Pity you couldn't have got her on her own, though.'

'Mmm. But it was pretty obvious there were things she didn't wanna talk about. I thought it would make her hostile if I pushed too hard.'

'But she did allude to some kind of illness, didn't she? Her sister's.' Matt glanced towards Evie, trying to assess her reaction. Phoebe's sister was, in fact, their grandmother. Was Evie's use of the phrase 'her sister' an attempt to distance herself from the relationship?

'Yeah. Libby's mom. Our grandmother.' He spelled it out. 'But there was nothing Phoebe said to indicate she was epileptic. *Difficult* was the word she used, as I recall.'

'So what does that mean?' Evie persisted. 'You didn't think to follow through?'

Matt cleared his throat.

'Better to take a softly-softly approach, methinks, than risk antagonising Aunt Phoebe,' he said, choosing his words with care. 'But of course, you're free to do what you think best.'

Evie shook her head. 'No. I'm sorry. This is your investigation, not mine. I've no right to interfere.'

Matt glanced sideways at the slight figure beside him. 'It may've bin me that started it,' he said, gently, 'but I do understand how unsettling it must be for you. I've had more time than you to get used to the idea. Evie, let's get one thing clear. The last thing I want is to upset you.'

'I'm sorry,' Evie said again. 'I'm being oversensitive. As you say, I just need a bit of time to get used to it all.'

'Course you do. I understand.'

With the flyover behind them, Matt put his foot to the floor. Crossing the bridge over the River Teign, he took a quick look out of the window at the mud flats and reed beds below, then down to the broad open reaches of the river's mouth and sea beyond.

Perhaps he'd expected too much in the way of unity from Evie? This was not her problem. And her concern, after all, was not for herself but for him. She was only trying to steer him in what she perceived as the right direction. But given Aunt Phoebe's initial reaction to his appearance on the scene, and especially to the revelation as to why Evie was accompanying him, he felt he'd taken the right approach. Better to leave the door open to future meetings than risk raising her ire and having them closed. Perhaps forever.

'I gotta admit,' he said turning briefly to Evie, 'I'm intrigued to know why Libby's mother – our grandmamma – was considered *difficult*. Not to mention a few other things. There sure are more questions than answers at this stage. Let's hope we get somewhere soon.'

Chapter Eight

Further Revelations

SOPHIE STOOD AT the window in her parents' lounge, staring down at the grey river below, reminiscing about the events of the day. As predicted, Liz had not put in an appearance. Which was a shame because, as the eldest, she must have lived through some of the experiences Matt and Evie had raised. She might, therefore, have been able to shed some light on various matters. Or not!

Why, for instance, was Aunt Beatrice deemed so difficult? What had caused the rift between her and the rest of the family? Why would no one speak of it? Sophie shook her head in disbelief. There was no point in denying it that she could see! Yet it was perfectly obvious that whenever Beatrice's name was raised, the subject was deftly put to one side. If it wasn't too fanciful a thought, one might almost suppose from various odd episodes throughout the day, that there was some kind of mystery afoot. The sort of dark, psychological thriller so loved by some of her pupils. She sighed.

Her mother put her head around the door, effectively putting an end to her reverie.

'Oh, there you are!' she said, with what Sophie took to be a certain displeasure in her voice. 'I'll be in the dining room putting things away if you need me.'

Riddled with guilt, Sophie turned. But before she could apologise for her inactivity, her mother added, pointedly, 'There's still a lot to do.'

'Would you like me to give you a hand in the dining room before I clear up here, Mummy?' Sophie asked, aware that her mother would be storing away her best silver, porcelain and glassware, all of which were reserved for special occasions such as today's hospitality for Matt and Evie.

Clearly satisfied, her mother nodded. 'If you wouldn't mind putting the photographs away. It's the heavy boxes I can't manage. And I can't trust your father to do it properly. I've left him emptying the coffee grounds in the garden, to feed the hydrangeas. Mind you, he probably won't know which plants are which! But no matter. They'll keep the slugs away, wherever he puts them.'

Leaving the door ajar, she departed, while Sophie set to in the lounge, plumping up cushions, retrieving the odd coffee cup that had been overlooked, and generally straightening things up. Then she turned to the boxes of photographs, replacing them in the cupboard under the stairs from which she'd taken them earlier in the day.

It was back-breaking work and, twenty minutes later, she was glad to be nearing the end. Picking up the last carton, a particularly heavy plastic storage box, she adjusted her hold, and was about to move off when a further album slipped from the coffee table to the floor. It must have been tucked out of sight beneath the container, she thought, though why that should be, she couldn't imagine.

Carefully, she deposited the box on one side of the table and picked up the errant album. A colour photograph protruded from the pages. A wedding photo. Sophie examined it, briefly. The bride and groom, standing outside a registry office, were unknown to her, as were the two witnesses. She turned it over. '*Mike Gore and Libby*', it read, in her mother's perfect looped handwriting, followed by the date.

Of course! She turned the photograph over again and studied the faces before her. She'd never actually met Mike Gore, and wasn't at all sure she'd come across Libby either. Her mother had always spoken warmly of the childhood friendship she and Libby had shared, but rarely mentioned her adult life. Other than the fact that Libby's husband was a town councillor in Sheffield, and that it had been an unhappy marriage, Sophie knew nothing more, though again a vague impression of secrecy hung in the air whenever their names were mentioned.

How, she wondered now, had the photograph been overlooked? Hadn't Mummy told Evie she didn't possess a photograph of Libby's wedding? So had she forgotten she had this one? Or had she set it on one side to show their guests, and it had inadvertently been hidden beneath the box? Sophie shrugged.

Mummy had obviously intended to show it to Evie, she surmised, because she wouldn't, otherwise, have set it apart from the others. There was no point in holding her to account for her omission. She'd take responsibility, herself, pop it in an envelope and take it in to Evie next time she was in Exeter. Sophie dropped the wedding photograph into her rucksack, picked up the box again, and stashed it away with the others in the depths of the hall cupboard.

'That's everything back as it should be,' she said to her mother, putting her head round the dining room door. 'If there's nothing else, I'll make a move now, Mummy. Don't want to miss the last ferry home.'

With obvious discomfort, Phoebe rose from her knees in front of the sideboard where she'd been replacing the china.

'Thank you, m'dear. See you next week for shopping, then.'
Sophie gave a silent sigh.

'Great day, today,' she said, making a deliberate and habitual attempt to counter any negative thoughts. 'Well done, Mummy. Hope you're pleased with how it all panned out?'

'Yes, I think it went well.' Phoebe's face and voice were expressionless.

'I'm sure Matt appreciated all you'd done for him. Evie too. And isn't it exciting that we've been invited to his book launch in London! Certainly something for you to brag about to your friends.'

The light in her mother's eyes said it all. Gratified, Sophie left for home.

Once again, I've been chatting with Scott who, I'm glad to say, will soon be returning from America to his London base in time for the new intake at the theological college where he lectures. Having filled him in with all the details about my newly extended family, or at least, as much as I'm permitted to reveal, I then tell him about Matt's invitation to his book launch in London.

'Not that I shall be able to go,' I say, sitting at my desk at the end of the working day.

'Because of the costs involved?' asks Scott, his eyebrows raised as I watch him on the screen.

'Well, with travel and accommodation –'

'Let me help. Please.'

Unused to such generosity, I find it difficult to accept.

'I've too many commitments,' I protest, shaking my head. 'No can do.'

'Pity!' says Scott, before ringing off. 'It would have been good to see you.'

It is, actually, a month or more to Matt's book launch. Inevitably, during that time, the ethical procedures of my profession demand that I speak to my supervisor but, before doing so, I want to talk things through with my counsellor-cum-mentor, Grace.

When I visit her in a small village just outside Exeter, she greets me and takes me through to her counselling room, a converted garage decorated in soothing blues and greens, adorned with an assortment of potted plants. I settle into the black leather swivel chair she provides for clients and those she mentors, and begin.

'It appears that I not only have an older brother I knew nothing about,' I tell her, without preamble, 'but it seems my mother might have been married before she met my dad!'

Grace raises an eyebrow then studies my face for a moment.

'How did you receive the news?' she asks.

I guess it must be obvious to Grace that I'm barely coping. Making a conscious effort to relax, I look into the distance and silently recite my transcendental meditation: *Peace, be still.* When I feel sufficiently at ease, I turn back to Grace, with a manufactured smile in place.

'Discovering that your mother has deceived you all your life is hardly the sort of thing that comes up every day,' I reply, evenly. 'Naturally, it was a shock when I found out.'

Grace nods, sympathy written on her features.

'And now? How do you feel about it since you've had time to

assimilate the information?'

These are the standard interrogation procedures of a counsellor, designed to bring a client to a point of clarity, recognition. Consequently, they come as no surprise to me and I give due consideration to my emotional response. Nevertheless, I find it hard to put into words.

'I – I find it difficult to believe. For a start, she was too young! I don't see how she could have had time to be married and divorced before meeting my dad.'

The conclusions this conjures up in me are horrendous. Bigamy? Adultery? I stare into the green depths of a Venus flytrap plant in the corner of the room, and close my mind to such thoughts. Grace, her face smooth and bland, waits for me to continue, but I've nothing to add.

'Do you think your father was aware your mother had another child?' she asks, patiently.

'Good question! That's exactly what I've been asking myself ever since Matt turned up on the doorstep. And the answer is, I haven't a clue. I've no idea what Dad knew, if anything.'

'Mmm. I see.'

'As you know, things got worse between him and me shortly before he died. Dad may have been aware of a previous marriage, or of a child born out of wedlock prior to his marriage to my Mum. Or it might have come as a complete shock to him after they were married. I don't suppose I'll ever know. And to tell the truth, even if my parents were still around now, I'm not sure I'd have had the nerve to raise the subject with either of them.'

'Yes, I can see that. So what does the new half-brother have to say?'

I fidget in my chair, reluctant to incriminate myself by admitting it was Phoebe Hamilton who had revealed the information about my mother, not Matt.

'He's very nice. Kind. Understanding. Affectionate. Typical American. I think, when we get to know one another better, we might become quite close. I like to think so, anyway.'

I'm being evasive, and I imagine Grace is aware of it. Sure enough, she persists in raising the matter.

'If he's uncovered an earlier marriage, he must know something more. What's he said?'

'Well –' I draw breath deep into my lungs. 'It wasn't actually he who told me.'

Grace lowers her chin, surveys me over the top of her glasses.

'Do you want to tell me about it?'

Not really, I think, knowing I have little option.

For the next half an hour, while she sits in silence, I fill her in with the events of the past few weeks: the circumstances of Phoebe Hamilton's appointment with me; my impromptu meeting with Matt McEwan in The Royal Clarence Hotel; his disclosures to me; my illicit visit to the home of the Hamiltons. Do my clients feel this uncomfortable, I wonder, fixing my eyes on the threadbare patch of carpet beneath my chair, evidence, surely, of the embarrassed scuffing of feet other than my own.

Grace continues to say nothing for some moments when I finish. I feel wretched.

'You're going to tell me I'm a disgrace to my profession; that I've breached every convention in the rule book; that you're going to have to report me, and I shall be struck off.'

Grace shakes her head.

'Evie! It's true, that you've done things you shouldn't have done and you've broken the rules, but would you do what you've suggested, if the boot were on the other foot? Would you report me? Would you think me deserving of being struck off?'

I shake my head, tears of misery and remorse welling in my eyes. I feel so foolish. All the years of training, of self-assessment, of cognitive restructuring. The term *physician heal thyself* again comes to mind.

'My guess is you had an inkling something was amiss when you first met Mrs Hamilton, and later your half-brother?'

'I s'pose. I was convinced I knew Phoebe. She looked so – familiar, somehow. I thought we must have met before. I even asked her if we had. Then, when Matt came to see me – no! Not instantly. Later. When he told me he was my half-brother, the penny dropped. It was like looking at myself in the mirror.'

'Exactly! You responded not as a practitioner but with a subconscious, primeval recognition that defied all normal responses. Are you in so low an emotional state that you really think I would condemn you?'

I am, by this time, properly in tears. Grace responds in the measured manner of all counsellors, passes me a box of tissues, and allows me to cry myself out.

'There,' she says, when my shame and embarrassment are spent. 'Give yourself some space now. Perhaps it might be an idea for you to see your GP, get yourself signed off work for a few weeks? Give yourself time to come to terms with everything. And next time we speak we can work through what you want to do next.'

The relief that floods through me, following my visit to Grace, is immeasurable. It's as if I've had a full-body-and-brain plaster-cast removed. A ridiculous analogy, I know, but it pretty well sums up the constraints I've felt in the past few weeks. I feel liberated. At least, in part. A consultation with my supervisor has followed and, although we've agreed that I don't need to take time off work unless I find it necessary, it's been made clear to me, as I already know, that my relationship with the Hamilton family must remain entirely non-professional from now on.

Matt, of course, despite a busy pre-launch schedule in London, has kept in touch with me throughout, and continues to do so. You might think his excitement at having discovered he has a sister would be infectious. In fact, it has the opposite effect on me. I find myself backing off. His enthusiasm is just too effusive. Typical of a gushing American, I tell myself, self-righteously.

And then the guilt kicks in. Professional and personal. How can I be so cynical? So judgemental? Particularly when he has good reason to be pursuing his quest for knowledge about his family. Am I averse to change, I ask myself when I return home at the end of each day? Overly protective of my privacy? Or is it that I'm too insecure to face the possibility that it might be my mother who's passed on the faulty gene that's caused Matt's daughter's condition?

Feeding Pumpkin one evening, I realise I have passed the first hurdle in behavioural modification! I have identified the problem: my insecurity. An underlying, deep-seated, anxiety about who I am. A foreboding that has its roots in my infancy. A dread that I might, one day, learn that all is not as it seems.

The clarity this brings me floods through my thought processes. Facing the truth, I realise I see Matt as the trigger. In my mind, he has taken the place of my father as the cause of my unease. In my mind! That's the key. It's not *de facto*.

Poor Matt! Evaluating my response to his appearance on the scene, I can see I've done him a disservice. In order to change my behaviour, I need to develop a better emotional outlook. I determine to relax, to be more welcoming to my half-brother, perhaps, even, to rejoice in my new status as a younger sister.

Gradually, over the next few weeks, I begin to look forward to his calls.

'You do realise our grandmother was struck out of her father's will?' I ask him one evening, when I'm curled up on the sofa with Pumpkin on my lap. 'Not that I've ever set eyes on it.'

'Yeah, I've been wondering about that. No reason was ever given for that decision. And I didn't like to ask if you knew anything more, because I can see how much this whole thing has upset you.'

Guilt kicks in, instantly.

'I'm sorry.' I fondle Pumpkin's neck, her silky ears. 'I've been a bit of a pain, haven't I?'

'Not at all. It's perfectly understandable.' Matt turns up the American accent. 'Neurotic *nouveau riche* Yank turns up on the doorstep seeking roots in Mother England, watcha gonna do? Run a mile, of course.'

I laugh, and a startled cat jumps from my lap, goes to the door and looks round at me to open it. Still holding the phone, I let her out into the garden.

He's right! I had run a mile. I closed down, emotionally. Shut him out. What must that have been like for him? Ejected from the family when he was still only a few months old. Taken from his native country and culture, raised by adoptive parents, and then cold-shouldered by me, his half-sister? I vow to make amends.

'Seems hard, doesn't it?' I return to the front room. 'There's Beatrice, our grandmother, deemed to be difficult by her sister, Phoebe, and she's given the ultimate rejection by her family. That must have hurt. Finding she was the only one to be cut out of the will.'

At the other end of the phone, Matt is silent. Then he says, 'You do realise I have a copy of the will, don't you?'

I do know, of course, but I'm unable to let on it was Phoebe who told me when she first came to my counselling rooms. Brother or not, I'm still bound by the ethics of confidentiality. It's just one of those things.

'A copy of our great-grandfather's will?' I ask.

'Yeah. But also our great-grandmother's. I won't say anymore now, but there's something I think you oughta see, Evie. When you come up to Town for the launch.'

I haven't yet had the courage to tell Matt I shall have to decline his invitation. Another hurdle to be overcome.

'I'm afraid I'm not going to be able to make it,' I begin, and there follows a debate as to the whys and wherefores. But as far as the matter of my grandmother's will is concerned, he won't be drawn, I realise that. So with Pumpkin jumping on the windowsill and asking to be let in again, I bid him goodbye, none the wiser.

Matt put the phone down, following his call with Evie, and immediately dialled Sophie's home number. Before his departure from the Hamiltons', they'd exchanged contact details in a hurried and somewhat shy manner, more reminiscent of adolescent romance than that of adult acquaintances. It had been a long time since he'd found himself so attracted to a woman. The celebrity status of authorship invited a constant flow of illicit sexual propositions, of course, all of which he rejected. And the hurt he still nursed since the break-up of his marriage, had, to date, proved an insurmountable obstacle to anything approaching a meaningful relationship.

Sophie's childlike innocence might, just possibly, he thought, have peeled back a corner of the barrier he'd erected, revealing to him the merest glimpse of a still-beating heart beneath. In stark contrast to the sophisticates who populated his life, she represented something fresh and new, her cut-glass English accent as perfect as her peaches and skin complexion, her virtue shining from clear blue eyes.

'So! How're you doin'?' he asked when she picked up the phone.

'Can't wait for the book launch,' she replied, with endearing enthusiasm. 'I shall be back at school, of course, but I only work part time so that's okay. I've cancelled my coaching lessons for that weekend, and I'm going to drive my parents up. We've booked into the hotel we usually stay in, at Marble Arch.'

Matt stood at the window of his first floor study, looking down through the leafy branches and peeling trunks of the London Plane trees growing on the pavement below. It was, actually, the second bedroom of the flat and was furnished with a sofa bed, but there was no way he could accommodate an extra three adults. Evie had initially declined the invitation he'd extended for the launch, citing work commitments. He guessed impoverishment might be a more accurate excuse, but hesitated to offer financial help for fear of demeaning her. So he'd offered her a room for the night – his own as it happened – and to his surprise, after some persuasion on his part and hesitation on hers, she'd accepted.

'Don't suppose you'd have space for one more in the car – cousin Evie?' he asked Sophie now, then immediately regretted it as he imagined her wrinkling her pretty little face apologetically, while she explained the dilemma of logistics – too many passengers, too much luggage, too small a car boot.

'I'm so sorry,' she finished, her voice filled with regret. 'If I could get Mummy to cut down on all the stuff she thinks she needs, I wouldn't hesitate.'

'Not to worry. We can make other arrangements.'

'Mummy's really looking forward to showing you round the properties Grandma used to own in London,' Sophie continued. 'We can meet you on the Friday morning, the day after the book launch. Is that all right with you?'

'Yeah. That's swell.'

Matt turned from the window, crossed the room and sat at his desk. Stretching his legs before him and leaning back on the chair, he said: 'Your mom was telling me about her sister. Beatrice? She'd be Evie's and my grandmother, of course.'

'Oh yes!' Sophie laughed. 'It's so confusing isn't it. My aunt. Your grandmother. Mummy's never really spoken much about her. Only that in the early years of her marriage, Aunt Bea gave Grandma a hard time. I think she kept leaving her husband for long stretches and would land herself in London for months on end. She never had any money to pay for her keep, apparently. It fell to my grandmother to take care of her. That's all I know. Before my time, of course.'

Matt pictured the scene. 'I guess she would have had Libby with her? My mother?'

'I suppose she would have. She couldn't very well have left her behind, could she?'

'So you never knew her yourself?'

'Libby? Or Aunt Bea?'

'Either. Both.'

'Not sure I ever met Libby, though I think my sisters, Liz and Fiona, knew her. And I only recall seeing Aunt Bea once. She was quite old by then, of course. It was one of those occasions never to be forgotten.'

Matt sat up, abruptly.

'Oh? Why was that?'

'Well, I was only a child, about five, six, I suppose, so I don't know how accurate my memory is. She came to our house. She couldn't have been visiting Grandma because she wouldn't have been around then. She died before I was born. Same year, I think.'

'Your grandmother died before you were born? So you would have been living in Kingswear when you saw Beatrice?'

'Yes. My parents moved down after I was born. Though Mummy sometimes gets muddled and says it was before.'

'And Beatrice stayed with you? With your mom?'

'I doubt it! I don't think she and Mummy ever saw eye to eye. I don't know where she would have stayed. Anyway, she came over to see Mummy one day. That I do know.'

'And what do you remember of her visit?' Matt asked, gripping the phone to his ear.

'I seem to think there was some sort of upset. A bit of a shouting match between Mummy and Auntie Bea. Something about money. It was always about money. Auntie Bea never seemed to have any. Mummy's feeling was that her husband should provide for her.'

Sophie fell silent.

'So what was the outcome?' Matt asked.

Sophie hesitated. 'Bear in mind I was quite young. But I seem to recall all this yelling going on, and then it stopped. Very suddenly. And there was Auntie Bea on the floor, shaking about and frothing at the mouth.'

Matt was on the edge of his seat.

'A fit?' he prompted.

'Could have been. I was too little to understand what was going on. But it was horrible. My mother had to move some of the furniture, I suppose in case Auntie Bea hurt herself, then she whisked me out of the room. I never saw my aunt again after that. I don't know if she went back to her husband in Scotland, or what. No idea. But I think she died soon afterwards.'

'That must have been pretty traumatic for a little girl to witness,' said Matt, thinking of his own 'little' girl, Sam, and the horrors she must have to endure.

'Yes. It still gives me the collywobbles when I think of it.'

I bet it does, thought Matt. He straightened the papers on his desk, bade Sophie goodbye, and rang off.

So there it was, he concluded, continuing to sit at his desk. Evidence, however nebulous, that his grandmother, Beatrice, poor woman, might well have been epileptic. Which, reluctant as he felt to admit it, would explain why his daughter, Sam, had inherited the condition.

'One up for you,' he said aloud, picturing the triumph of his ex-wife once she came to know.

Outside, on the street below, a car alarm sounded off, a cacophony of noise. Matt jumped from his seat and went to look from the window. A neighbour appeared on the pavement below, pointed and pressed his key fob at the car, and the flashing lights and horn desisted. If only it were that easy, thought Matt, in respect of his daughter's illness. He turned from the window and left the room.

Chapter Nine

Where There's a Will There's a Way

A FEW WEEKS later, Matt lay on the sofa bed in his study, contemplating the coming days. Unlike a conventional afternoon book-signing at, say, Waterstones, the launch of *Murder in Madagascar* was an evening do at the Bloomsbury Hotel, near Covent Garden. Laid on by his publishers, the room would be set up with small tables as if for a social event, rather than in lecture-room style, and all he had to do was to turn up, stand at a lectern and read selected portions of the book. Questions from the floor would follow, then he'd sit and autograph the pile of hardback copies on a table at the front of the room, and endure countless photographs taken by fans, mostly female.

It was as much part of the job as was sitting on his backside creating the characters, conflicts and conclusions in the first place. He knew that. The following evening, though, would be special. With his sister, Evie, cousin Sophie, Aunt Phoebe, and Phil in the audience, how could it be anything else?

He turned his mind back to the previous day. Evie had come up by train. Ignoring her protestations, he'd sent the return ticket himself, first class so she could travel in style. To begin with, she'd resisted like mad, but eventually, she'd caved in.

'You're spoiling me,' she'd complained.

'Gee, it feels good to have a sister to spoil,' he'd responded. 'Indulge me?'

He'd met her, himself, at Paddington station, rearranging his schedule to do so. He'd then taken her to his apartment in Pimlico, noting with pleasure her wide-eyed appreciation of the white stucco

Regency terraces, four stories high; the broad streets; and the grand garden squares.

'Winston Churchill lived in these parts,' he said, 'and your Welsh designer, Laura Ashley.'

The first floor flat was older and grander than his apartment in Manhattan, though somewhat smaller. Furnished with cream leather sofas, pale rugs on the solid oak flooring, and an assortment of watercolour paintings on the ivory walls, the lounge was light and sunny. It was clear that Evie was bowled over, unused to the comfort and wealth he took for granted, and he felt a pang of remorse. Here he was, the adopted sibling, deprived of his biological mother, but raised in a manner Evie could only dream of.

He'd given up his room for her – hence his occupation of the sofa bed in the study – and he'd made it clear how much it meant to him to have her stay. They'd dined in that first evening, Matt showing off his culinary skills, Evie displaying her ignorance of such things in a way he found endearingly honest.

'We've a lot of catching up to do, Sis. We know so little of each other. What was it like growing up with Libby as your mother?'

'Nothing like this,' she said, sitting bolt upright on the sofa as if on tenterhooks, when he served coffee after the meal. 'We lived on fish and chips, convenience foods, something from a tin on toast.'

On the other side of the room, Matt grinned. 'Fast foods. Not so different from a million Americans then. So where did you live as a child?'

He knew, of course, from his research into Libby's past, but he wanted to encourage Evie to talk, to get to know her.

'I grew up in Sheffield. Once a wealthy steel producing city. Now –' She shrugged.

'Yeah. Isn't that near the Derbyshire Peak District? Supposed to be pretty awesome countryside and good walking terrain?'

Evie nodded. 'It's stunning. But we rarely went on outings as a family. Don't think my parents had that sort of relationship. My dad was Chairman of the Council. When he wasn't at work he was otherwise involved. Always at meetings. Always busy. All I ever knew was the city.'

Matt leaned back, one foot resting on the other knee.

'And Libby? Your mother? *Our* mother! She accepted that?'

Evie's face crumpled into a grimace. 'I don't think she had much choice. My dad was as much the chairman at home as he was at work.'

Matt hesitated. He wanted to learn as much as he could about his biological mother, but he could see it was distressing for Evie. However, before he could bring his interrogation to an end, she continued her discourse.

'Mum never spoke much about her childhood. But from what Phoebe said when we visited her, it doesn't sound as if it was a very happy or settled period of her life. Up and down from Glasgow to London with her mother. Leaving her father behind and living with her grandmother for weeks on end. Then back again to Glasgow. Don't suppose she got much schooling or stability.'

'Yeah. Didn't Aunt Phoebe suggest it was Libby's dad who kept shunting them off to London? And her grandmamma who booted them back to Glasgow. Poor Beatrice. And poor Libby. Makes them sound like footballs. Or shuttlecocks.'

Evie shook her head.

'I can't understand it. My Glasgow grandparents must have been reasonably well off. He was a draper, I think. Had his own business in the city. I never knew him. Too far for us to go to visit.'

She fell silent for a moment and, as Matt watched, he saw a flicker of recognition pass across her face.

'I never thought about it before,' she said, 'because, of course, I didn't know about Mum's awful childhood until Phoebe said. But perhaps with that behind her, and my father's indifference – perhaps that's why she drank.'

Matt stiffened.

'She drank?'

Evie looked across at him and grimaced.

'Like a fish. That's what killed her in the end. Sorry. I didn't mean to shock you. All this reminiscing, it just, sort of, came out.'

They fell silent for a moment. Then Matt rose to pour more coffee.

'And our grandmother? Beatrice?' he asked. 'What of her?'

'I only remember meeting her once. When I was in my teens, I think. As far as I know, she died soon afterwards.'

'So you would have met her some years before Sophie saw her?'

'Sophie saw her?'

Matt recognised the same incredulity in Evie's voice that he'd felt on hearing the news.

'So she told me. But she would only have been a kid. Five-ish?' Evie set her coffee cup down on the table.

'And where was this supposed to have taken place?'

'Kingswear, I guess.'

'I wonder what would have brought my grandmother all the way down from Glasgow to Kingswear? I thought, by the time Sophie was around, relationships were a bit strained?'

'Could've been after your great-grandmother's funeral,' said Matt, casually. Aware that Evie probably knew less than he did, given the research he'd undertaken, he felt the need for caution.

Evie frowned, staring across the room as if trying to bring things to mind.

'Yes. I suppose that would make sense,' she said. 'As far as I know, my great-grandmother died round about – my thirteenth birthday, I suppose. Not that I knew her that well. But I seem to remember my parents talking about it. And it would have been soon after that I saw my grandmother, Beatrice.'

Matt leaned forward, lifted the coffee pot and hovered over Evie's cup, refilling his own when she raised her hand to indicate she'd had sufficient.

'According to Sophie,' he said, resuming an upright position, 'and bearing in mind that she was very young so might not have accurate recall, there was a bit of a spat. A row between our grandmother Beatrice, and her sister, Aunt Phoebe. Know what that was about?'

'No idea! You have to remember, Matt, we had very little to do with any of the family. If anything! I've never thought about it before, but looking back, it was almost as if there was a rift. As if my mother had cut herself off. Or *vice versa*. So what do you know about it? Do tell me.'

'Well, I can't be sure. But it looks to me as if it might be to do with this,' Matt turned in his seat, opened a drawer in his desk, and produced a folded photocopy of a handwritten document.

He passed it to Evie.

'The will our grandmother was written out of,' he said. 'The one that was drawn up only a few days before our great-grandmother's death.'

Sophie sat in the back of the car reflecting on recent events. Much to her delight, Liz had decided to join them on the London trip. Whether she'd been persuaded to do so by their mother, or whether it was the lure of a shopping excursion was unclear, but Sophie's unspoken hope was that she might be able to fill in the gaps their mother chose not to recall.

They'd travelled up in their parents' car, a Ford from the luxury end of the market, but now showing its age. Liz had insisted on driving, with Phoebe in the front passenger seat, leaving Sophie in the back with her father. Which, of course, was only natural, she told herself. Liz was the eldest and was, therefore, deserving of respect.

What was of far greater importance, as far as she was concerned, were the days ahead in Liz's company. Time spent with her sister was a rarity which, given their biological and geographical proximity at home in Dartmouth, was a puzzle. What Sophie was hoping for was that, despite the polarisation in their personalities and lifestyles, this might be an opportunity for bonding. For getting to know one another better. For learning to value the other's strengths and weaknesses in such a way as to enrich their own and each other's lives.

Staring out of the car window at the English countryside rolling past beside the motorway, she thought of the relationship between her sister and herself in terms of the estuary at home, where the incoming tide met the outflowing plume of the River Dart. Aided and abetted by moon, wind and gradient, the conflicting forces created what was known as a tide race. The resulting turbulence might be more, or less, acute at certain times of the day throughout the year. But as each element battled to maintain its natural flow, it concluded, ultimately, in a merger of salt water with fresh. And that was exactly what she hoped she and Liz would achieve, a merging of affection and interests.

She turned her head towards her sister and found, to her surprise, a meeting of their eyes in the rear view mirror.

'You okay?' Liz asked. 'Not feeling car-sick?'

'No, I'm fine, thanks.' Sophie shook her head, touched by the unusual display of sisterly concern for a condition she'd suffered from as a child. She made a similar enquiry of her father, at her side.

'Are you all right, Daddy?'

He nodded, smiled, and reached for her hand to give it a squeeze.

With the inevitable convenience stops required by her parents, the journey took longer than expected and they didn't arrive in London until mid-afternoon. A relative stranger to the metropolis, herself, Sophie was impressed with Liz's driving skills, given the high volume of traffic in the city centre and around Hyde Park.

'I'm glad you know where you're going,' she said, in tribute to her sister.

As soon as they arrived at The Cumberland Hotel, Marble Arch, Sophie set about seeing that their luggage was offloaded, then took her parents into the foyer – a vast open area – while Liz took the car to the designated multi-storey car park, nearby. Hardly daring to do anything until Liz's return, Sophie gazed around her at the contemporary surroundings, feeling as if she were an alien on another planet.

Returning eventually, and clucking with disapproval at Sophie's ineptitude, Liz checked them in with the receptionist and they were then shown to their respective accommodation, two twin-bedded rooms on opposite sides of the same corridor. Once installed, Sophie began unpacking her suitcase while Liz tested the beds.

'Rock hard,' she pronounced. 'I'll take the one near the window. You can have the one next to the bathroom. Okay?'

'Fine!' As the youngest sib by far, Sophie was well used to being relegated to whatever suited everyone else. It really didn't bother her, especially as the entire experience was a bonus by comparison with her usual meagre lifestyle, whereas it was far-from for Liz.

'It's a pity you weren't able to meet Matt and Evie when they were down visiting Mummy last month,' she said, eyeing her sister in the mirror as she took various items of clothing from her suitcase and placed them in drawers.

'I really can't be doing with all this intrigue,' Liz replied.

Sophie turned and perched her bottom against the dressing table.

'What intrigue, exactly? Please tell me, Liz. I feel as if I'm the only one who doesn't know what's going on.'

Her voice was full of pleading, her desire to understand eating at her like a voracious animal.

Liz sighed, then raised herself on the bed and leant back against the fancy glass bedhead.

'I suppose you've as much right to know as anyone else,' she admitted, reluctantly. 'Goodness me! Mother treats you like a baby all the time.'

Sophie frowned, perplexed, cocking her head to one side, trying to make adjustment to her usual mental perceptions.

'She's only being kind, isn't she? I'm not sure I know what you mean?'

'You don't think she mollycoddles you?'

Sophie's confusion grew, a cocktail of indignation splashed with guilt, and sprinkled with a light dusting of hurt.

'I do try to do my best for her – for them both, you know. It's just that with work and well, other things, I don't have a lot of time. Do you think Mummy needs more help? What are you saying?'

'Oh, never mind.' Liz sounded brisk, almost terse. 'What is it you want to know about the situation?'

Reluctantly, Sophie let Liz's original comment go. She shrugged, her enthusiasm for the opportunities these few days presented momentarily abated.

'I suppose I'd like some background knowledge of my relatives. I mean how come Matt was adopted? Couldn't his mother have kept him?'

'That I don't know,' Liz admitted. 'But what I do know is that Libby was very reluctant to give him up for adoption.'

'Well you would be, wouldn't you? Any mother would, surely?'

Liz turned her head away, looked towards the window and said nothing.

'So what *do* you know, Liz?' Sophie pleaded. 'I mean, it was all before my time.'

'Mine too.' Liz bent her fingers towards her, examined the frosted purple varnish on her nails, then pushed at a cuticle. 'I was only a tiny tot when Matthew was born. But I remember hearing Mother and Father discussing it once, years later. As far as I know, Libby only signed the adoption papers when Matt was about eight months old.'

'So you're right.' Sophie nodded. 'That does suggest she didn't want to let him go. But in that case, what on earth prompted her to do so after so long?'

Liz looked exasperated. 'Well it's obvious isn't it! She must have been married and expecting Evie by then.'

Sophie pressed her lips together as realisation dawned. 'Of course! Silly me. I hadn't thought of that. Gosh, she was quick off the mark.'

Liz nodded. 'Absolutely! There could only have been a matter of months between the two events.'

Sophie shook her head in disbelief, and they both lapsed into silence. Then Sophie flexed her shoulders.

'I still don't understand. If, as you say, there was so little time between Matt's birth and his mother's marriage, why didn't she keep him?'

'You could hardly expect the new husband to take on the first baby,' Liz retorted.

Sophie frowned. 'So you think Matt wasn't his? Seems strange, doesn't it? Libby has an affair which leads to a pregnancy, and ultimately to Matt's birth, then out of the blue she marries someone entirely different and has a second baby, Evie.'

Liz shrugged, clearly unable, or unwilling, to answer her query.

'So do you think the husband was even aware of Matt's existence?'

'Who knows? I wouldn't have thought so. But even if he did know, you could hardly expect him to take on another's man's child, could you? Though from what I gather, pressure of some sort had to be brought to bear to remind Libby of that. Now if you don't mind, I'd rather not talk about it anymore. As I said, I hate all this conspiracy.'

Resisting the temptation to question what sort of pressure might have been put on Libby, and the use of the word 'conspiracy', Sophie launched herself from the edge of the dressing table, hung up the last item from her suitcase, closed the lid and turned to face her sister once more.

'So why *did* you come?' she enquired.

Liz looked at her, one eyebrow raised in an expression of – what? Was she trying to suggest she'd had no choice, Sophie wondered?

'You forget that Fiona and I grew up in London.' Liz assumed an air of nonchalance. 'This was our place of birth; all our childhood memories are here.'

Sophie sat on the edge of the bed and eyed Liz up. People always said they were incredibly alike – the same blonde hair and peaches and cream complexions, the same height and slight build, the same dress size. They even took the same size shoes – all to Sophie's benefit, as Liz was in the habit of passing unwanted items on to her from time to time.

'So where exactly did you live?' Sophie asked. 'And where did you and Fiona go to school?'

'You'll see when we show Matt and Evie around,' Liz said, swinging her legs to the floor and rising from her semi-recumbent position to take her turn at unpacking.

Sophie promptly threw herself down on the bed her sister had vacated and bounced on the mattress.

'Rock hard?' she said, full of scorn and humour. 'Gosh, Liz, you must be made of gossamer. This bed's as comfy as they come.'

'Just as well,' Liz replied. 'We're going to be doing a fair bit of walking over the next few days.'

She then proceeded, as Sophie watched, to shove all Sophie's things in one drawer so she might have the use of all those that remained.

Waking in Matt's luxurious apartment the morning after my arrival, I can't recall a more exciting period of my life. It certainly eclipses my wedding to Pete. And fond though I am of Scott, even time spent with him. Who would have thought I would ever travel first class on a train to London? Or taste fresh crab, accompanied by real champagne as a starter for dinner? Let alone stay in so sumptuous an apartment?

I gaze around the room, at the king-sized bed on which I'm lying; the thick, smooth, Egyptian cotton sheets that feel like whipped cream against my skin; the pale oak flooring scattered with deep pile rugs; the uncluttered simplicity around me. Despite my well-worn attitudes of derision that run contrary to such a privileged existence, I finally have to admit they are a sham. Matt may be from an élite class of society I could never attain to. Nor would want to, I tell myself, immediately acknowledging this as a matter of habit. But he is one of the kindest and most genuine people you could ever hope to meet. And his lifestyle is quite simply amazing.

He knocks on the door, and covered only in a short white towelling dressing gown, much to my embarrassment, delivers a cup of tea to my bedside.

'Sleep well?' he asks. And without waiting for an answer tells me there's no rush to get up.

An hour later, showered, dressed and fed – smoked salmon for breakfast! – I insist on stacking the dishwasher and hand-washing the items that can't go in, despite Matt's protestations. I simply can't get over the way he's spoiling me, and with such obvious pleasure.

'You've no idea how good it feels to have a sister,' he says, earnestly, tea towel in his hands. 'My adoptive parents were real good to me. Made a thing about how I was *chosen*. But because of the problems they had in starting a family, and the little'un my mom had lost, I always felt I owed 'em. Being an only child isn't all it's cracked up to be. Is it?'

'No!' I turn towards him, surprised at his perspicacity, impatient with myself for entertaining such a thought. 'Though it was very different for me,' I continue. 'My dad had no time for me or my mum. I know she loved me, but I grew up believing I must be this horrible, naughty child. Because her love for me created tension between her and my dad. She stood up for me, I reasoned, therefore I must have been the cause of all the disagreements and unhappiness between the two of them.'

I fall silent. I've never admitted to any of this before except, of course, to Grace. But standing at the kitchen sink with Matt, it seems strangely natural to be discussing such things with him.

'How awful for you,' Matt says, his face creased with the full horror of his understanding.

His reaction brings tears to my eyes.

'I suppose the worst thing was never having anyone else to share with,' I say, surreptitiously wiping my eyes with the back of my hand while emptying the washing up bowl and sponging down the black granite counter tops. 'As you say, the perils of being an only child. But then it must have been just as difficult for Mum being the only one.'

Matt waits until I've washed and dried my hands, then leads me from the kitchen to his living room.

'Interesting you should say that,' he says, indicating that I should take a seat at the glass topped table where we'd breakfasted. He seats himself opposite me, with a pile of papers in front of him. Taking one of the documents, he spreads it before me. It's the copy of our great-grandmother's will he'd shown me the previous evening.

'Notice anything strange about it?' he asks.

'You mean other than that Phoebe and her one surviving brother at the time were the only two beneficiaries?' I ask. 'And our grandmother, Beatrice, doesn't get a mention.' I turn the multi-folded document back and forth.

'Anything else?' Matt asks.

The sun is breaking through the tall sash window, and I'm struck, again, by the grandeur of my surroundings. Without a trace of envy or malice, I ponder my adopted half-brother's good fortune. The sunshine touches on a silver cup on the dresser – an award of some sort – glinting off the surface and reflecting on the ceiling above. There is an absence of illumination, however, when it comes to answering Matt's question. Raising my eyebrows, pursing my lips, I shake my head.

'I didn't want to raise the matter yesterday evening,' Matt says, 'in case it gave you a sleepless night.'

'So come on,' I grin. 'What's with all the suspense?'

'Look at the date,' Matt tells me.

I take a look, but see nothing amiss.

Matt tugs at the hair on top of his head. 'It's only a week before great-grandmamma died,' he declares, pointing to the relevant lettering.

'Y-e-s,' I say, slowly, trying to see the relevance of what he's saying.

'You don't think that's strange?'

'I remember your telling me it was just before she died. But I suppose, if she was ill, she'd want to make sure her last wishes were recorded.'

'I take it you're not aware she already had a will in place then?'

'No. Why should I be? So what are you saying, Matt?'

Once again he tugs at his hair, before unfolding another of the papers in the pile before him.

'Take a look at this. This was the earlier will.'

Making every effort to concentrate, I compare the two documents. It's clear that the earlier one was made years before the most recent one. Also glaringly obvious is that 'all such offspring as shall survive me' are included as beneficiaries in the earlier one. Our grandmother would, therefore, have inherited from her mother at this stage.

'Take another look at the date of the earlier will,' Matt urges me. I read it aloud.

'Exactly,' he says. 'This will was made when Beatrice, and her sibs were still children. And it continued to stand until a week before her mother died. That was soon after Libby's birth. Now take a look at the signature.'

Obediently, I scrutinise the signature on the original document.

'And the other one,' says Matt.

I lay the two wills on the table, side by side, with both signatures visible.

'Oh, my goodness!'

Matt nods, vigorously. I look across the table at him for a moment, before returning my gaze to the documents.

'How did I fail to see this?' I ask.

'How indeed,' Matt says. 'More to the point, how did it get through probate?'

It is, truly, unbelievable. My eyes swivel from side to side between the two wills. I can't take my gaze away from them. For on the earlier will, there is – as you'd expect – a single signature. On the later will, made just a week before my great-grandmother's death, three attempts have been made. And each is slightly different from the others.

Chapter Ten

A Give Away

SOPHIE STOOD FOR a moment, looking around her at the room set aside for Matt's book launch at the Bloomsbury Hotel. Deeply carpeted and dotted with small circular tables beneath the chandeliers, it was beginning to fill with guests. An air of hushed excitement permeated the proceedings as people streamed in, each gazing at the large table at the front, which was piled high with Matt's latest books. A microphone stood to one side, and through the tall sash windows behind it, each festooned with fuchsia pink blinds, Sophie could see the street lamps glinting through the trees outside. Spotting Evie, seated alone at a table near the front, she headed straight for her, deliberately leaving Liz with no alternative but to escort their parents.

It felt good to relax. She'd spent most of the day shepherding Daddy around the shops, while Mummy and Liz went off on a spending spree. Not given to shopping therapy, herself, and without the income to support it anyway, she had to admit she'd found it a tiring experience. Watching over Daddy so he didn't get lost in the crowds must rank among the most difficult of tasks, she thought.

Lost in the crowd was how she felt right now! Liz's accusation, for that was how she'd thought of it since the previous evening, had replayed in her mind throughout the day. Mollycoddled! Was that really how her sister perceived her? It was a travesty of the truth. The weekly shopping trips, the help with hospitality, the emotional support – did it all count for nothing? As far as Liz was concerned she, Sophie, was a spoiled baby, a pampered and over-protected prima donna.

Determined to put it out of her mind, to enjoy what was to come, she approached Evie.

'May I?' she asked, one hand on the back of the chair next to her. Evie looked up. 'Of course! I'd be glad of the company.'

Sophie pulled the gilded chair out from beneath the table. It was gratifying to see the pleasure on Evie's face as she seated herself. At least someone seemed to relish her presence. She returned her smile.

'So what have you been up to with Matt?' she asked. 'Anything exciting?'

Evie was attired in what Sophie thought was probably her best dress, that of a well-known couturier, similar to something Liz had once owned and discarded some years back. Without doubt the soft violet colouring suited Evie but, sadly, if she was hoping to impress the élite among whom they were seated, Sophie suspected she would fall well short of the mark. As if that mattered, she told herself, aware that she, too, was wearing a skirt and jacket she'd picked up for a song in a charity shop. They were kindred spirits, she and Evie – poor, and proud of it.

Evie smiled again. 'Oh, this and that,' she replied. 'This is a first for me, so it's all pretty exciting. And you?'

Sophie grimaced. 'We're staying at the Cumberland Hotel at Marble Arch, so I'm sure you don't need me to tell you what we've been up to all day.'

Evie looked puzzled, clearly unaware of the significance of their whereabouts.

'Shopping. On Oxford Street,' Sophie enlightened her. 'Not my favourite pastime.'

'Nor mine,' Evie confessed. 'Matt took me on the London Eye this morning. That was an amazing experience. You can see right over the Thames to the Houses of Parliament and – oh, I don't know. Everywhere. Otherwise, we've just been walking around, sitting drinking coffee, catching up, getting to know one another.'

Sophie put her handbag on the floor at her feet. Getting to know one another! The questions she'd put to Liz about Matt's adoption the previous evening flooded back into her mind on a tide of compassion and understanding.

'It's sad, isn't it, to think you and Matt might have grown up together if things had been different,' she said.

A waiter approached their table with a tray of what looked like Prosecco. She waited until Evie had taken a glass, then took one herself and clinked it against Evie's as a toast, before drinking.

'Very sad,' Evie responded. 'Though I doubt that Matt would have achieved all this had he grown up in my family. There wasn't much in the way of money or encouragement.'

'He has done well for himself, hasn't he?' Sophie concurred. 'But even so, it's hard to understand why your parents didn't keep him, isn't it.'

Evie looked at her over the top of her glass, an expression of surprise on her face.

'I guess my dad didn't want to bring up another man's child,' she said, emphatically.

Sophie nodded. 'That's what Liz reckoned. Not that she's old enough to remember what went on then. She's only, what, three or four years older than Matt? Four at most?'

Evie shrugged. 'Well I certainly wasn't around then. Matt's older than I am. About fourteen months I think. He was a September baby. And I was November the following year.'

'Not a big gap between you then. That must be nice. There are as many years between me and my middle sister, Fiona, as there are months between you and Matt.'

Evie's face was a picture of surprise and sympathy.

'Funny how the generations get so mixed up, isn't it,' Sophie added.

She looked around the room. Her parents and Liz appeared to have seated themselves at a table on the far side near the back. Probably because Daddy would need easy access to the loo, she surmised. Oh, well, Liz could cope with his needs for once in her life. Sophie stifled the sense of guilt that rose, unbidden, in her mind, and turned her attention back to Evie.

'Oh, by the way,' she said as Matt appeared and began to approach the rostrum. 'I nearly forgot. This is for you.'

She bent down to the large handbag at her feet and produced a brown envelope. It contained the photograph of Evie's parents' wedding. The one her mother had left out on the coffee table for her, when Matt and Evie had visited. Passing it across the table to her, now, she smiled, warmly. And as Evie took the envelope, and Matt greeted his audience, a ripple of applause broke out from around the room. Sophie settled back in her seat, prepared to enjoy what the evening had to offer.

Sipping my glass of bubbly and listening to Matt expounding on his trip to the Indian Ocean island off the South-East coast of Africa, and the background research he's undertaken in respect of his latest book, *Murder in Madagascar*, I feel all-but overwhelmed with the sense of privilege this evening has afforded me. I'm touched, too, that Sophie appears to have abandoned her family and singled me out for company. Equally, I'm glad of the opportunity to get to know her better. Despite her immaturity, she has a generosity of spirit that I admire.

I'm increasingly aware, however, as the evening progresses in a series of readings from Matt's novel, that a sense of wistfulness pervades her being. As a result, I find myself glancing, surreptitiously, in her direction throughout the proceedings, in an attempt to analyse what lies beneath the pretty façade. However compelling Matt's fictitious narrative might be, it's Sophie's real-life circumstances that mesmerise me.

'Don't you just love the way Matt writes,' she enthuses, more as a statement than a question when he finishes the readings and is thanked by whoever is hosting the evening, presumably his publishers. And I'm struck by the light that radiates from her eyes. The more so when, at the end of the evening, Sophie duly collects a hardback copy of *Murder in Madagascar*, and joins the queue at Matt's table at the front to have it signed. Is this, as I surmised when first they met, the blossoming of a one-sided infatuation? Or is it a genuine, two-way, romance?

'I'm looking forward to tomorrow,' I tell Sophie when she joins me again. 'And I know Matt is, too.'

'You're not the only ones,' Sophie responds. 'I've never been on a tour of Grandma's properties before, though I've heard plenty about them, of course.'

'And will Liz be with us?' I turn away from Sophie to pick up my bag and am immediately aware of her hesitation.

'Is everything okay?' I ask spinning round and seeing the distress on her face.

She draws a deep breath. 'Yes. I'm sure it is. Probably just me over-reacting.'

'Sisters, eh?' I touch her arm briefly in a gesture of comfort and friendship. 'Not that I would know, never having had any.'

A broad grin lights Sophie's face.

'Liz will be with us tomorrow,' she confirms as we begin to walk towards the foyer where I've arranged to meet Matt. 'She's looking forward to it. As she reminded me yesterday, she and Fiona grew up here, in London, before my parents moved us all down to Devon.'

'Well, that's good. I'm hoping she'll be able to fill me in with a few gaps in the family history. And I'm sure you'll be able to do the same for Matt, won't you?'

Sophie's smile tells me she appreciates the hidden agenda behind what I'm saying.

Liz steps into view as we approach the doorway.

'What on earth's taken you so long? I've had to leave Mother standing outside the gents, on guard in case Father comes out and gets lost.'

'Sorry.' Sophie turns, gives me a quick and unexpected peck on the cheek, then scurries off to relieve her mother of her sentry duties while her sister ducks into the ladies' room, no doubt to powder her delicately sculpted nose.

'And I must find Matt,' I say to no one in particular, lifting my hand to indicate my whereabouts when I see him emerge from the room we've vacated.

We're on our way back to his Pimlico apartment before I have a real chance to congratulate him on the book launch.

'Well done! Great event.' I lean towards him in the back of the taxi and, for the first time without the slightest sense of embarrassment, kiss him on the cheek.

'Gee, thanks, Sis. Means a lot coming from you.'

'It was an excellent evening. Most enjoyable. Not that I'm by any means an expert.'

He laughs. 'Nor me.'

'Oh, go on! Book launches. Readings. All the adulation. Must be ten a penny for you.'

Matt purses his lips. 'Not at all! The fear of failure never ceases to gnaw at an author's insides. *Will this book be as well received as those before? Is this gonna be the end?*'

I shake my head in disbelief. The paradigm of human insecurity is well documented in various psychological tomes. Cited as symptomatic of underlying neuroses – usually low self-esteem – rather than a condition in itself, it seems to be prevalent in varying degrees throughout the human race. Yet why someone of Matt's talent, achievement and fortune should not have the confidence and psychological resilience to overcome temporary feelings of inadequacy is a mystery to me. Unless, of course, it has something to do with the circumstances surrounding his adoption?

'Pity we didn't get to meet Liz properly,' he says, and in the darkness of the cab I sense, rather than see, his disappointment.

'I thought I saw her take her parents upfront to have you sign a book for them?'

'Yeah. But that was it.'

'Sophie did say Phil couldn't cope with late nights and crowds,' I tell Matt. 'That's probably why they left so promptly, without saying goodbye.'

Matt nods. 'Oh, well. Can't be helped. Didn't see much of Sophie, either.'

This time, his disappointment comes across loud and clear.

'I know she's looking forward to tomorrow.' I say, encouragingly. 'But I got the impression that she felt guilty because she'd sat next to me all evening and left Liz looking after their parents. I think there was a bit of a spat between the two sisters, and they left soon afterwards.'

Matt holds onto the handle beside him as the taxi swings around a corner, while I'm taken by surprise and fall against him. Murmuring apologies, I right myself.

'Probably just as well we didn't get the opportunity to chat for long,' Matt says. 'Must admit, I'm feelin' pretty bushed now. And as you say, I guess we'll see plenty of them tomorrow.'

Matt's tiredness is understandable given the demands made of him all evening. I deliberately fall silent to give him space, and gaze out of the taxi window at the lights and the street names, trying to get my bearings – and failing. I know why, of course! My concentration is shot to pieces. Because the one thing I want to discern eludes me.

My mind returns to this morning in Matt's apartment, when we'd sat at his glass-topped table after breakfast. Following the revelation of the signatures on our great-grandmother's will, we'd spent some time discussing the ramifications and possible reasons for the discrepancies.

'Do you think the will could have been forged?' I asked Matt, with a sense of disbelief. 'I mean, the signatures look completely different.'

'Forged by whom?' he asked. 'And why?'

In all honesty, I could think of no reason why anyone would forge a will, other than to augment the inheritance of the beneficiaries, in this case Phoebe and her brother, now deceased. Disclosing my theory, however, was quite beyond me. After all, brother or not, I barely knew Matt. I'd no way of knowing how far he would take it were I to make my suspicions known. Moving to seat myself on one of Matt's cream leather sofas, I stretched my legs out in front of me and admitted to the only known fact.

'I don't suppose there's any way of finding out who signed the will. But it's perfectly clear that our grandmother, Beatrice, was not one of the named beneficiaries.'

'Darned right, she wasn't,' Matt tugged at his hair. 'And given that the earlier will included her, the only valid conclusion is that she was cut out. Deliberately.'

I shuffled, uncomfortably on the sofa, while Matt sat on at the table finishing his coffee.

'I know for a fact she was cut out,' I told him. 'I was about thirteen when our great-grandmother died. I remember, soon afterwards, my father carrying on about the will and yelling at my mother that her family were nothing but a no-good bunch of hypocrites.'

There had been more. Much more. Verbal abuse hurled at my mother – *our* mother – which I couldn't, wouldn't, repeat to Matt. A period of being sent to Coventry had followed, and financial deprivation that had led to Mum having to eke out the food we consumed as if we were on war-time rations, while Dad absented himself each evening and dined out.

Why my father despised my mother's family so much was a mystery. But he clearly felt justified in doing so when it came to my grandmother having been disinherited.

'Given all the practice signatures, I can't believe there could have been a grant of probate,' I said. 'Surely, the solicitors would have queried it?'

'You'd have thought so,' Matt agreed. 'But perhaps the witnesses to the signature were able to verify it?'

I sat up straight. 'Who were the witnesses?' I asked. 'Anyone we know? Someone in the family, perhaps?'

Matt stood, stretched his arms above his head and yawned. Dressed informally in navy jogging pants and loafers, he looked younger than his forty or so years, and I was struck again with the marvel that this was my brother! Blinking hard to stem my disbelief, I wondered, again, at the reality. Matt continued to stand.

'Nope,' he said, in answer to my question. 'I checked. No one in the family witnessed the will. Would that be permitted? I think you'll find, lookin' at the addresses, it was just next-door neighbours. But I guess if there was any doubt about the testator's signature, the probate office would have summonsed the witnesses to ask if they could vouch for the identity of the signatory.'

'So you think it was *bona fide*?'

Matt shrugged. 'Who knows? Is Aunt Phoebe likely to tell us? I doubt it! Phil? Nope.'

It was clear from his demeanour and tone of voice that, despite his fame and fortune, the process on which he'd embarked was taking its toll. Childless as I was, I couldn't begin to imagine how distressing that must be for him. To be seeking an acquaintanceship with your biological relatives, not for familial purposes, but to ascertain the roots of your daughter's medical condition must bring about a mixed bag of emotions.

Metaphorically, I shook my head. Was this why he kept tugging at his hair? Was it a childhood habit, developed, perhaps, as a result of being abandoned in an orphanage for eight months until his mother signed the adoption papers? Could it be that the self-confident image I saw before me was no more than a façade? Or that the writing skills had developed as a result of the boy in him needing to find himself? The self-pity in which I found myself consumed from time to time was all very well, I thought, but it didn't bear comparison with Matt's state of mind. A surge of empathy and affection for my brother engulfed me .

I looked across the room at him and attempted a smile. It was unobserved as he stood, yawned again, and joined me on the sofa. Aware that I was occupying his bed, I felt a stab of guilt. Was he not sleeping well on the sofa bed in the study, I wondered? Before I could enquire, the telephone rang, Matt's publishers from what I could deduce from the conversation, and the moment was lost. Walking across to the window, I looked down at the broad street below. Then I took myself off to the bathroom to clean my teeth.

In the taxi on the way back from the book launch, I'm brought back to the present by a touch on my arm. It's Matt.

'Look,' he says, and pulling me from my dark memories, he points out of the window at the lights sparkling against the night sky and London buildings. I take a look at the street names and see we've left The Strand and are now turning into the Victoria Embankment alongside the River Thames. In the distance, The London Eye, where we'd spent the morning, is a spectacular arc of iridescent blue, its image shimmering in the water beneath it like spilled paint.

'I'd take the tube, normally,' says Matt, 'but I thought you'd like to see the magical qualities of the capital by night.'

In what I take to be an attempt to give me some sense of direction which, actually, leaves me more confused, he then indicates St James' Park, beyond which lies The Mall, Westminster Bridge, The Florence Nightingale Museum and Lambeth Palace Gardens on the far side of the river until, eventually, we turn into what he tells me is Parliament Square. The wide open spaciousness of the grassy, tree-lined area, the mellow yellow of Big Ben's spot-lit stonework, and the shadowy beauty of Westminster Abbey take me by surprise.

'You're right! It is magical. And to think I'd always thought of London as somewhere noisy, crowded and dirty,' I confess to Matt.

'It's all of those things, too,' he says, a grin of pleasure lighting his face. 'But as with everything, you just have to know where to look. And how to screen out the ugliness.'

His remark seems oddly significant, given my earlier thoughts. Whatever discrepancies lie behind the making of our great-grandmother's will and are now clamouring for attention, they have to be screened out. However ugly the truth might be, it's the present on which we now need to focus.

The taxi turns a corner and, recognising the awesome Eccleston Square Gardens as we draw up at the kerb before Matt's apartment, I feel at peace. He holds the door open for me to alight, pays off the cabbie and ushers me up the broad white steps of the building. It's not until I've divested myself of coat and shoes in the bedroom, that I remember the envelope Sophie gave me earlier. Taking it from my bag, I join Matt in his living room.

'Something Sophie gave me at your book launch,' I say, taking a seat and squinting at what she's written on the outside of the envelope. 'It says here that she found this after we visited her parents in Kingswear.'

Matt pours two glasses of wine and passes one to me. I take a sip, then place the glass on a side table. Ripping open the envelope, I pull out the contents. It's a photograph. Black and white. And unless I'm mistaken, it looks like my parents, all dressed up, seated behind a table. Before them lies an open book, and my father is holding a pen.

'Must be their wedding day,' I say, leaning forward the better to see it. 'I'm sure that's the same outfit my mother was wearing in the photo I have at home.'

'So this is a different picture to the one you have?' Matt asks from behind me, adding, when I nod, 'Gee that's great, isn't it?'

It is! I've so little photographic evidence of my mother's life, and to have been given this is something special.'

The only puzzle, I reflect, is why Phoebe had this picture in the first place, when there was no sign of a duplicate among my parents' possessions? Nor any evidence of Phil and Phoebe having been at the wedding.

'Looks as if they're signing the register,' I say, recalling that they'd married in a registry office.

'May I?' Hesitantly, Matt reaches out.

'Of course!' I remind myself that this may be my parents' wedding photo, but it's a picture of his mother, too.

He moves around the back of the chair to sit beside me, skewing his head so he can see the picture on my lap.

'Gee, she doesn't look much older than my daughter, Sam,' he says.

We both fall silent as we study the photograph, then Matt says, 'May I?' again, and takes it from me.

He continues to look at it for a moment while I wonder what he's seen that I've missed.

'What is it?' I ask.

He hesitates, then says, 'Isn't that Phil Hamilton standing behind the bride and groom? Was he a witness at the wedding?'

Astonished, I grab at the photograph and it falls to the floor face down. It's then that I see someone has written on the back of it, naming the bride and groom, the venue, the day, month and year of the event.

I pick it up. Stare at it. Reel as the writing blurs. I'm aware that Matt is watching me, intently. My heart lurches. For the date of my parents' wedding does not tally with what I had previously been told. And it's perfectly obvious to me that Matt already knows.

Chapter Eleven

A Picture of the Past

MATT WOKE NEXT morning feeling decidedly groggy. He'd hardly slept, tossing and turning on the narrow sofa bed in his study, wishing that his quest to find his biological family wasn't so disruptive. Wishing that the reason for it was non-existent. Wishing he could make things right for Evie.

'You knew, didn't you!' she'd exclaimed the evening before, her tone of voice full of accusation as if he'd contrived the situation in order to hurt her.

She'd soon relented, saying she realised that just because he'd known she was wrong about the date of her parents' marriage did not mean he was implicated in the deception. Then she'd burst into tears.

'I'm sorry, Sis,' he'd said and, because he was still sitting next to her on the sofa, he'd put his arm around her shoulders and gently pulled her towards him so she could weep on his shoulder.

Without in any way being judgemental, he'd found himself wondering how she coped with counselling her clients. She was not the cool, calm, collected woman he'd supposed her to be, but was full of passion. And hurt! It was plain as a pike-staff she'd not had an easy ride. And though he'd Googled her name and researched all he could about her in the archives of Somerset House before making contact with her, he had little idea about the construct of her life. The emotional events. The part of her that lay beyond the bounds of controlled responses. The hidden depths.

When she'd at last quietened down, he'd handed her a box of tissues, passed the glass of wine he'd poured her earlier, and given her some space.

'This has obviously come as a shock to you,' he said, standing and moving across the living room to seat himself at the table. 'I quite understand. That's why I didn't wanna push it when the subject came up in Devon.'

'I'm sorry,' Evie whispered through her tears. 'I remember you told me a different date, then. But I just didn't want to hear it. I felt angry with you.'

'That's what big bros are for,' Matt said, trying to lighten her mood. 'Punch bags to be pummelled when you're feelin' down.'

Evie made an obvious attempt at a smile.

'Why should I feel so angry?' she asked, wiping her eyes and blowing her nose. 'I must have known, deep down, you were right. But I didn't want to have to admit it. Nor to think about what lies behind it. Do you mind if we leave it at that for the time being?'

What, indeed, lay behind the deceit Matt thought now, the following morning. He rose from the sofa bed in his study, tiptoed across the hall to the bathroom, shut the door and switched on the power shower. Beneath the steady onslaught of water pounding his skin, he pondered the matter further. This, after all, was the same kinda problem he would set himself in one of his novels. Create a character whose date of birth was crucial to some mystery, some fraudulent activity in the past perhaps, and – bingo – you had the basis of a plot-line for a thriller. He soaped his head, torso and limbs, shut his eyes and allowed the jet to sluice away the previous day's dirt.

So what reason could there have been for Evie's parents to have deceived their daughter, he wondered? Evie had been born in November, exactly fourteen months after his own birth. Given that he had not been adopted until he was eight months old, Libby must already have been three months pregnant with Evie. Which begged answers to several questions. He listed them in his mind, as if preparing them for a manuscript:

• Who was his father, and at what point had he disappeared from the scene?

• Had his dad known about the second pregnancy? And just how promiscuous had his mother, Libby, been?

• And how come Evie's father had not known about Libby's first-born? Himself!

• Was it Evie's dad who had insisted on Matt's adoption as a pre-requisite of marrying Libby?

• And was the fact that Evie had been conceived out of wedlock the reason for the deception about the wedding date?

He turned the shower to cold. Gee! His adoptive mother had made out he was a 'chosen' child. But her opportunity to make that choice had to mean he'd been rejected by his birth mother. He'd hardly been chosen by her. Cheated more like. He gasped as the water hit him, the cold jets biting, razor-sharp, into his flesh. Then he turned off the shower, stepped out and began to towel himself dry. Remembering Evie's tears the previous evening, he had every sympathy for her.

'It's not so much that they deceived me about their wedding date,' she'd said, straightening up and drying her eyes. 'What upsets me is that their relationship was so venomous. I have to ask myself 'Why?' Was I the reason for their marriage? Had someone forced them into it? And was I, therefore, the sole cause of their unhappiness?'

Matt had no answers for his sister.

He picked up his razor and began the ritual removal of the accumulated bristle. What a mess! What a hot-pot he'd stirred up. He visualised streaks of tongue-burning toxic emotions rising to the surface, then disappearing beneath the black sauce of grief-stricken relationships, peppered with more than a hint of callous deception.

Rubbing shaving balm into his jaw, he gave himself a quick inspection in the mirror, then pulled on his clothes. Leaving behind the thoughts of the last few weeks and the book launch of the previous evening, he projected his mind forward to the day ahead; a day of exploring the family property around London in the company of Phoebe, Phil and their two daughters.

Given the hidden secrets of the past, what was the likelihood of any answers in the future, he wondered? He unlocked the bathroom door and stepped out into the hall. If only, he thought, for his own sake, for that of his sister, Evie, and his daughter, Sam, if only it were as easy to unlock the enigmas surrounding them all. Somehow, he doubted they'd learn much today.

I'm lying in Matt's king-size bed when I hear the bathroom door open and, moments later, the shower. Suddenly, my mobile rings. Retrieving it from my backpack, I wonder who on earth is trying to make contact with me at this hour. With some surprise, I find it's Scott.

'I'm back,' he says, the excitement evident in his voice. 'Back in the UK, I mean.'

'I thought you weren't due home until the end of the week.'

'Couldn't stay away, could I? Especially knowing you're in London and that I might be able to see something of you. How are things?' The sound of his voice, his wish to see me, his concern, all-but overwhelms me.

'Okay,' I answer croakily.

'What's happened, Babe?'

Before I can stop myself, I launch into the detail of the previous few days: Matt's warmth and generosity to me, the novelty and excitement of attending his book launch, the way in which Sophie reached out to me in friendship, and then – the devastation of finding the photograph she gave me.

'I now know, without a shadow of a doubt, that I wasn't wanted,' I tell Scott.

'Oh, come on now –'

'It's perfectly clear from the photograph!' I interrupt. 'Phil Hamilton was a witness at my parents' wedding. And the date of the marriage, which was printed on the back of the photo, was three months later than the date my parents used to tell me. It's pretty obvious that I was conceived before my parents got married. In fact, I'm beginning to think they must have been forced into marriage, and that's why they had no time for each other.'

'Look, why don't we try and meet to talk this through?' The calm in Scott's voice makes me realise how agitated I've become. 'That's what I was ringing for, anyway. To see if there was any chance of meeting up.'

'I don't know,' I make myself breathe deep, and slow down. 'I'm a guest at Matt's apartment. I don't want to be rude.'

'Two Yanks together,' says Scott. 'What more could a gal want? Give it a go. See what he says.'

Hearing the bathroom door open, I bid Scott a hasty goodbye and ring off. Then knowing that Matt will be cooking me a special breakfast again, I make ready for my ablutions, wondering what further revelations the day will bring forth as we look around the Hamilton family's properties.

Sophie shuddered, the clamour of London traffic an incessant demand upon her senses; the rush of those on foot a seemingly mindless passage of flight that took no heed of others.

'You okay?' Matt asked, appearing at her side.

She turned towards him, a smile on her face.

'I suppose you're used to all this. But to a country girl like me –'

He grinned, and she felt her heart hammer on her ribs.

'Not so sure about that,' he retorted. 'I'd say the suburbs, where we are now, are worse than the city centre where I live. Perhaps you need to visit the metropolis more often. Get used to it. I could show you around. What d'you say?'

Sophie felt herself blush. Was this a proposition? A date? Before she could think of a suitable riposte, her mother intervened.

'Sophie! You mustn't monopolise our guest. He wants to discover his roots. Find out where his family originated from. Isn't that right Matthew?'

Sophie exchanged a glance with Matt as her mother led him away.

The tour of the London properties owned by Grandma had begun that morning when the four of them – she, Liz, and their parents – had taken a taxi to Clapham South, where they'd arranged to rendezvous with Matt and Evie, who had travelled in by tube. As agreed, they were meeting at the entrance of the underground station, where they were standing now. Having dressed casually in jeans and T-shirt, Sophie was glad to see she did not look out of place when Matt and Evie emerged into the sunshine. Liz and her parents, all more formally clad in smart suits, stood to one side; and once the usual greetings had taken place everyone looked to her parents for guidance as to how they were to proceed.

'This is where my father started his hotel business,' her mother said.

Aware that everyone was looking puzzled and that Mummy was playing to the crowd, Sophie said, 'But this is the tube station.'

'Exactly! But once upon a time this was a respectable hotel. Tinturn.'

It was difficult to imagine, as all heads turned to look at the entrance, where hundreds of commuters streamed back and forth.

'So what happened?' Oozing charm and attentiveness, Matt picked up the gauntlet Phoebe had thrown down.

Revelling in the drama, she turned towards him, a smile on her face.

'The hotel was compulsorily purchased and knocked down to build the underground station,' she said, triumphantly. 'Then, during the war, when London was bombed, the government constructed a deep level shelter just around the corner here. In fact, I think my mother had to take refuge here with one of my sisters, when she was a baby.'

'Gee, that must have been frightening!' It was clear from the expression on Matt's face that his horror was genuine, and looking at Mummy, Sophie could see that she was positively glowing with satisfaction and pride in having impressed her audience.

'Well, I wasn't born, of course,' she simpered. 'but I believe my parents were living too far away for my mother to run all the way back there pushing a pram when the sirens went off.'

'So they were no longer in the hotel business?' Matt asked.

'Oh they were! With the money they realised from the sale of the hotel to London Transport, they then purchased the Malwood Hotel, round the corner.'

Liz, who had been preoccupied with their father all morning, now spoke up.

'Didn't Grandma once own the cinema on Balham Hill, as well? You used to tell Fiona and me that you went to Saturday morning pictures there.'

Sophie felt a pang of exclusion. Being so much younger than her sisters, there were large tranches of family life she'd missed out on. She'd shared none of these London experiences. It was almost as if she were a stranger in the midst of her family.

Her mother laughed at the memories Liz had evoked.

'Oh, yes! They had an organ that came up out of the depths and we'd all have a singalong, with the words of the song projected on the screen and a little bouncy ball showing us which word to sing. It was so much fun. Come on. This way and I'll show you.'

Led by Aunt Phoebe, they began to walk away from the tube station towards the deep level shelter. Now classified as a listed building, it appeared, to Sophie, to be remarkably similar in appearance to a French *pissoir*. Or a circular concrete pillbox! They walked on down the road until they reached what had clearly been a cinema. Sophie looked up at the distinctive architecture, with its white stone frontage and tower effect roof, trying to imagine what it must have been like in her mother's childhood. Liz turned to their mother.

'It was the Odeon Cinema in your day, wasn't it?' she asked. 'And didn't you say it used to be all lit up with strip neon lights?'

'It was indeed. And they're still there. I believe it opened in the 1930s – before my time, of course. But as you can see, it's now a wine store. However, it's still a listed building. Can't remember who built it, but it was someone famous.'

Matt looked impressed. And you still own it?' he asked.

'We never owned the cinema outright. Only the freehold on the land. But my mother owned a good deal of property around here. Plus, of course, Rosegreen on Nightingale Lane, where I was born.'

'I remember going there with you once, when I was a small girl,' said Liz. 'Isn't that also a listed building? I seem to recall a domed ceiling painted like the Sistine Chapel. Very grand, it was.'

Phoebe nodded. 'And all the doors had hand-painted murals on them. They had to be covered with hardboard to protect them when Wandsworth Borough Council requisitioned it as a nursery during the war. So my mother told me.'

'Why was it requisitioned?' Sophie asked.

'The government needed women to help in the war effort,' her mother replied. 'Obviously, they had to provide somewhere for them to leave their preschool children.

'There was a gatekeeper's cottage at the front of the property, so we moved in there temporarily, and then into one of the other properties my parents owned. It was a bit of a comedown, but there you are. Everyone had to do their bit.'

'And your parents?' Matt asked. 'What did they do?'

'At one time they had two hotels on Balham Hill. The residents tended to be there for the long term. There was such a chronic housing shortage after the Blitz. My father ran one and my mother the other. But my father died when I was very young. My mother had no option but to soldier on, on her own. Wonderful woman she was.'

Sophie noted the pride on her mother's face but before she could comment, Daddy, who had been silent all morning, intervened, his face and voice full of excitement.

'That's when I met you,' he said, 'In the hotel your mother was running. Fell in love with you. Best girl in London. Best girl in the world.'

'You met Mummy here?' Sophie asked. 'What were you doing staying in a hotel?'

'Moved here from Scotland, didn't I! Got my first job as a doctor in the city, and I had to have digs somewhere. Couldn't have been better with the tube so handy. A godsend.'

'So what made you choose here, Daddy? I mean, if you were working in the city –'

'Chay Rae, of course. Knew his family in Scotland, didn't I. He'd stayed here at the hotel, so they put me in touch with –'

Sophie gasped as her mother turned abruptly and grasped her father by the arm.

'Be quiet, Phil!' she hissed. 'No one wants to hear about your past. Come on! Let's get a taxi and take a look at Rosegreen and my old school.'

Sophie felt rooted to the spot as her mother, accompanied by Liz, marched her father away from them all. She turned to apologise to their guests. Then she saw the look on Matt's face. And the penny dropped.

Matt closed his mouth, suddenly aware that his jaw, quite literally, had dropped. Unable to move, he stared at the retreating figures before him: Aunt Phoebe marching fiercely up the road; Phil, his arm involuntarily linked with hers, stumbling along beside her. As he watched, Liz intervened and brought the pair to a halt. He turned his head. Sophie was staring, not at her parents, but at him. On the other side, stood Evie. She, too, looked wide-eyed and aghast. So he was not alone in having picked up on Phil's revelation!

'Good grief!' he exclaimed. 'Did I hear that right?'

Evie moved towards him. 'Rae. He said Chay Rae, didn't he?'

Matt frowned. He felt utterly perplexed.

'You don't think we misheard?'

Sophie joined them. 'Please, please don't make a scene,' she begged. 'I mean, I know you've every right to be angry. But, please. Daddy doesn't mean to be difficult.'

Matt shook his head to clear his mind. Around him, the traffic noise seemed to have increased to a deafening crescendo. He looked at Sophie.

'So you heard him, too?'

Even to his own ears, his voice sounded hoarse. What the hell was going on? What did Phil know? What was Phoebe concealing? More to the point, why?

Evie slipped her arm through his and addressed herself to Sophie.

'We didn't imagine it, did we? Your father did say he knew someone called Chay Rae? You do realise the implications? That this could be the person named on Matt's adoption papers?'

Sophie looked close to tears.

'Yes. But I've never heard Daddy mention that name before. Or anyone with a name like that. It must be being back on old territory that's triggered his memories.'

'And you don't think your mother would have remembered?'

'I don't know. I'm sorry. I just don't know.'

Matt put his hand on Evie's to silence her, then reached out to take hold of Sophie's arm.

'Look, it's no good us falling out about this. You're right, Sophie. There's obviously something going on here that needs investigation. But this is not your father's fault. Nor is it yours. And this is neither the time nor the place for me to have it out with your mother. So let's leave it for now, shall we?'

Ahead of them, a taxi drew up to the pavement. As they stood together, a tight knit trio, they saw Liz open the door and usher her parents inside. She raised a hand to the side of her head, her thumb and little finger extended to indicate she would ring them, then she too boarded the vehicle. Shackled with the chains of helplessness and frustration, Matt watched as the cab pulled out to join the slowly moving queue of traffic.

Chapter Twelve

Revealing and Concealing

WATCHING THE RETREATING taxi bearing Phil, Phoebe and Liz to a destination unknown, I can see that it's down to me to take charge of the situation. Seeing a Costa Coffee shop on the far side of the road, I urge Matt and Sophie to follow me.

'This is a caffeine moment if ever there was one,' I tell them, wondering, immediately afterwards, if Matt might have thought it more of a whisky moment.

Together, we cross the road and dive into the corner café, seating ourselves at a table in a relatively quiet spot away from the door.

'I'm so sorry,' Sophie says, repeatedly, when the waitress has delivered two frothy cappuccinos for the two of us, and an Americano for Matt. 'Your day has been spoiled. Ruined.'

Her fragile English rose beauty looks crushed, her blue eyes crumpled with the pain of imagined fault and remorse. It's hard to imagine what has induced this sense of blame within her but I'm aware that I need to expunge it.

'Now listen, Sophie,' I reach across the table and take her hands in mine to focus her attention on what I'm about to say. 'This is not your doing. There's obviously a mystery here. And equally obviously Matt has every right to hope that it will be solved. But you don't need to take this on yourself.'

'But you've come all this way up to London, and you've hardly seen any of Grandma's properties,' Sophie protests.

'It doesn't matter. Your mother mentioned Rosegreen and her convent school, and we can ask for directions and make our own way there without her, if we want to.' I glance at Matt for corroboration, but he continues to look stunned. Or at least, deep in thought.

'I've only ever seen them from the outside,' Sophie persists, her voice full of guilt. 'And then there are all the other houses that Grandma rented out.'

'You never knew your grandmother did you?' I ask, in an attempt to divert her.

Sophie pursed her lips and shook her head.

'She died the year I was born. Liz and Fiona knew her well, of course. They would have been in their teens. Fiona used to tell me she loved playing games. Cards. Board games. Sounds as if they had lots of fun together. But I missed out on all of that.'

Matt sips his coffee. 'You said earlier you'd only ever seen your gran's properties from the outside?'

Sophie nodded. 'Yes. I never went in any of them. I'd have loved to have seen Rosegreen. It sounds stunning from the way Liz described it.'

'So does your mom still own all the properties?'

Sophie looked puzzled.

'Good question! I don't think so. As far as I know, she and my uncle inherited whatever Grandma left. I believe he died soon afterwards. What happened to it all then, I've no idea.'

The café is filling fast, mostly with young mothers meeting friends. Facing into the room, I can't help being drawn to watch the scene behind Matt, nor to form an unfavourable opinion of what I see. Heads bent, eyes glued, as the women conduct their screen-oriented lives, their toddlers appear to be nothing more to them than little bodies and limbs restrained in buggies, or little mouths and voices silenced with sugary drinks.

Unbidden memories of my own lost baby flood – a dull and desperate ache – into my heart and mind. How can I not compare what I see before me with the love, the mother-skills, the life-lessons I'd yearned to impart to my unborn babe?

Hearing my name mentioned, I refocus, turning my attention back to where it belongs. Across the table from me, Matt is still quizzing Sophie.

'I was telling Evie about the row between your mom and Aunt

Bea. Can you add any more to that?'

Sophie looks down at her hands.

'I've been trying to visualise the scene ever since I told you about it, Matt, and I'm now quite sure it was about Grandma's will. Because I also remember Mummy carrying on at Daddy about it again, when you first contacted her.'

'Just before our visit to Kingswear, then?' I ask.

Sophie nods. 'It didn't mean much at the time, and it's only now that I realise the connection. I think Daddy was trying to say that Aunt Bea should never have been cut out of Grandma's will. And Mummy was saying there was good reason for it. I probably shouldn't tell you this, but she seemed to think you were going to contest the will.' She looks at Matt. 'She was in quite a state about it. Hence the panic attack.'

Matt shoots a look of excitement across at me.

'I don't think I shall be doing that,' he reassures her.

'But do you know what reason your mother gave for her sister being cut out?' I ask.

Sophie purses her lips. 'No I don't,' she says. 'All I know is that Daddy seemed to think it had stirred up a hornet's nest. And I seem to remember it had something to do with this Chay Rae. I'd forgotten until Daddy mentioned him this afternoon.'

Matt shakes his head in what looks like disbelief.

'Amazing that he has such lucid memories, given his dementia,' he says. 'So what...'

My mobile phone alerts me to an incoming call. Fumbling to retrieve it from my backpack, I drop it on the floor. At the same moment, Sophie's phone rings. By the time I surface from beneath the table, she's answered it, and it's clear, from the look of consternation on her face, that all is not well.

'Where are you?' she asks, anxiously stuffing a strand of blonde hair behind her ear. 'Yes. We'll come immediately. We'll get a taxi.'

She rings off, clutches her shoulder bag, her face taut with fear. 'That was Liz. She wants us – well, you, Evie – to go back to the hotel. I've said we would. Do you mind?'

'What's happened, Sophie?' I think I have a pretty good idea, but

I want to hear it from her.

'Mummy. Another panic attack. I think we ought to go. Do you mind?'

In reality, I suspect it would have been more sensible for Liz to summon the duty manager to ask for a medic to attend her mother, but somehow I doubt that this is a real emergency. Besides, it's an opportunity to see if Phoebe will be more forthcoming about Phil's revelations. I begin to gather my things together.

'Of course we'll go. Are you ready, Matt?'

Emerging from the café, we cross the road again and walk briskly back towards the underground station, where we hail a cab and make our way to Marble Arch. Conversation, if you can call it that, is limited. I guess we're all dealing with the various facets of the morning's events and the tumultuous thoughts these have thrown at us. It's only as we approach the hotel that I remember my forgotten phone call.

Glancing at the screen, I see it was from Scott, a follow-up, presumably, on his call earlier that morning. Quickly I tap out a text, @ *Cumberland Hotel* and send it off in reply. I hope he'll realise I'm otherwise engaged and will have to get back to him later. Poor chap! He's left his family and homeland and returned to the UK early in the hope of seeing me, and now this!

Liz, it would appear when we arrive at the hotel and take the lift up to her parents' room, has taken charge of the situation. I am to see Phoebe, alone, in her room, she tells me, while room service provide lunch for Liz and her father in the room she is sharing with Sophie. The inference is that Sophie and Matt should make themselves scarce.

'Not to worry,' says Matt, resuming his usual affable self, 'Sophie and I can lunch in the bar. Unless you have other plans?'

It's clear from the suffusion flooding across Sophie's face, that Matt's solution is more than amenable to her. My tummy rumbles in protest, but hey, I know my place.

Everyone departs, and I'm left alone with Phoebe, who appears to have got over the worst of her attack and is sitting on the only easy chair in the room with her eyes shut. I pull out the upright dressing table chair and seat myself.

'Would you like to talk, Phoebe? I can assure you that anything you have to say to me in this room will remain confidential. Despite the family gathering, I shall view this time together in a professional capacity.'

Phoebe draws a shuddering breath. Is it my imagination, or is it a tad over-dramatic, as if there's something not quite real about her response?

'There's no rush,' I continue. 'Would you like me to make you some tea?'

Phoebe nods. 'That would be nice,' she whispers.

I proceed to fill the kettle from the tap in the *en suite* bathroom, and set it to boil in the bedroom.

'Milk and sugar?'

Phoebe nods, then falls silent again.

From the first floor window, I can see the *mêlée* of London traffic and pedestrians beneath me. Scurrying about with a precision and intention that is more perceptible from above than when one is embroiled in it, a pattern seems to emerge. It's a little like this family, I can't help thinking. Beneath the veneer of normal, affable relationships, mysteries abound. What is it they're so intent upon hiding, I wonder?

When the tea is made and I've set a cup on a small table beside Phoebe, I move the upright chair opposite her and seat myself again. She's removed the jacket of her suit and, unless I'm mistaken, has undone the button above the zip on her skirt. Evidence of her panic attack is apparent in the twisted nature of her silk blouse, some of which has escaped from her waistband. Before I can say a word, she launches forth, her tone rasping and accusing.

'It was Sophie's plan, coming to London to see the property. A ridiculous idea!'

'I think it was she who suggested it but you who encouraged it,' I correct her, mildly. 'And I must say, we've all enjoyed it. It's quite something to hear that your family owned a property that was compulsorily purchased to become a tube station.'

'And a deep shelter!' The pride in Phoebe's voice is evident despite her condition.

'And a deep shelter,' I acknowledge. 'Just think of the lives that must have saved.'

Phoebe lifts her cup to her lips. 'It was all my mother's doing, of course. Wonderful woman she was.'

Despite my earlier promise to Phoebe of professionalism, it's hard to remain impartial when the circumstances under discussion are part and parcel of one's own life. I find myself unable to resist the temptation to discover more.

'So, if it's not too impertinent a question, how did she finance all the property? I thought Matt said she came from a somewhat impoverished background?'

'Oh, well' – it's clear I've touched a nerve – 'my father's family were wealthy landowners. Country folk. Farmers. But it was my mother's idea to invest in London property. And her hard work that made the business so successful.'

'She sounds wonderful,' I respond, quick to placate Phoebe. 'Certainly someone to feel proud of.'

Phoebe's elation in response to my praise for her mother is exactly what I'd hoped for.

'So what upset you this morning?' I ask her.

She shuffles in her seat. 'It's Phil! He gets carried away. Goes off on one of his flights of fancy.'

She falls silent again.

'It must be distressing – difficult – living with someone with dementia.' I set my empty cup down on the tray next to the kettle, and take Phoebe's from her. 'I don't suppose your husband remembers what's happened from one minute to the next, does he?'

'It's enough to drive you mad. You ask him to take the dustbins to the gate on collection day, and find him an hour later wandering about the garden with them, not knowing what he's supposed to be doing. Or he's put them in the shed.'

I nod to convey my sympathy, and Phoebe continues.

'He's not the man I married. Not that he was ever a driving force – a macho-man. Is that what they say? So yes, it's difficult.'

'But they do say, also, that long term memory isn't affected in the same way as short term, don't they? And I understand that it's good to prompt dementia sufferers to recall events from long ago.'

'So they say!' Phoebe looks away, her tone of voice disparaging.

Unmoved, I continue on the same tack.

'I suppose seeing all the old haunts and hearing familiar road names, I guess that's what triggered the memories for Phil about his friend. Chay Rae, wasn't it?'

Phoebe glowers. 'I told Phil to be quiet. I never want to hear that name again, I said. Nasty piece of work he was.'

I'm aware that time is going on and that lunchtime is fast approaching. If Phoebe's hunger pangs are as acute as mine she might, at any moment, bring our ruminations to a close. Having got this far, I don't want to lose the opportunity to encourage her to open up further. Perhaps to press her on the photograph Sophie gave me of my parents' wedding, and the dispute about the date of their marriage in relation to my birth? But for now, the need to push forward on what has upset her is paramount.

'Is it possible that this Chay Rae, could be the reason for your panic attack this morning?' I ask.

Without hesitation, Phoebe bursts out, 'Oh, I'm sure it could. After all, he was the reason for the eventual demise of my parents' business. It's his fault we lost – had to get rid of – all the London property.'

The phone rings on the bedside table. Phoebe jumps in her seat but makes no attempt to answer it.

'Shall I?' I ask. 'It could be your daughter.'

She nods. I cross the room and pick up the phone. It is, indeed, Phoebe's daughter. But not, I discover, the one I'd expected it to be.

Matt put his mobile phone back in his trouser pocket and looked across the table at Sophie. Lunch, in the hotel bar without the influence of 'Mummy and Daddy' and the rest of the family, had been a particularly enjoyable experience. He felt he'd had a chance to get to know the real Sophie. A Sophie whose love of reading and depth of knowledge belied the merely skin deep beauty of first impression.

A Sophie whose yearning for more, far surpassed the little-girl-lost image she conveyed. A Sophie held back, he suspected, by an aura of false-guilt imposed upon her by her mother. Which made it all the more difficult to have to go along with the suggestion that had just been put to him.

'That was your sister, Liz, on the phone,' he said. 'She wants to meet up with Evie and me. On our own.'

Sophie's plump red lips broke into a smile. 'I suppose that means I'd better go and look after Mummy and Daddy then.'

There was no rancour in her voice, Matt noted, nor any hint of resignation. He marvelled at her resilience.

'Gee, I'm so sorry.'

He continued to sit at the table, reluctant to bring his time with her to an end. 'It's been great. I can't tell you what's it's meant to me to have a chance to get to know you better.'

'Me too. I've really enjoyed it. It's not often I get to eat crab salad. Especially in the company of a famous author! Thank you.'

Matt grinned and stood up.

'My pleasure.'

He waited until Sophie rose from her chair. 'I hope we can do it again,' he said, aware of a sudden earnestness in his voice. 'In the not too distant future?'

Sophie blushed and lowered her eyelids, her lashes thick and long against her cheeks. Unable to resist, he leaned towards her and pulled her into his arms. Her face was soft against his, her body supple and yielding. He pulled away. This was a cousin. And he was in the midst of a complicated situation. No call to complicate it further.

'Better go and find my parents,' said Sophie, her cheeks rosy, her eyes still lowered. 'Where are you seeing Liz?'

'She's suggested we meet in the lounge. Bit too noisy in here, I think. I don't know what it's all about but, as I said, she's asked Evie, too. Hence you havin' to babysit your ma and pa. Sorry.'

Sophie shook her head. 'No problem,' she said. 'Thank you, again, for lunch.'

Matt waited until she'd left, paid a convenience call to the bathroom, then made his way across the concourse to the lounge. Cosy it was not. A sparse open space in contemporary style, in which cream leather chairs and brown mock suede sofas were arranged in groups around individual coffee tables, it was the epitome of minimalism.

He seated himself in a quiet corner facing the entrance to await Liz and Evie's arrival. On the far side of the room sat a well-to-do Asian family and, as he watched, a young waitress brought them a tray of tea. Good idea! He raised a hand to beckon the girl over, put in an order for a pot of tea for three and paid for it. He'd no sooner finished than Evie appeared. He stood and waved, gave her a peck on the cheek when she joined him, and waited until she had seated herself on the sofa adjacent to his chair before seating himself again.

'No Liz?' he asked.

'She won't be a moment,' Evie replied, running her fingers through her dark curly hair and lifting her head, briefly, to inspect the result in the mirror behind her. 'I left her giving instructions to Sophie as to what to do with their parents.'

She turned to Matt, raising her eyebrows in what was, clearly, an indication of her views on the matter. Matt inclined his head to show his understanding and agreement.

'Do you know what this is all about?' he asked.

'Haven't a clue.'

'And how's Phoebe?'

Evie shrugged. 'She's calmed down.'

Knowing there would be issues of confidentiality in Evie's lack of detail, Matt didn't press her.

Liz appeared on the far side of the lounge and made her way across to them, her heels clicking on the tiled floor. Matt stood to greet her. She looked somewhat flustered, he thought. Her hair, normally a sleek and immaculate bob, was ruffled, and her peplum top, which he recognised as Armani, was askew. Perhaps, unlike Sophie, she found it difficult dealing with her father?

Rather than seat herself on the sofa beside Evie, it seemed to Matt that Liz eyed up the possibilities before choosing an easy chair on the opposite side of the coffee table. Unable to stop himself, the

147

author in him began to make various conjectures. Was her choice of seating motivated simply for ease of discourse? Because she felt uncomfortable with her new-found relatives and wanted to distance herself? Or was it a mark of leadership, to show Evie and him that *she* was the one who had convened the meeting, so it followed that *she* was the one who was in charge? As if to confirm the last of his assumptions, she began, without any of the usual prevarications demanded by etiquette, to address the two of them.

'This has to stop,' she said, leaning forward, her well-manicured hands clasped in her lap. 'I don't mean to sound rude, but my parents are elderly and they can't cope with it.'

Matt shifted, uncomfortably aware it was he who had begun the investigation Liz was referring to. Before he could say anything, however, Evie spoke up, her voice calm and reasoned, in the manner one might expect of a therapist like herself.

'What exactly is it that they can't cope with, Liz?'

Liz sat back, abruptly. It was almost, thought Matt, as if she imagined she'd been slapped in the face. She shrugged and lifted one hand, briefly, as if to fend off any further assault.

The young waitress brought the tea Matt had ordered and began to lay it out on the coffee table before them.

'Hope this is okay with everyone?' he asked. 'Anyone prefer a coffee or soft drink?'

Both women shook their heads.

'Thank you,' Evie proceeded to pour. Liz accepted the cup she put before her, sat back and clasped her hands together.

'All this dragging up the past,' she said in clipped tones. 'It's just not on. You must know full well in your line of work, Evie, that there are memories – events – that are distressing and best forgotten. You must have seen for yourself that Mother can't handle this sort of thing.'

'That's what I'm trying to get at Liz. What *sort of thing* are you referring to?'

Liz threw her hands up in the air.

'This whole trip was a mistake! I should never have allowed Mother to be talked into it.'

Matt leaned forward into the conversation.

'But it was her idea,' he said. 'She wanted to show us the London properties. She said so when Evie and I first met her in Devon.'

'Only because Sophie put it to her.'

'Well, it may have been Sophie's idea originally,' Evie intervened, her voice soft and even. 'But your mother certainly went along with it, as we all did. She's obviously very proud of what her parents achieved. Particularly her mother. And rightly so. But the thing is, Liz, you can't expect us to be sensitive to your mother's needs unless we're privy to what's upsetting her?'

Matt nodded in agreement. And visibly unable to find fault with Evie's argument, Liz reluctantly followed suit. Evie continued.

'Don't you think, also, Liz, that Matt might want – need – to learn more about his family?'

Liz looked contrite. 'I do understand your need to find out about the family. But perhaps it might be better to do so through me? At least, as much as possible. After all, I grew up in London. As I've already said, I knew most of the properties.'

'So you'd be able to furnish us with a list?' Matt asked. 'And I could then do some research without having to bother you or your mom.'

'I could do,' Liz said. 'Or you could simply ask me what you need to know.'

'Let's be honest about this,' said Evie. 'It wasn't the property that upset your mother, was it Liz? It was your father's mention of this man, Chay Rae. Do you know why that was? And do you understand the significance as far as Matt's concerned?'

Matt held his breath. Evie's skills were amazing. He would never have had the gall to raise the subject himself, yet here she was –

Liz sighed. 'Yes,' she said. 'I know all there is to know about Chay Rae.'

Matt felt the wall of his chest tighten as his breath was expelled. He tugged at his hair. Then an unknown voice was heard.

'Oh, there you are!'

Across the room, behind Liz and to one side of Evie, a scene had been unfolding before Matt's eyes. A man, tall and, unless he was mistaken, American, was being escorted into the Club Lounge by the waitress who had served them with tea, earlier. She was, even now, pointing in their direction.

Matt focused more keenly on the duo, then nodded in recognition. Evie had mentioned to him when they'd travelled on the tube to meet with the Hamiltons, that morning, that her boyfriend, Scott, was in London and was hoping to see her. She'd voiced a sense of guilt at the concept of his intruding upon the family gathering – an emotion he'd quickly quelled, as he'd encouraged her to ask him over to the apartment the following day.

It seemed, however, that Scott had tracked Evie down to the Cumberland Hotel. How, was unclear. But the fact was that he was here. Now. Matt rose and stretched out his hand to greet the advancing stranger. At the same moment, Evie, red-faced and unmistakably embarrassed, turned in his direction.

Chapter Thirteen

History: Fact or Perception?

SOPHIE LEFT HER parents' room and made her way down the corridor. It seemed she could please no one. Summonsed by Liz to look after Mummy and Daddy, while she went down to the lounge to meet with Matt and Evie, she had then been summarily dismissed by her mother.

'Daddy and I are going to have a rest. We don't need babysitting.'

Sophie inserted the key card in the door of the room she was sharing with Liz, and went in. The chambermaid had done her job of bed-making, straightening up the room, and washing teacups, and had left fresh bottled water on the tray beside the tea-making facilities. Knowing Liz's preference for the sparkling variety, Sophie selected the bottle of still water, opened it and drank from it, directly. Mummy would not approve, but –

The room felt cold. She shivered, and stared out of the window at the street far below. It was in shadow, no sunlight penetrating the tall buildings. Following through on her earlier thought, she threw herself into the easy chair and began to weep. Mummy's approval, it seemed, was beyond reach.

'Fancy letting Daddy get into such a state,' she'd said, earlier, her face skewed into a picture of exasperation. 'You should know better, Sophie, than to encourage him.'

Sophie hadn't been aware of encouraging him in anything at that point. She leaned forward in the chair, her arms clutching her tummy as if to alleviate the ache she felt. As far as she could recall, Daddy had volunteered the information that he'd met Mummy when he'd been staying in Grandma's hotel. All she'd done was to ask him to elaborate, to tell them how it had come about that he was staying in that particular place at that particular time. It was his disclosure that had caused such consternation. And not simply with Mummy. Matt, too, had been affected.

Should she have known that Daddy had learned about Grandma's hotel from this man, Chay Rae? Perhaps she should have done? Perhaps Mummy was right in her assumption that Sophie would know the family history and she was to blame for the furore that had so rudely interrupted the purpose of this visit to London? Certainly Liz appeared to think so.

'For goodness sake, Sophie!' she'd said earlier. 'You know full well how Mother feels about this intrusion into family affairs. You were the one who arranged for her to have counselling in the first place. And then you go and find someone – Evie – who also claims to be a relative. Really!'

Liz was right. What a coincidence! It could only happen to her. 'You're a magnet for disaster,' Liz had told her.

Liz! She would probably be returning to their room soon when she'd finished her meeting with Evie and Matt. Was she *au fait* with Chay Rae's identity? And if so, was she intending to pass on what she knew? Sophie stood, and again went to the window, looking up over the rooftops to the sliver of sky above.

She had so enjoyed her time alone with Matt over lunch. His kindness and the interest he had shown in her was quite unlike anything she normally experienced.

'So what took you into teaching?' he'd asked, leaning towards her across the table and fixing his peaty brown eyes upon her as if she were the only person in the busy bar.

She'd shrugged, embarrassed to be the centre of attention.

'I suppose I felt it was the only thing open to me.'

'From the little I've seen of you, I'd say there was more to it than that. You're a born encourager, Sophie.'

Sophie paused over her crab salad and gave his remark her consideration.

'Well, given the hours I work during term, plus the holiday periods, I suppose it gives me more time to help my parents,' she admitted.

Matt shook his head. 'I wasn't thinkin' of your mom and dad. I can just see you inspiring the children you teach to reach their potential. You're a woman of passion, Sophie.'

She'd felt herself blush, hot and uncomfortable, and he'd laughed, reached across the table, and put his hand, briefly, on hers.

'Passionate about imparting your skills to those in your charge is what I mean. I wouldn't know about your passions in any other sense of the word.'

Did she possess any passion in any other sense of the word? Thinking about it now, she somewhat doubted it. Boyfriends had come and gone, and she was currently unattached. Was that normal given that she'd reached the ripe old age of twenty-six? It wasn't that she was devoid of feeling. True, she'd not thought about such things for a while. But if she was honest – and given that he was a cousin it wasn't a comfortable thought – she had to admit to finding Matt rather attractive.

They'd gone on to discuss all sorts of topics dear to her heart, literature, the arts, sport, and then he'd shared a little about his own life and work. She'd marvelled at the contrast between his preferred introverted life of writing, and the necessity for an extrovert persona when dealing with the public at book launches and the like; the creativity and innovation of story-telling, versus the administrative monotony required for proofing, editing and scheduling speaking engagements.

She'd been caught up in a world that was magical, far above the mundane and sometimes difficult matters of home and family – rather like the fluffy white clouds that were visible now from the window. Then the phone call from Liz had broken the spell.

Before they'd parted company, Matt had expressed a wish to see her again. It could only have been a polite termination of their time together, of course, rather than a real desire on his part. Then he'd hugged her, and she'd felt her heart hammering against her ribs.

Before she could regain her balance, he'd pulled away. And she'd realised then – and now – that his tactile nature was, just that. A gesture born of his American culture. No more than the conventions of his personality and upbringing.

She looked around the featureless hotel bedroom.

'Pull yourself together, Sophie,' she told herself.

Moving away from her spot at the window, she went into the bathroom to wash her face. Then, knowing she would not be welcome in the Club Lounge where Liz was holding forth with Matt and Evie, she went downstairs to the reception area to ask if it would be possible to have a newspaper delivered next morning.

I return from the ladies' room to the Club Lounge in the Cumberland Hotel, where I've left Matt and Scott talking together. Scott's appearance on the scene, half an hour earlier, was both surprising and exciting but, at the same time, oh so frustrating and embarrassing! What timing! Just as Liz had been about to impart what she knew of Chay Rae. Catching sight of the vexation in Matt's face, I couldn't help feeling for him.

'What are you doing here?' I asked Scott, painfully aware that my voice was conveying exasperation rather than pleasure.

He looked uncertainly from one to the other of us.

'Well you texted me to say you were gonna be here, at the Cumberland –'

My eyes closed for a moment as I recalled my hurried text message in the taxi, in response to the call I'd missed from him. He'd obviously taken it to be an invitation to join us, when my intention had been to let him know I was busy. *Mea culpa*! Why should he have known? I opened my eyes, smiled, broadly, and lifted my face to receive his kiss of greeting.

'Just hadn't expected you to be here so soon,' I said. 'How did you find us?'

'I was asking at Reception – said I was a friend of Evie Adams – when who should I bump into but your cousin, Sophie, ordering a newspaper. She overheard me and introduced herself. We had quite a chat together. Then she told me where you were.'

I turned to introduce Scott to Liz. She was already gathering her things together and, after a brief handshake and exchange of the minimum greeting required by etiquette, she indicated her need to get back upstairs to her parents. Matt, however, made every effort to welcome Scott and, despite my initial discomfort at having been the cause of the disruption, the three of us engaged in a pleasant exchange of dialogue.

I realise, now, half an hour later, that I can hardly expect to monopolise Matt's time, but am at a loss to know how to draw our threesome to a close. As it turns out, I have no need to worry.

'Look, why don't you two make the most of what remains of the day, while I head home?' Matt says when I reappear from the loo. 'You can get a taxi back to the apartment whenever you're ready, Evie.'

I'm torn, the longing to be alone with Scott tugging against the etiquette of excluding my host. Matt, sensitive guy that he is, immediately picks up on my dilemma.

'Truth be told, I could do with couple of hours to sort some stuff out,' he says, in an obvious attempt to let me off the hook.

'You're sure you don't mind?' I shrug my backpack onto my shoulder.

'I need to contact my publishers,' Matt says. 'You two go off and get some sightseeing in. I'm very aware of how little you've seen since you came to town. How about a boat trip on the river?'

The two men shake hands and Scott and I head off. A trip on the Thames appeals to us both as the ideal solution to sightseeing without exhausting ourselves, as well as giving us the opportunity to sit and talk together. We make our way to St Katharine's Dock with its fabulous restaurants in sight of Tower Bridge, and a mere stone's throw from The Tower of London, and from there we take the ferry down to Greenwich, birthplace of Henry VIII and Elizabeth I, and ultimately, the Thames Barrier.

'I've missed you like crazy,' Scott says as we seat ourselves on the upper deck. Oblivious to all the other tourists, he turns and, missing my cheek, kisses me on my ear. A thrill of desire runs through my veins and I lower my eyes as I feel the blood-rush suffuse my face and neck.

'Me, too,' I respond, conscious that this is not entirely true given the hectic schedule of the last few days, but equally aware of the pleasure his company now instils in me.

'So what's been happening?' Scott asks, taking my hand in his.

'What indeed!'

I haven't the heart to tell him that his arrival prevented an important disclosure from Liz about Chay Rae, whoever he is, but I feel I owe him some explanation.

'There's certainly something weird going on in this family,' I begin, launching forth into an account of the morning's events.

Scott shakes his head. 'Gee! What a mess.'

The tour guide's voice over the tannoy interrupts our conversation as he announces our whereabouts.

'Ahead of you, on the left bank, is Canary Wharf,' he booms. 'Now home to approximately fourteen million square feet of office and retail space, and one of London's two major financial centres, it was once the West India Docks, and many of the imports were from the Canary Islands. Hence the name.'

Obediently, and with a good deal of interest, we take in the scene before us.

'We're now skirting around The Isle of Dogs,' the guide continues. 'One of the poorest areas of London, anyone living there was seen as having *gone to the dogs*. A good deal of controversy exists about how the name came about. One of the earliest written records we have was by King Henry VIII, who in 1519, or thereabouts, mentioned the purchase of a hose from the Isle of Dogs for 10d – the *d* being old pence. Then we have Samuel Pepys, who in the 17th Century referred to it as the *unlucky Isle of Dogs*.

'But although there's no written record, it's thought that King Edward III, who predates Henry VIII by two hundred years, was supposed to have kept his greyhounds here, and that's why it was given its name. Who knows? It's anyone's guess.'

Scott grins and turns to look at me.

'Interesting. One of the concepts I lecture on at theological college is that history is often not fact but perception.'

I nod in agreement.

'In fact,' Scott continues, 'I'd go so far as to say that although we know truth is absolute, perceptions of truth are often relative. I'm thinking of your family situation, here. While you were in the bathroom, Matt filled me in on today's aborted attempt to look at the family property.'

I'm feeling quite tired after the day's exertions, so Scott's philosophical explanation of things goes over my head. I frown, perplexed.

'Not sure I follow you?'

'Phil's take on his friend Chay Rae versus Phoebe's perceptions of him as an arch-enemy,' Scott persists. 'It could be that neither is the truth; that he's neither friend nor foe. I suggested to Matt that he could try doing some research of his own, either online or through the local newspaper archives. If there was some sort of falling out – perhaps over the hotel business – it could be that it made the news.'

'What a brilliant idea!' I lean my head, briefly, on Scott's shoulder.

'Anyway, enough of my family,' I continue, straightening up as the ferry loops the loop and the O2 arena comes into view, a shallow dome that looks a little like a sponge cake with birthday candles on top. 'What's your news?'

Scott looks down at me, his eyes alight with an excitement that's evident despite the advancing evening.

'Funny you should ask that,' he says. 'I do have something to tell you – an answer to prayer. And something to ask you. I'm just not sure this is the right moment.'

As if to confirm his doubts, the clipper's horn sounds to warn a small dinghy of its approach. I'm left wondering how many more mysteries I can take. Then Scott leans over and – for the first time ever – kisses me full on the mouth.

Matt did, indeed, have good reason to ring his publishers, but that was not the prime purpose of his return. Having left Evie and Scott to enjoy some down time together, he entered his apartment with a quiet enthusiasm. Something Scott had said to him had resonated, and he was intent, now, on following it through.

Nice guy, Scott, he thought as he opened his front door, removed his jacket and kicked off his shoes. Not that they'd had long to become acquainted. Evie's embarrassment when he'd turned up had been patently obvious. And he had to admit to a certain amount of

157

irritation, himself. What timing, dammit! Just as Cousin Liz had been about to reveal all. Or at least as much as she knew about the elusive Chay Rae.

Making his way to his study, Matt sat himself at the desk and switched on his PC. An image of Sophie sprang to mind while the machine fired up, and he shut his eyes, the scent and softness of her assailing his senses with dizzy recall. He allowed himself a moment or two of bliss, then returned to the matter in hand.

Chay Rae, he typed into the search box and hit the return button on the keyboard. Instantly, a list of possible URLs appeared on the screen: Facebook and Twitter profiles, LinkedIn and YouTube, Pinterest and Instagram. Matt gripped his chin, thinking through the implications. Phil Hamilton had described Chay's family in Scotland as friends, so did that suggest he would now be in his late seventies, as Phil was? In which case, was it likely he'd be using social media such as Facebook or Twitter? Matt thought not. Much less Pinterest and Instagram.

LinkedIn might serve him better. If this man had been a professional, he could well have had staff who used the medium to advertise his skills. Retrieving his mouse, Matt scrolled down and clicked on the link. A dozen or more profiles were listed: a construction engineer, a dentist's surgery, a wannabee writer, and a professional wedding photographer. Doubtful of any success, he clicked on each in turn, trying to imagine how and why a connection might be made with Phil and Phoebe Hamilton.

Half an hour later, after a frustrating and unproductive search, he abandoned LinkedIn and Chay Rae, and keyed in a new topic for investigation, the name of the local newspapers in the Borough of Wandsworth and Lambeth. Doubtful that he would be able to study the archives online, he made a note of them with the intention of researching them in the public library. It might, also, he thought, be useful to have contact details for the current editor.

It was while he was metaphorically turning the pages of the current edition on screen that he struck gold. Bingo! There, on the newspaper's business pages, was an advertisement for Chay Rae, solicitors. Instantly, he typed the name into his search box.

Established in 1937, he read. He'd have been too old, in that case, to have been a friend of Phil Hamilton's, but he might well have had a son of a similar age.

The telephone rang. It was Matt's publishers. Hell! He'd gotten so caught up in the mystery of Chay Rae he'd forgotten to ring them. How unprofessional!

'Gee, I'm sorry,' he said into the receiver. Hastily, he rummaged around in his in-tray and retrieved the printed cover of his yet-to-be published novel.

'Yeah, it looks great. As always. There's just one little query I have in respect of the blurb –'

I return to Matt's apartment that evening to find his study-bedroom door open, his computer on, and his desk and sofa-bed scattered with papers.

'Guess what?' he says, leaving me in no doubt about the extent of his excitement. 'Oh, sorry! Did you have a good time with Scott?'

He opens the living room door and switches on the light so I can go in. It's clear that my news will have to take second place to whatever it is that he's learned.

'Great thanks.' I reply. 'But never mind that. What's happened?'

I seat myself on the sofa and Matt sits opposite.

'Drum roll,' he says, simulating the action.

'Oh, go on,' I laugh. 'Don't keep me in suspense.'

His face becomes more serious and I'm itching to know what he's discovered.

'I've found out – at least, I think I've found out – who Chay Rae is.'

Lit by one of the table lamps, Matt's face is a picture of elation, albeit overshadowed with doubt. I'm aware that his discovery, if it can be authenticated, might hold the key to his roots, though it has little to do with me. I lean back on the sofa and prepare to put on my counselling hat.

'So what are the known facts?' I ask.

Matt jumps to his feet and begins to pace the floor.

'Facts? You want facts?' He grins. 'The fact is that there's a solicitors' office in the vicinity of where we were this morning, which goes under the name Chay Rae. Equally certain is that the business was established in 1937.'

I must say I'm impressed.

'Wow! That's excellent news. So what might we surmise from that?'

Matt stops pacing, picks up his iPad from the dining table and seats himself next to me on the sofa.

'I've been going through all the research I did before setting out to find the family – birth certificates etc – and I've created a time-line as far as I'm able.' He taps the screen and turns it in my direction.

'We've no way of knowing when Aunt Phoebe's dad acquired his first hotel, of course. But given that her mom was born in 1919 and had our grandmamma in 1937 –'

'Goodness me! And Beatrice wasn't her first child! She must have been a teenage bride.'

'I've found no evidence of her having been a bride at all,' he says. 'At least, not yet.'

'You mean she may not have been married?'

Matt shrugs. 'Who knows? But the point is, our grandmamma's birth certificate shows her to have been born in the Borough of Wandsworth so we can be pretty sure Phoebe's parents were living in the vicinity when Chay Rae appeared on the scene and started the business.'

'The solicitors, you mean?'

'Yeah! So it's perfectly plausible he and Phoebe's dad would have known one another. Phil said earlier that he knew the Rae family in Scotland and that Chay had stayed at one of the family hotels. I suspect he boarded there until he set up the business and found himself somewhere to live.'

I pause again, trying to see where this is leading.

'So do you think Phoebe's father might have used Chay Rae as his solicitor?'

Matt jumps to his feet again.

'Too right I do! I think we can safely assume it could have bin for the conveyancing of some of the properties they purchased.'

'Of course! Phoebe said they had two hotels, didn't she.'

'It doesn't go anywhere near explaining why they fell out, Chay and Phoebe's dad, but it does give me something to work on. Phoebe mentioned the Malwood Hotel. That's gonna be my next bit of research. And then I'll be paying Chay Rae's solicitors a visit. See what I can glean from them.'

I stifle a yawn. It's been a long day and it's definitely past my bedtime. My train home leaves mid-morning tomorrow, and I still have my packing to do.

'Gee, I'm sorry, Sis.' Matt suddenly comes to. 'You must be worn out. All that trailing around the properties, and then having to look out for me when Phil let slip he knew Chay Rae. Not to mention having to look out for Phoebe too.'

I smile and get wearily to my feet.

'I am quite tired,' I admit. 'Think I'm ready for bed if you don't mind.'

Matt reaches out and gives me a hug.

'It's so good to have you as my sister. Can't tell you what it means to me.' He releases me, but continues to hold me by my shoulders, at arm's length. 'I'm sorry I've bin so self-absorbed,' he says, gazing at me. 'And I haven't even asked how your evening went. All well with Scott? How are things between you?'

I smile and lower my eyes, unable to face Matt's scrutiny.

'We had a wonderful evening, thank you.' Releasing myself from Matt's restraint, I cross the room and open the door. 'He had some news for me, but I'll fill you in another time if you don't mind.'

I turn and make my way to bed, shutting the door behind me.

162

Chapter Fourteen

A Change of View

IT IS WITH mixed feelings that I return home. Much to my surprise, saying goodbye to Matt almost reduces me to tears. Considering how short a time I've known him, and the depth of my antagonism in respect of his pronouncements about our mother at times, I simply hadn't expected to have forged what I now recognise as a deepening affection for my new brother.

'See you again soon, Sis,' he promises, giving me a bear hug before seeing me onto the train. 'And we'll keep in touch.'

It isn't only Matt who occupies my thoughts as I deposit my suitcase in the luggage rack and take my seat in first class, which he has paid for. My mind returns to the boat trip Scott and I took on the River Thames the previous day.

'I have something to tell you and something to ask you,' he'd said, adding that he wasn't sure if the timing was appropriate.

Naturally, I was unable to leave it there. The suspense was too great! Was the news he had to impart going to be good or bad, as far as I was concerned? Tortuously, I turned over the different scenarios in my mind as we rounded the bend in the river and drew nearer to the O2 arena.

Possibility number one was that Scott would be returning to his ex-wife in America, and that would be the end of us. Option number two was that he'd lost his job at the theological college in north London. The ramifications of that prospect eluded me. And option three was that he would be returning to America and wanted me to accompany him. This, strangely, represented the most frightening scenario. How, I asked myself, would I feel about that? My humble home in Exeter took on an unexpected grandeur in my heart and mind.

In the end, without answering any but the first of my theories, Scott kissed me – a tender, loving meeting of our lips that rendered my heart aflutter.

From my first class seat on the train, I stare out of the window at the gently undulating countryside of middle England, and envision the boat scene once more.

'I've been head-hunted,' Scott said, without an inkling of conceit. 'By a conference centre.'

So that negates option number two, I'd thought *and makes my third supposition more likely. Is he going to be leaving the country and will he be asking me to go with him?*

The boat's klaxon sounded again, and ahead of us a small boat veered, suddenly, to starboard. My heart lurched and my breathing felt laboured. The yearning to spend my days with this man was overwhelming, yet at the same time, the prospect terrified me. Given my past failings – shaky childhood, divorce, childlessness – was I up to such change, such upheaval? Could I commit?

Recognising the symptoms of a panic attack, my trembling hands, shortness of breath and racing thoughts, I reined myself in and put into practice the cognitive behaviour therapy I use to help clients. In doing so, I was reminded of what Scott had said earlier about fact and perception, for this is the basis of CBT. *Focus only on what you know, Evie,* I told myself, *and not on the negative perceptions you have.*

'Where?' I was able to ask Scott.

He took my hands in his, his eyes searching mine.

'It's at Brunel Manor, in Torbay. I'd be managing the centre. It's a fabulous place, and a great opportunity. It's also a lot closer to Exeter than where I am now. We'd be able to see so much more of one another. But I recognise that we each have a past that needs time to heal. I'm not suggesting for one moment that we rush into anything. I just want to know how you –? Do you think, given time, you might feel for me what I do for you?'

The remainder, or at least the detail, of his appeal was lost to me as once again the clipper's horn blasted a warning, in an attempt to avert a collision with what now appeared to be an empty vessel, drifting, rudderless, on the current. The diversion, as fellow passengers rushed to the rails to watch the spectacle on the water below, sending our own vessel listing to one side, brought the matter to a close, and it wasn't until our return, upstream, that Scott raised it again.

'I want to spend time with you, Evie,' he said when we alighted from the boat and walked, hand in hand, beside the still waters of St Katharine's Dock. 'To get to know you better.'

Ahead of us, a pure, clean, mirror image of the floodlit buildings around the dock reflected what seemed to me to be a symbol of our relationship.

'It would be so easy to ask you now to take this further,' Scott continued. 'But I want you to be sure. No rush. No pressure. Above all, I want you to know, and to experience, the depth and breadth of my feelings for you.'

Now, on the train, gazing out of the window across the flood plains that announce the imminence of my destination, I realise I have spent the entire journey from Paddington to Exeter mulling it over. Recalling, with delight, the recognition of our shared philosophy on life, but recognising, also, our differences. The fact that Scott understands my reservations. No! More than that. His empathy. Because he, too, has experienced similar trauma in his relationships. Our mutual desire for one another. The muted restraint we place on the heat of our passion. Our overriding need to refrain from hurting one another.

On Scott's insistence, I have given him no answer as yet.

'How can you?' he asked, as we prepared to part. 'You've enough to think about.'

'But you'll have to let them know if you're going to accept the post,' I protest. 'And give notice at the college where you are now.'

'True. But I've alerted the college and asked Brunel for a few days to think it through. I need to be sure this would be right for me, for you, for all of us. They understand that. It's a big step.'

It is! Alighting from the train in Exeter, I recall a counselling seminar I once attended at Brunel. A more inspiring environment would be hard to find. By the time I reach home, and open the door, to find a wealth of mail on the mat and a purring Pumpkin cat – well fed by my next-door neighbour's son, Jason, who waves an enthusiastic greeting to me – I know what my answer will be. Idly, I wonder how Sophie's romance with Matt is faring?

Sophie sat at the table in the window of her living room, looking out at the advancing evening. Dartmouth was a popular resort for most of the year. The summer, particularly, would be heaving, and the cobbled pavement onto which the cottage fronted would be alive with visitors – 'grockles', as they were known – making their way to and from the harbour and the River Dart.

Most of them engaged in some sort of water-sport and owned the appropriate vessels: sailing dinghies, speedboats, motor-cruisers, gin palaces. The amount of money that must be moored up in the marina was, in Sophie's opinion, beyond belief. Not that she felt in any way judgemental, she chided herself. It was up to each individual how they spent their money. And spend it they did! Trade in the bistros and boutiques of the town was phenomenal.

On a part-time teacher's salary, Sophie could never have afforded to live here. The cottage, bestowed upon her by her parents was, they'd made clear, all that remained of Grandma's estate. Full of gratitude, she had unfailingly expressed a sense of privilege that she lived in this beautiful place all year round.

Now, however, with the October half-term over and the nights drawing in, a vague sense of depression had settled upon her. Here she was back into her usual regime, part-time teaching, evening tutoring, and caring for her parents. A pile of marking lay on the table before her, and she lacked her usual enthusiasm to tackle the task.

Matt had rung her a couple of times since her return from London with Liz and their parents, and suggested she might like to go up alone at some point.

'We could see a show in the West End, and spend some time together as a twosome,' he said. 'Get to know one another without the family entourage.'

'I'd love to,' she'd responded, thrilled, but doubtful of a successful outcome. 'But it would have to be during holiday time because of work. And I don't know if Mummy could spare me before Christmas. There's always so much to do.'

She hadn't liked to add that, given her lack of funds, the cost would probably be prohibitive. But as if he'd sensed her hesitation and the reason for it, Matt had immediately offered to pay for her transport, had pointed out that she could have her own room at his place and, as if that were not enough, had made it sound as though she would be doing him a favour.

'It would be swell to have your company,' he said. 'You could come up to stay when they switch on the Christmas lights. It's not much fun doing these things on your own. It would be great to have someone to share the pleasure with.'

Full of longing, she'd again pointed out her commitments and made a faltering attempt to defer any decision.

'I'm sure your mom and pop would understand your need to have some time to yourself,' Matt had said.

That statement had continued to resonate in her mind. Along with the upset she'd felt when Liz had accused her of being mollycoddled. Plus the indictment levelled against her by Liz and Mummy, of having encouraged Daddy to reveal too much about this person, Chay Rae. It was all so unfair! And completely untrue.

She thought of Evie, comparing her life of independence with the tedium of her own limitations. And suddenly, with the same determination that had seen her abandon her parents to Liz's care for the duration of Matt's book launch, she decided she had to take control of her life. She had to learn to stand up for herself.

Abandoning the school marking on the table, she crossed the room, picked up the phone, and rang Evie.

'I really enjoyed getting to know you,' she said, shyly, once they'd exchanged greetings.

'Same here,' Evie responded. 'I still can't quite believe, after all these years of living alone, that I have this extended family. And some of them, like you, right on the doorstep.'

'Well, that's why I'm ringing. I wondered if you'd like to come for lunch on Sunday. And then I thought we could go over on the ferry to my parents' and see if we can unearth any more information about your mother. That's if you'd like to, of course.'

Evie didn't hesitate. 'I'd love to, Sophie! How kind of you.'

Swiftly, so as not to lose impetus, Sophie pressed on.

'And I wondered, Evie, if you don't mind, if you'd give me a bit of advice? Not proper counselling, of course, but – I don't know – woman to woman.'

'Of course! No need to be formal, is there? That's what friends and family are for.'

'It's just that … I don't know. You say that's what family's for, but I feel I hardly have a proper relationships with my sister Liz. It's as if … almost as if she resents me.'

'R-i-ght. And does she have any reason to do so?'

Noting the way Evie strung out her response, Sophie wondered if it had any significance.

'None that I know of!' she said, shaking her head as if she were in Evie's presence. 'Except that she seems to think I'm spoiled. "Mollycoddled" was the word she used.'

'Mollycoddled! That's a strong word. In what context do you think she means it?'

'Well it can't be to do with money or possessions,' Sophie exclaimed, 'because if anyone is indulged in that respect, it's Liz!'

At the other end of the phone, Evie gave a murmur of recognition. 'Okay,' she said. 'So is it possible that your parents give you more of their time and attention than they do Liz, and she feels put out?'

Sophie snorted. 'She's welcome to spend more time with them! She can do all the running around, shopping, looking after them. But she doesn't! She's hardly ever there. Too busy shopping for herself. And I don't mean the necessities of life.'

Full of pent-up anger, Sophie immediately felt ashamed of her outburst.

'I'm sorry,' Evie exclaimed. 'I shouldn't have asked. I didn't mean to upset you. It's probably not a good idea talking about these things over the phone. Shall we wait until we meet for lunch?'

Alone in the darkening room, Sophie nodded.

'I'm sorry,' she said, stiffly. 'I didn't mean to sound off like that. It's just that – she's never been like this before with me. Liz, I mean. It's weird. The way she's been behaving ever since this business came up. You'd think she had something personal against this Chay Rae as well as Mummy. Or that she's afraid of some secret being uncovered. I shall be so glad when we get it all sorted out.'

'Me too,' Evie breathed down the phone. 'Can't wait. And I'm sure Matt must feel the same.'

Nodding again to the empty room as she put down the phone, Sophie could only agree.

Seated at his computer in the study, Matt sighed. His concentration was shot to pieces. Frustrated, he slammed his hand down on his desk.

The situation was dire. His main character, Alban Goodman, the protagonist in his last three books, was about to uncover a sinister infiltration of the UK Cabinet by Islamist extremists, and he hadn't a clue how Goodman was going to pull it off without leaving himself wide open to certain assassination. In short, he didn't know how the hell he was going to spin out the plot to fill the remaining fifty-thousand words of this particular book, plus a further hundred and twenty thousand for the next.

His usual *modus operandi*, to get his first draft down in the shortest possible time, regardless of spelling, grammar or literary merit, had failed him. And since revision and re-writes to knock out the dents at a later date presupposed an existing text, he was stumped. He closed his eyes and thought about Alban Goodman, willing himself into character. Instead, his head was filled with one, Chay Rae.

Impatient with himself, he slapped his hand on his thigh then stood up and walked across to the window of the study. It was on the first floor, level with the canopy of plane trees along either side of the road. An early Fall was unfolding before his eyes as the leaves, brown and crinkled at the edges, threatened to be stripped from the branches by the unseasonable – or should one now say newly-seasonal – weather. Whatever conclusion you reached about the *causes* of global warming, he reflected, its effects seemed indisputable.

He turned and went through to his bedroom. No evidence of Evie's occupation remained, and an unaccustomed loneliness stabbed him. He missed her. Hell, he missed Sophie, too.

Put your mind to other things, he commanded himself. He stood in front of the wardrobe, examining his reflection in the mirror. He'd debated long and hard since Evie's departure, about how he should present himself in his search for Chay Rae. Having tracked down the solicitors' office while she was with him, he was about to carry through his intention and ring to make an appointment. But should he do so as Matt McEwan, well-known American author? Or as the unknown, but perhaps controversial, Dean Rae?

He tried to imagine the scene as if he were writing the characters into one of his thrillers. And failed! Reality – the lessons learned from past behaviour – was more conducive. Or was it? He'd told Phoebe Hamilton his mother was Elizabeth Rae, which would make him her nephew, and where had that got him? Initially hostility. But ultimately?

'This is absurd,' he said aloud in the empty room.

Striding into the living room, he picked up the phone, rang the solicitors' number and arranged an appointment.

Two days later, he found himself being ushered into the senior partner's office in the centre of Clapham, less than a mile from what had been The Odeon Cinema.

'Mr McEwan for you, sir,' the secretary announced, shutting the door behind her.

A man, in his mid-sixties by Matt's reckoning, stood to greet him. 'Matt McEwan, celebrity author, I understand,' he smiled. 'I believe you asked for the senior partner, and that's me. Andrew Bartholomew, at your service.'

They shook hands, and seated themselves on opposite sides of the desk.

'So what can I do for you, Mr McEwan? Not in trouble with Detective Inspector Alban Goodman, I hope? Yes – my wife and I are ardent followers of yours. We were both sorry to have missed the launch of *Death in Madagascar* due to other commitments.'

Matt grinned, well used to the treatment doled out to those with celebrity status.

'I'll have to make sure Mrs Bartholomew gets a signed copy,' he said.

'Oh, she would be delighted. Can I get my secretary to bring you a coffee?'

Matt lifted his hand. 'No. I'm fine, thanks. The senior partner is not a Mr Rae, then?'

'Afraid not. Chay died – what – forty years ago? Didn't even make his seventies. I'm his son-in-law. Kept on the family name because it was well-known in these parts.'

'So he had no son of his own?' Matt asked.

'No.'

Matt could see from the reserve that clouded Bartholomew's face that he'd overstepped the mark.

'Sorry,' he said. 'Typical American, too nosy by half, wanting to know all the history of the old country. Just thought there'd be someone carrying on the family name.'

Bartholomew smiled. As Matt had hoped, in denouncing the manners of his countrymen, he'd disabled the awkward moment.

'Only a nephew,' said Bartholomew, opening up again. 'Charlie Rae. Emigrated some years ago. Australia, I think. So! How may I help you?'

Elated to hear about the nephew – another possible line of enquiry – Matt stifled the urge to ask more.

'I'm thinking of revising my will,' he began, and he launched forth into a deliberately lengthy and detailed description of his divorce and his daughter's illness. 'I'd be grateful if you could advise me as to how I could go about protecting her interests,' he finished.

'Of course. Not a problem.'

Nearly an hour later, as Matt had hoped, the two of them had dealt with the serious business pertaining to his new will, and were laughing and joking about how DI Alban Goodman might have gone about resolving the matter of inheritance, following divorce.

'Should have a draft of the will ready for you in – let's say a couple of weeks,' said the solicitor. 'My secretary will post it to you so you can see if you require any amendments. And then we can arrange a date for you to come in and sign it. Meantime, if there's anything else I can help you with – ?'

Matt continued to sit. A thought had occurred to him.

'I don't suppose you know anything about Rosegreen on Nightingale Lane?' he asked. 'Just wondered if the owner might be interested in selling. Who would you suggest I approach to find out more?'

Was there a slight stiffening of Bartholomew's shoulders, he wondered? Or had he imagined it?

'No chance,' Bartholomew rose to his feet. 'Besides the place has been converted into luxury apartments. All occupied, I'm afraid.'

Matt frowned, and stood up.

'I thought it was a listed building?'

'It is. The conversion was carried out with the utmost care. With the consent of the Heritage Protection Board of course.'

'Of course!'

'So – how did you happen across the property?' Bartholomew asked.

'Oh,' Matt stooped to retrieve his brief case, 'I believe it was owned at one time by an acquaintance of mine. Phoebe Hamilton? Daughter of Eliza Jones.' He looked up quickly, just in time to see to see the alarm etched on Bartholomew's face. 'Not to worry. I should think it would be out of my reach anyway. Impoverished lot, we authors.'

He straightened up, extended his hand, and bade the dumbstruck Mr Bartholomew goodbye.

Chapter Fifteen

Chained

MY INVITATION TO Sophie's for Sunday lunch is still three days away, two of which I shall have to spend in catching up with clients and office work. On my first day back at work after the London trip, I make sure I arrive early enough to meet with my colleague, Guy Sampson, for a coffee. Removing a pile of magazines – his room is not the tidiest of places – I take a seat while he sets about making the brew, one of his morning rituals. As he measures out the coffee grounds, he fills me in on what's been going on while I was away, and asks me how things went at the book launch.

With that topic exhausted and the coffee now made, I suppose it's only natural that he should focus his attention on the subject of Scott. He is, after all, Guy's nephew by marriage, and it was he and Nancy who first introduced us.

'I gather he came back early from the States?' he asks, sitting opposite me at his desk, while sipping from his mug and scrutinising me intently beneath his bushy eyebrows.

I avert my eyes, unwilling to divulge too much. I presume that Nancy must have heard this from her sister in America. However, I'm not at all sure what, if anything, they know about Scott's plans for the future, or the offer made to him by Brunel Manor. A degree of discretion is called for on my part.

'Yes. It was while I was in London for Matt's book launch. Scott got in touch with me and we had a river boat trip down the Thames,' I respond. 'It was great. Never done that before.'

'Sounds good! He obviously enjoys your company. Can't bear to be away from you for too long, I'd say.'

Guy uses a paper towel to wipe the coffee froth from his beard, but not, I notice, the grin from his mouth. Softly, nonchalantly, he starts to hum the Barbara Streisand tune, *Matchmaker, Matchmaker* –

I feel myself blush.

'We get on well.'

Guy raises an eyebrow, but says nothing. We've developed a good friendship over the years we've worked together, and a degree of ribbing one another is a given. But I'm not sure I'm ready to be teased just yet about my relationship with Scott.

'Everything else ok?' asks Guy, changing the subject, much to my relief. 'Any further on with the family investigation?'

I shrug. The faint sound of an organ recital drifts across The Green from the cathedral, prompting me to stand up and walk over to the window to hear it better.

'We're still left with masses of unanswered questions,' I reply.

Thanking him for the coffee, I cross the landing and return to my room. The phone is ringing as I unlock the door. A client? Already? With an inward sigh, I pick up the receiver.

'Hi, Evie. Matt here.'

My sigh is replaced with pleasure.

'Oh, I was just thinking about you. No further on with your research, I suppose?'

'Gee, you'd be amazed just how far I've got.'

'Well go on. Do tell.'

Standing at the stone-mullioned window looking down again at the Cathedral Green, I listen intently as Matt fills me in with his visit to the solicitors in Clapham.

'You're kidding!' I exclaim when he tells me that the senior partner, Andrew Bartholomew, is Chay Rae's son-in-law.

'No kidding, Sis. And what's more, it appears there's a Charlie Rae. A nephew of Chay Rae. Seems he worked at the firm for a short while but has since emigrated to Australia.'

'Matt! That's amazing.' Bowled over, I plonk myself down at my desk. 'Do you think he could be –?'

'I dunno.'

I had been going to ask if he could possibly be Matt's father, but this is clearly a step too far.

'Don't want to speculate,' he says, confirming my thought. 'I'm gonna do some more research. See if I can come up with a birth certificate. See how old he is. And how that would tally with Libby's age at the time. P'raps find out what he did at the solicitors and when he was there. It would be good to know if he was down this way when Libby was around.'

I nod to the empty room, then bite my lip. Of course such affirmation would be excellent news for Matt. I'm just not so sure that I want to think about what my mother was up to so near the time when she married my dad. Once again, I'm reminded of my little friend, Jason, who lives next door, and the secret he shared with me about the *other daddy wot put a baby in his friend's mummy's tummy.*

Sophie dressed carefully that morning in slacks and a decent smock top, as a visit to Mummy's demanded, telling herself she didn't often have guests, and that she owed it to Evie to take a little more care than usual. She was glad to see that Evie, too, was clothed in a manner Mummy would approve of. Given the progress Sophie was hoping for in the search for Matt's family and Evie's past when the two of them visited her parents later in the day, it wouldn't do to alienate her mother.

She carved the roast chicken she'd prepared, and put it on the plates she'd heated in the oven for Evie and herself, together with a rasher of bacon, a chipolata and some packet-made sage and onion stuffing.

'Sorry about the plated meal,' she said. 'My dining table isn't big enough to take serving dishes as well. Would you like to help yourself to potatoes and veg here, and then I'll put it all back in the oven to keep warm.'

'Not a problem.' Evie served herself as instructed, then took her meal over to the table in the window. 'What a lovely spot you have here. Puts my place in the shade.'

'I am lucky,' Sophie admitted taking a seat opposite Evie. 'Though I had wanted to work in Exeter when I left college. But my parents bought the cottage with what was left of Grandma's estate, and told me it was mine if I stayed.'

'No brainer, I'd say.' Evie tucked into her lunch, and, not for the first time, it hit Sophie how different her life might have been had she followed through on her original goal.

'No regrets, have you?' Evie asked, as if picking up on her reticence.

Sophie hesitated. One of the maxims she'd been brought up with, drummed into her by Mummy, was that nice people don't wash their dirty linen in public. But then could Evie be deemed to be *public*? Hardly! Besides, Mummy, herself, had been to see her for counselling. And wasn't that what Sophie was after now, Evie's professional expertise, albeit in an informal and *gratis* manner?

'Well, actually,' Sophie began, head down, 'that's what I wanted to talk to you about. Do you think – how much of an obligation do you think a person should have towards their parents? I mean, you must come across this sort of thing, in your line of work.'

She glanced up, aware that she was being watched, Evie's brown eyes full of hidden depth as she finished chewing what was in her mouth.

'Good question,' Evie replied, when she'd swallowed her food. 'And no easy answers, I'm afraid. In general terms, I'd say it's probably a matter of love and commitment rather than obligation. Only my opinion, of course! Once upon a time, when families cohabited across the generations, the responsibility was shared. They say it takes a village to raise a child, and I suppose the same could be said for the care of the elderly.'

Struggling to stem the flow of tears that rose in her eyes and threatened to spill down her cheeks, Sophie nodded, politely, and Evie continued.

'But with people living longer, and health issues like dementia and diabetes on the rise, it's all much harder, nowadays, isn't it. And carers need to guard against burnout. That's one of the big issues that needs to be highlighted. But am I to take it that this is *you* we're talking about, Sophie, and not just a general topic of conversation?'

The tears spilled, unbidden.

'I feel so guilty. All the time. As if whatever I do, it's never enough.'

Evie put down her knife and fork, leaned across the table and put her hand on Sophie's.

'Oh, my dear! I can see how hard it must be for you. I think you need to try and stand back and ask yourself is this because you genuinely feel you're not doing enough? Or is it because you've been made to feel that way?'

Sophie gulped, and dabbed at her eyes with her paper napkin.

'I don't know! I do what I can to support my parents but it's not as if they live with me. I shouldn't be grumbling. I'm not in constant demand. It's just –' she shook her head. 'I feel as if I'm under an obligation to show eternal gratitude. That I'm not entitled to a life of my own. And I don't understand why.'

Evie squeezed her hand.

'So – back to where we started. Who makes you feel like this? Is it your parents? Or is it something in you, yourself?'

Powerless to identify the answer to Evie's questions, and aware that she was on the brink of tears again, Sophie shook her head, unable to speak.

Evie appeared to think for a moment, then she picked up her utensils again.

'Okay. Let's look at this from a different angle,' she said, spearing a piece of chicken. 'You told me you don't have a very good relationship with your sister. And that she said you're mollycoddled? Is that right?'

Sophie nodded. 'We've never been close, Liz and I,' she whispered. 'I mean, we just have a completely different handle on life. But when we were in London, it was worse than that. It wasn't just about having nothing in common. She seemed to be – quite hostile towards me.'

A couple of seagulls began to squabble on the lane outside, their squawking an intrusion on Sophie's thinking. Uncharacteristically, she banged her hand on the window, expecting them to fly off. Instead, with what she supposed was the temerity one might anticipate in a wild animal that knows it is a protected species, they merely strutted further up the road, as if in search of a more appreciative audience.

Evie returned to the topic in hand.

'I think we have to unpack that word *mollycoddled*. It means spoiled, doesn't it. Or pampered. Or babied. So why is it that Liz considers you're being spoiled or pampered?'

Sophie shook her head.

'I suppose she may be right. I know I have a lot to be thankful for. I didn't want for anything as a child. Or since.'

'So – forgive me, but I think it's important that you identify the root cause. Who do you think Liz believes is spoiling you?'

'Well that's it! She seems to think it's my parents. But the fact is, I do more for them than they do for me these days. And certainly more than Liz does for them.'

Instantly, Sophie regretted her outburst. She put her hand to her mouth and looked across the table to see how her guest had taken it. Evie sat there impassively, her face full of kindness and concern beneath her dark, curly hair.

'So does that suggest that she feels resentful?' Evie asked. 'Could it be that she feels they've done more for you, now, and/or in the past, than for her?'

'Well I don't know what she has to feel resentful about,' Sophie said. 'I mean, she's far better off financially than I am. I'm not sure I understand what you're saying.'

Evie cocked her head on one side and looked up as if searching for an explanation. 'Sometimes it's not what we *have* that matters,' she said. 'It's what we'd *like* to have. So if Liz felt your parents had given you something she would have liked – perhaps love and attention rather than something tangible like your cottage? Sorry. I'm thinking out loud.'

Sophie threw herself back on the chair.

'Liz and Fiona know they're going to be compensated in Mummy and Daddy's wills, so it can't be that they're miffed because I have the cottage.'

'No. I shouldn't have said that. But what about your parents' love? I mean – forgive me – but I've noticed that you address them as Mummy and Daddy. That suggests to me that there's some warmth and affection that's lingered on from childhood. But what about Liz?

Did she have a happy upbringing?'

Sophie could feel the heat in her face. 'I call them Mummy and Daddy without thinking. It's what I've always called them. But I suppose it sounds babyish to you.'

Evie shrugged. 'Each to their own. But I have noticed your mother refers to your father as Daddy when speaking to you. And I think he does likewise. Though neither of them does so with Liz.'

'Well she's the eldest! And they wouldn't would they? I mean, she doesn't call them Mummy and Daddy. They're Mother and Father to her. But I'm not sure what any of this has to do with anything?'

Evie sighed. 'Only, as I say, that if someone feels there's something lacking in their life, and then they see that self-same thing being given to someone else, it can make them feel even more deprived. As if they've been robbed.

'Sometimes, for instance, bereavement can be easier to handle than adultery. Or adoption. Yes, you've still lost that person, their companionship, their love, their care for you. But at least you know your loss isn't because of someone else's gain. Does that make sense?'

Sophie nodded. What Evie had said had triggered a memory. Something she'd heard, long ago. Something that had made no sense at the time.

'You may be right,' she said to Evie, in a small voice. 'I've often wondered why Liz never had a family. I always thought it must be because she didn't want to share Gordon with anyone else. Or that she was too lazy, or self-centred, to be bothered with the demands of bringing up a child. Or that she didn't want to risk losing her figure, of course!'

She laughed, a short, hoarse sound.

'And now?' Evie asked. 'What's changed your thinking?'

Sophie began to scrape the leftovers from one plate to another so she could stack them and take them over to the sink.

'It's just a vague memory I have,' she said. 'Or it might even be fantasy on my part.'

Evie poured herself a glass of water and took a sip as Sophie continued.

'I remember once, long ago, hearing Daddy, in his capacity as

179

a doctor, telling Mummy that Liz's problem – some health issue, I think it was – had arisen because she'd had such a bad labour when she'd had *The Baby*.'

Coughing and spluttering, Evie set down her glass of water and clutched her throat.

'Went down the wrong way,' she croaked.

Sophie rose and began to pat her on the back, wondering, as she did so, whether it was her story about Liz that had caused Evie to choke? And if so why? Outside the window, the seagulls, once again, began their squawking, in their usual brash competition for attention. Still patting Evie's back, Sophie resisted the temptation to bang on the window a second time.

My first thought when Sophie shares the story about Liz? *Not another mysterious birth! How many more in this family?*

Eventually, with Sophie's help, I bring my choking episode under control, but there's no time to follow through on what Sophie has disclosed. She makes it clear to me that we either need to have a yogurt or apple for desert immediately, or wait for the inevitable cake at Mummy's. We're unanimous in choosing the second option. But there's more.

'I don't know what you want to do,' she says. 'We can either go across the river as foot passengers, which is the cheaper option if you don't mind a fair old walk either end. Or, what I would suggest, is that we go in your car on the lower ferry so you can go straight off home, when we've had tea, without having to come back here again. You'd go on the ring road, past Paignton and Torquay, instead of going through Totnes.'

'And what about you? How would you get back?' I ask.

'Oh, I can walk down the hill to the passenger ferry from Mummy's quite easily. And it's no great distance to get home on this side of the river.'

It's a done deal and we set off together in my car, driving through the town, past what Sophie tells me used to be the bookshop owned by the real Christopher Robin, son of A. A. Milne, now replaced by a community not-for-profit shop elsewhere in town, and on to where the car ferry docks.

'Do you want to talk any more about things?' I ask switching off the engine while we wait in the queue.

Sophie nods without actually saying anything. I turn towards her.

'So have you any further thoughts on what we were talking about earlier? Do you think the way you address your parents might diminish you in your mind? And perhaps in theirs? And possibly Liz's, too?'

'How do you mean?' Sophie looks down and picks at one of her nails.

I draw a breath and think for a moment how I might best explain what I'm saying.

'I just wonder if it might have a subconscious influence on your self-perception,' I begin, and immediately realise my mistake. 'Sorry. That sounds a bit abstract. What I mean is, could it possibly make you feel like a little girl who's answerable to her parents? In other words, are you trying so hard to be the *good little girl* for them, that you're not giving yourself enough freedom simply to be *you*?'

Privately, I wonder if Phoebe has been manipulating just this very scenario, but I'm certainly not about to divulge that.

Sophie's head snaps up and round to look at me as I'm speaking.

'I've never thought of it like that before.'

'And now?'

She frowns and pauses for a moment.

'I think you're absolutely right! I can't believe I haven't seen it for myself.'

She falls silent again, and I give her space to ruminate.

'It's exactly what I was trying to put into words earlier,' she says, at last. 'About feeling obligated. But I – I just couldn't think it through properly. Looking back, I can see now, I've spent my whole life trying to be 'a good girl', as you said. I almost feel as if it's been instilled into me. As if – I don't know – as if I've been trained to believe I have a duty. As if – as if I owe something to my parents. Something more than is normal. Does that sound too far-fetched?'

The ferry has docked, and is offloading passengers and vehicles. In front of me, I can see that other drivers are starting up their engines.

'It isn't what I think that matters,' I say, switching on and edging forwards. 'But it might explain Liz's recent perception of things. Something to think about!'

We move ahead onto the ferry and park on the deck, as indicated by a man in uniform. I'm bowled over by the spectacular beauty of the river and surrounding countryside, the gentle swell on the water, and the riverbanks rising steeply on either side up stream. As we begin our short voyage to the other side, I'm reminded of my first visit to the Hamiltons' with Matt, when we'd walked down through their garden to the water's edge and watched the higher ferry plying to and fro. Known as the floating bridge, it is not self-propelled but is dragged across the river on chains tethered to the bank on each side, which also prevent it slipping downstream.

It seems to me, as we sit in the car, that this might be a picture of some people's lives. And not just children chained to their parents expectations, but sometimes, perhaps, parents to those of their children – or partners to one another? Back and forth, back and forth they ply, driven by an outside force; tethered to a lifestyle that inhibits freedom. Could this be true of Sophie, I wonder? I glance in her direction. She's deep in thought, and I wish with all my heart I might see her cut free, self-propelled. Resolutely, I make up my mind to make it my mission. In my opinion, it appears Phoebe Hamilton might have a lot to answer for.

Chapter Sixteen

A Falling Out of Friends

STRAIGHT AFTER LUNCH, in the gathering gloom of the winter afternoon, Matt took himself off to the study of his London apartment. Staring at his blank computer screen, he reviewed the situation to date. Ever since his visit to the solicitors, Chay Rae in Clapham, he'd not stopped.

The disclosure made by Andrew Bartholomew, revealing that there was a nephew by the name of Charlie Rae and that he had worked, briefly, for the firm before emigrating to Australia, was exactly the sort of lead Matt had been hoping for. And Mr Bartholomew's startled response when he'd asked about Rosegreen spoke volumes. As did the antipathy he'd encountered on mentioning Phoebe Hamilton by name. Without a doubt, there was some history between the two families. Something had to have happened to generate such hostility.

Bidding Andrew Bartholomew goodbye, he'd returned to his Pimlico apartment on a high. The moment he'd got home, he'd embarked on a lengthy and scrupulous investigation for one, Charlie Rae.

That was some days ago now. Well used to such procedures when researching the background material required for his novels, he'd begun by typing the name into the internet search bar on his computer. Top of the list that came up was a young female street singer-turned-star, from San Diego. Having taken Charlie to be an abbreviated version of Charles, it was – stupidly, he supposed – a surprise. In this case it would, of course, be short for Charlotte! Unable to resist the temptation before moving on, he'd listened to the young woman's performance and was blown away by the melodic quality of her voice.

Refining his search, he'd added the location Andrew Bartholomew had mentioned, and it hadn't taken long before he'd discovered a Charlie Rae who, it appeared, had been practising law in Australia since the early eighties. The timing, he thought, would be spot on. Via LinkedIn, he'd then learned, only a few moments ago, that the lawyer was a Scot, born in Bridge of Don, Aberdeen. The connection with Phil Hamilton, via their shared nationality, was too great to be a coincidence.

Matt's fingers and toes were charged with fear and excitement. Could this man be the link that would explain why he'd been known as Dean Rae in the orphanage? Was it possible that Charlie Rae might have known his biological mother, Libby, all those years ago? That he might, in fact, have fathered Matt?

Bounding from his seat, Matt strode back and forth, tugging at his hair; aimlessly picking up papers and discarding them, pens and paperclips likewise. Touring the narrow dimensions of the book-lined room, he ran a blunt finger nail lightly against the spines of his own publications in all their many editions, formats and translations. This was ridiculous! He felt a sudden angry impatience with his current reticence. Finding Charlie Rae was as crucial to his endeavours as contact with Phoebe Hamilton had been. For Sam's sake, if no one else's, he had to keep going. No matter how long it took.

Determined, but still in need of fortification, he headed off to the kitchen to make a coffee. Ten minutes later, steaming mug in hand, he returned to the study, standing at the window and looking out at the drizzle and waning light. The plane trees were shedding their leaves revealing the extraordinary beauty of their mottled, exfoliated trunks. A couple of years earlier, not far from his own apartment, a huge tree, still in full leaf, had been uprooted by a gale and smashed down on two cars parked on the roadside. Recalling the event, he couldn't help but compare it with the ill-wind that had blown into Sam's life, and thence his own. Nor the seismic shift that had followed, shattering his usual peace and equilibrium.

The Power of Positive Thinking. That's what his mom, Bonnie, would have urged upon him had she still been around.

'I have to do this, come what may,' he said aloud to the empty room. 'It's the least I can do for my daughter. For every positive act you decline to take forward, Matthew McEwan, you choose a negative path.'

He looked at his watch. By his reckoning, it would by now be midnight, or the early hours of Monday morning, in New South Wales. Given that the only contact details he had for Charlie Rae were via the firm of Australian solicitors, phoning was out of the question. Besides, even if it were possible, he could just imagine the conversation:

G'day. How may I help you?
May I please speak to Mr Charlie Rae.
Who's calling, sir?
Well, I think I may be his son.
Sorry sir, Mr Rae doesn't have a son.

Matt laughed. Worse still, he thought, if he substituted something like *I have news for him.* What sort of response would that evoke?

Oh, yeah? And what would that be? A billion dollar deposit in some foreign bank account? No thank you. We get scammers like you all the time. G'day!

Turning from the window, Matt plonked his empty coffee mug on his desk. There was nothing for it: he would have to write. And perhaps, to make himself heard, this was one occasion when, more than ever before, he'd have to plug his celebrity status. He seated himself at his desk, opened and saved a blank document on the computer screen, and began to type.

Sophie and I arrive at her parents' home on the other side of the River Dart, mid-afternoon. It's now nearly three months since my last visit here with Matt, and I've forgotten quite how imposing the house is, not to mention its location. Standing for a moment in the broad sweep of the drive, I take in the pillars and porch at the front entrance; the balcony above it looking out from what must, once, surely, have been the master bedroom; and the circular turret facing down river at one end of the building. It's certainly grand! And boy, it must have cost a bomb in upkeep when the Hamiltons inhabited it in its entirety. How the other half lives!

'Which was your room when you were a girl?' I ask Sophie, closing the door of my clapped out little car.

She points to a small window on the upward, landside of the house.

'No river view for you then! I thought you'd have been in the turret.'

'That was Liz's room when we moved here. When she left home it became the guest room.'

'Did she go to college, then?'

There's a chill wind blowing in from the direction of the sea, but I want to pursue this conversation before we go in. I clutch the collar of my jacket around my neck.

'No. She went into nursing. That's how she met her husband, Gordon.'

Sophie's voice sounds flat, and her face is expressionless. I hope I haven't upset her with what I had to say on the ferry, earlier. She'd seemed willing enough at the time to consider my suggestion that she might need to cut loose and give herself the freedom to find out who she really was. Perhaps we need to talk some more. Meanwhile –

'I suppose Liz would have left school soon after you moved here?' I persist. 'You said she was about sixteen when you were born?'

'I guess so. I don't remember any of that, of course. I was too young.' Of course you were, I think. And then an unthinkable thought occurs to me. Before it can develop, Phoebe appears at the front door.

'Come on in,' she calls in imperious tones. 'The kettle's on.'

Obediently, Sophie and I turn towards her. It's not hard to see why Sophie succumbs so easily to her mother's wishes. Together we walk towards the front door.

The twinset and pearls are still very much in evidence in Phoebe's attire, and though I've made every attempt to dress in what I hope will be an acceptable manner – woollen skirt, blouse and cardi – I nevertheless feel lacking. Phoebe honours me with a peck on the cheek as I step over the threshold, and I marvel, once again, at the art gallery hanging on the baronial style walls of the hall.

Phil is dozing in a chair when we're shown into the sitting room. He jumps when Phoebe remonstrates with him, then leaps to his feet to greet us. It's clear that whatever his age or mental infirmity, he remains lithe in body and limb.

'Libby,' he says, evidently believing I'm my mother again, and causing the usual protest from Phoebe with which I'm now becoming familiar.

A fire burns in the grate of the marble fireplace, and the room is suffocatingly warm.

'I'll make the tea,' says Sophie to her mother, 'so you can sit and chat with Evie.'

She disappears from the room, and I'm left wondering how I'm going to approach the various matters to which I'd like answers. As if she's read my mind, Phoebe jumps straight in.

'I hope you enjoyed the London trip. It's a pity we didn't get the opportunity to see Rosegreen, where I was born. It was such a grand house. You'd have loved it.'

We've been standing at the French doors, where Phoebe's led me, though whether that is to admire the view or to give space between herself and Phil is unclear. It's immaterial, because looking down over the garden to the river, I'm more than happy to express my appreciation and awe at the scene before me, and am gratified when both are well received. It's so easy to see how Phoebe might manipulate and exert her influence over Sophie. Turning away with a smile on her face, she preens her hair and indicates that I should seat myself on the sofa, while she takes up residence in the easy chair next to Phil's.

'It sounds wonderful, from what I've heard.' I respond. 'Fancy growing up in an historic listed building! So was my grandmother born there, as well?'

Phoebe looks horrified at the suggestion.

'Beatrice? Goodness me, no! She was far older than me. You forget she had Libby, your mother, when I was only a little girl. Besides, my parents only acquired the property shortly before I came into the world.'

'But she would have lived there with you at some point, wouldn't she? Before Mum was born?'

Is it my imagination, or does Phoebe look a little shifty?

'Evelyn – should I call you Evelyn? – what you have to understand is that my sister, Beatrice, was not well. She did, indeed, live with my mother until she married. And even then, I'm afraid she spent a good deal of time imposing upon my mother. Which was lovely for me, of course, because, as I've told you before, it meant that Libby and I spent a good deal of time together. As children. And later as young women.'

I'm confused, but am determined to push ahead in an effort to clarify matters.

'I'm sorry. I don't understand. You said my grandmother, Beatrice, wasn't well. What was the matter with her?'

'She had fits.' Phoebe spits the words out as if they are poison; an affliction designed to harm those around.

Phil, who has been silent until now, suddenly comes to life.

'Elipeptic. She was elipileptic.'

'Epileptic!' Phoebe corrects him. 'Yes, we know, Phil.'

I grip my hands together on my lap. It's all I can do not to exclaim out loud. So Matt's ex-wife was right. His daughter's epilepsy did originate on his side of the family.

'But she still married?' I ask, aware that my probing will certainly be viewed as impudence, and that I need to tone it down. 'And had a child? My mother. How did her husband feel about that? Did he know she had epilepsy, before they married?'

'Of course he did!' Phoebe explodes. 'He may have said otherwise when he kept sending her back. But I'm quite sure my parents would have told him before they married her off.'

I'm flabbergasted! What the heck are the implications behind that statement? It hardly bears thinking about. Before I can collect my thoughts together to ask the next question, about the date of my parents' wedding, the door opens and in comes Sophie, pushing a trolley laid with the best crockery, tea and a Victoria sponge cake on a silver cake stand, no less.

'Teatime,' she says, gaily.

With a distinct look of relief on her face, Phoebe gets to her feet and the moment is lost to me. At least for now.

In the kitchen, alone while Evie chatted with Mummy, Sophie filled the kettle and put it on the Aga, found the cake, doilies and cake stand in their usual locations, and laid the trolley with an embroidered tray cloth beneath the best porcelain cups, saucers and plates. Pouring near-boiling water into the silver teapot to heat it, she then looked out the sugar lumps her mother insisted upon, even though few people used them these days. Finally, after emptying the pot, she measured out the tea leaves and poured on the boiling water from the kettle, then put milk into the jug while the tea infused.

Since disembarking from the ferry, she had been deep in thought about what Evie had had to say in respect of her demeanour with her parents, a conclusion with which – now it had been pointed out to her – she could only agree. How come she'd never seen that for herself? Never understood the self-deprecation she'd subjected herself to? Never made the comparison – now glaringly obvious – between the way friends and acquaintances referred to their parents, and the terminology she used in addressing her own?

Silently, she vowed never again to use self-effacing language like *Mummy and Daddy*. Nor to think of herself as in any way beholden to her parents. She looked at herself in the large mirror hanging on the wall by the door which led out to the backyard and herb garden. Dressed formally in skirt and jacket, there was no doubting she had the appearance and decorum of a young woman in her late twenties. She was an adult. And she would behave like one!

That didn't mean she would no longer love and care for her parents. Merely that she would do so on her own terms. As far as possible she was going to adhere to an old Chinese proverb she'd read somewhere: *Know your enemy and know yourself, and you can fight a hundred battles without disaster.* Not that *my mother and father* are the enemy, she thought, emphasising her new way of thinking so as to retrain her mind. It was more likely to be her own attitude that she needed to know and change. It wouldn't be easy, she had to admit. And it might well require further conversation with Evie in order to achieve her aims.

But for now, she was going to do one thing she ought to have done two or three months ago. Hurriedly, she crept out into the hall and, with a furtive glance at the door of the sitting room, she opened the cupboard under what had once been the staircase, before the house had been converted into flats, and switched on the light. As quietly as she possibly could, she pulled out one of the boxes of photographs at the back of the cupboard, one she'd been instructed to leave untouched the last time the contents of the cupboard had seen the light of day.

'What about this one?' she'd asked her mother the day Matt had first met them all last August Bank Holiday weekend.

'No, no. There's nothing in there that's of interest to Matthew or anyone else,' her mother had said.

'Are you sure, Mummy? It looks to me as if there might well be photographs in here.

'I said no, Sophie, and I meant no. It's not relevant. So put it back and bring the others out, there's a good girl.'

Sophie flinched at the memory. How long had she been subjected to put-downs like that from her mother? How long had she endured them without even noticing? Without doing anything but accepting them as the norm?

She hauled the box to the front of the cupboard, her determination strengthened. Lifting it onto her hip, she looked again towards the door of the sitting room. Hearing her mother's voice, she switched off the cupboard light and crept out into the hall. A sense of guilt assailed her. It was one thing vowing not to be the little girl her mother so clearly wanted her to be. Quite another to be – was *stealing* too strong a word?

I'm only borrowing these, Mummy – Mother – she whispered to herself as she teetered silently across the hallway with her heavy burden, and opened the front door.

Evie's car was parked in one of the designated areas, alongside the altogether sleeker model of that belonging to the tenants in the first floor apartment. *Please, please, don't let her have locked it,* she prayed, and breathed a sigh of relief as the door yielded to her touch. Heaving the box from where she'd balanced it on her hip, she threw it onto the back seat and covered it with an old car rug she found lying there. Softly, she shut the door again, retraced her footsteps and reached the kitchen before letting out the breath she was unaware she'd been holding.

A request to allow Matt and Evie to see the photographs she'd taken would, she knew, have resulted in a refusal to cooperate. Mummy – her mother – had made it quite clear that she, Sophie, was expected to work with her in this, as in all things. But why? Because there was further evidence of Matt's mother's past? Photographs of her with someone else? His father, perhaps?

It had become increasingly evident to Sophie that there was enormous prejudice on her mother's part; a resistance to Matt's research into his past. Yet how, she asked herself, could it be deemed morally ethical to keep Matt in the dark about his past? Taking the banned box of photos from the cupboard would, at one time, have been unthinkable. But now – now that she had had her eyes opened to her mother's manoeuvrings. Well! She simply wanted to help Matt in his objectives. Surely everyone had the right to know where they came from?

So engrossed was she as she pushed the laden tea trolley across the hall, opened the door of the lounge and stepped over the threshold, that she almost missed the atmosphere in there. Almost! She might not be the brightest spark in the family, but even so, it was clear that something momentous appeared to have passed.

She looked from one to the other of the occupants of the room. Her father had that excited look on his face that told her he'd recalled something from long ago. Her mother looked furious. Was it Daddy's – her father's – memory that had infuriated her mother? Quite likely! And one glance at the stunned expression on Evie's face confirmed it for her. She'd never seen her look so dazed.

'Teatime,' she announced, with a deliberate but false tone of gaiety. Inside, she was trying to make sense of what she thought she had heard as she'd entered the room. Who on earth could it be that had been *married off*? And if so, Why? To whom? And by whom?

192

Chapter Seventeen

What Else Lies Hidden?

'YOU WOULDN'T BELIEVE it!' I tell Matt on the phone, when I reach home after my visit to the Hamiltons. 'I'm so gobsmacked I don't know where to begin.'

He laughs. 'Gee, Sis! You better start talkin' or I might not let on what I've bin up to.'

It feels so good to have a brother to tease me and laugh with me, and I can barely believe my good fortune. At the same time, I still grieve for the lost years, though I doubt he does given the difference in our circumstances. Outside, the sky has darkened as the day draws to a close, and I draw the curtains to shut it out. By the time I resume my seat, swinging my legs up on the sofa, Pumpkin has made her presence known, jumping up on my lap and purring loudly. Fondling her, I attempt to collect my thoughts together.

'Seriously, I don't know where to begin,' I say again. 'I had a great time at Sophie's. We got on really well together. And Dartmouth is fabulous.'

'Yeah. I remember we saw Britannia Naval College and Dartmouth Castle from the other side of the river, when we visited the Hamiltons.'

'Oh, but it's so much more than that. Such a quaint town. Narrow streets, some of them cobbled, full of boutiques and bistros. You'd love it.'

'Sounds like every American's dream,' says Matt. 'Shopping. Food. Grand buildings. And a bit of history thrown in. You'll have to take me some day. Meantime, you sure are stringing out the news you have to tell me.'

'Sorry!' I laugh. 'Got a bit carried away. Anyway, the point is that Sophie's cottage is smack bang in the middle of what is one of the most popular tourist resorts in Britain. Don't you find that extraordinary?'

I pick at a pulled thread in my jeans, suddenly aware that what I've said must come across to Matt as judgemental.

'I don't mean that to sound critical,' I exclaim, eager to correct any negative impression I might have given. 'But I couldn't help wondering how she could afford it on a teacher's salary. Turns out, her parents purchased the cottage for her.'

'Nice gesture,' says Matt. 'I suppose it's every parent's dream to provide for their offspring.'

I feel myself flinch. He's obviously not aware that the pain of being childless never completely recedes.

'But it's not just that. It made me wonder if all this business of *losing* the London property is merely a ruse on Phoebe's part? Could it be that the Hamiltons actually *sold* what they had, and reinvested elsewhere? I realise this is all conjecture. But I'm trying to make sense of why our grandmother was disinherited.'

Matt is silent for a moment, probably thinking through what I've said.

'Yeah! You've got a point there, Sis,' he says. 'P'raps the family's better off than they're letting on. Definitely somethin' fishy goin' on, what with the three signatures on the will, and what Sophie had to say about Aunt Phoebe thinkin' I might contest it. Don't suppose you had a chance to follow up on that, did you?'

'I'm not sure she knows any more than she told us. After all, as far as we know she's never seen the will.'

I pick again at the thread on my jeans, rolling it into a ball. I'm aware I've been sidestepping what I have to say. And I know why. Realising the impact it's going to have on Matt, I've been wrestling with this conversation ever since I left Kingswear.

And then there are the ethics. I keep telling myself I'm right in being reluctant to divulge details of my conversation with Sophie and the manipulation I believe she's suffering at the hands of her mother. After all, what Sophie shared with me, deserves the confidentiality reserved between friends. Neither does it have any bearing on Matt's search.

I don't think, however, that professional etiquette need come into it, as far as Phoebe's recent disclosures about her sister are concerned. I know Guy is always reminding me – albeit teasingly by alluding to my name and nature – to watch myself when it comes to adhering to the rules of my profession. But this, surely, comes into a different category altogether? For one thing, Beatrice is Matt's and my grandmother, and the matter of her being disinherited is, therefore, very much our business. For another, what Phoebe had to say about her was merely in the context of a social occasion, not a professional counsellor-cum-client session.

Next door's washing machine starts its spin cycle somewhat earlier than its normal economy seven electricity programme, but with the usual thump, thump, thump. Absent-mindedly, I find myself pulling on Pumpkin's ears somewhat harder than would be comfortable for her. She leaps from my lap to the floor. Jumping to my feet, I cease my endless inner argument around the integrity of what I'm about to do, and determine to break the news to Matt, although with a certain amount of discomfort.

'I think you might find – and this is an observation made with my professional hat on – that there was no love lost between Phoebe and her sister, Beatrice,' I begin. 'She made that quite clear when Sophie and I went there for tea.'

'Yeah, that rings true,' Matt says. 'I've nothing concrete to base my supposition on but I think I got the same impression as you.'

'What's more –' I cross the room and, for no good reason, part the curtains and peer through the window at the empty street outside. 'What's more,' I continue, 'I'd say the same was true between poor old Bea and her parents. She seems to have been the pariah of the family.'

'I agree,' says Matt. 'Sounds as if you got evidence for that conclusion?'

I nod, though there's no one there to see me, and picture the scene at the Hamiltons' house in Kingswear.

'Phoebe let slip that our grandmother had been *married off*. In other words, the marriage was not her choice.'

'Wow! That's some admission. Thought you were gonna say it was Phil who let the side down again.'

'Not this time. Poor man.'

'So how come Phoebe 'fessed up?'

'She got angry. I'd been questioning her. Pushing her a bit, I suppose. And she didn't like it.'

Matt falls silent again for a moment, wrestling with the ramifications I would guess.

'What sort of parents would marry their daughter off against her will?' he asks at last.

'Exactly! And why?'

'It can only be because she was already pregnant with our mom, Libby,' says Matt. 'I can't think of any other reason, can you? I'll take another look at the birth and marriage certificates. See if the dates can confirm that.'

'Good idea.'

'So how did you raise the subject with Phoebe? What were you questioning her about? You said she was angry?'

I swallow hard, scoop Pumpkin up from the floor and plonk myself on the sofa again. This is the bit I'm going to find difficult. Having to break bad news to Matt.

'Yes. She was angry. But not with me, I don't think. Her anger was – I think it was because of the circumstances, the stigma – she let slip, and this was confirmed by Phil, that Beatrice was epileptic.' Matt's sharp intake of breath whistles down the phone. Then he falls silent.

Sophie rang Evie the moment she reached home after the visit to her parents. But all she heard was the engaged tone. Again. And again. It was so frustrating. She'd had no chance to point out the box of photographs she'd placed in the back of Evie's car, and she was concerned Evie might think her mother had given them to her. Perhaps she was on the phone to – Mum – right now? Thanking her for something she knew nothing about? Something Sophie didn't want her to know.

Phone in hand, she strode up and down the room, tried to sit and read *The Radio Times* to see what was on TV that evening, jumped up and resorted to striding again.

'That wasn't my mother you were speaking to, was it?' she asked, her heart racing when she eventually made contact with Evie.

'No. Are you okay, Sophie?'

Evie's concern was palpable. Sophie ignored it. She let out her breath and sat down, hard, on one of the chairs at the table in the window.

'Did you find it? The box in the back of your car?' she asked.

'Box? What box?'

'Under the rug on the back seat. I put it there when I made tea at – Mum's.'

Mum's, not Mummy's! It didn't come easy remembering your vow to change the habit of a lifetime, when you were feeling agitated about other things. Had Evie noticed, she wondered? Disconcerted, she picked up a pepper pot that had been left there since the last meal, and tapped it repeatedly on the table top.

'I didn't see it, Sophie. I'm sorry. Are you sure you're all right? Nothing's happened to upset you, has it?'

Outside, it had begun to rain, a heavy downfall that would, inevitably, lead to a small river gushing down each side of the land outside the cottage. Sophie made herself draw breath again, then she walked across the room and threw herself down on the sofa, laughing uncontrollably.

'I'm sorry,' she gasped, at last. 'It's just that I've never done anything like this before. They used to taunt me at school for being a goodie-goodie. That was my nickname. Goodie-Two-Shoes. When all my class-mates were off scrumping apples, or pinching other people's dinghies to row round to the beach – well – you get the picture.'

Memories of the bullying she'd encountered came back to haunt her. The runt of the family, she'd been known as. Some of the name-callers had even intimated, in a way that implied she was the talk of the town, that she must be the milkman's daughter. It had been a miserable and painful experience, but one she had never let on to anyone before. At the other end of the phone, Evie's voice came over quietly and calmly.

'I'm sure you were a star-pupil. Nothing wrong with not allowing yourself to be led astray.'

Sophie laughed, a strangled and awkward squawk that expressed the discomfort she felt.

'Not sure my teachers, or my parents would agree with you there.'

'Don't take it to heart,' said Evie. 'We all have aspects of ourselves we'd rather not admit to.'

Sophie laughed again. The room was in darkness, lit only by the street lamp outside.

'So let me get this straight,' Evie continued. 'You put a box in the back of my car without your mother knowing? Is that what I'm to conclude?'

Sophie sat up, her laughter gone, the full impact of what she'd done weighing upon her.

'Yes. I know! It sounds terrible, doesn't it. I probably shouldn't have done it, but I just felt that Mumm... my mother might be keeping things from you and Matt.'

She switched on the overhead lights and drew the curtains.

'Mum was adamant that I shouldn't take this last box out of the cupboard when you and Matt came down to visit,' she said, recalling the event and the anger her mother had expressed when Sophie had dared to query the decision. 'She kept saying it wasn't relevant. But I think there may be something in there that you should see.

'Taking it behind Mum's back was a spur of the moment thing. And I feel bad about it now. Even so, I don't want to waste the opportunity. So I wondered, would it be all right with you if I came up one day this week, after school, and picked it up? I could go through it, then, and see if there's anything significant. What do you think?'

Evie didn't hesitate.

'Of course, Sophie. In fact, why don't you stay and have some supper with me?'

She was so kind, Sophie thought. And so understanding. Happily accepting the invitation, she rang off.

I have to confess to a degree of concern about what Sophie has told me. Taking her mother's property without her permission is tantamount to theft. Well, it would be construed as such by some people. The point is that putting it in my car implicates me, too. The repercussions could be embarrassing to say the least.

Naturally, I have no option but to go along with Sophie's wishes at this stage. Accordingly, I remove the box from the car and place it, unopened, in my front room at one end of the sofa. At least she's agreed to stay for supper, so I'll have a chance to talk it through with her.

Sophie arrives at my little terraced house the following Tuesday afternoon at the end of the school day.

'I'm useless at finding my way around,' she confesses, when I open the front door to let her in. 'It took me ages to find you. I've never been in this part of Exeter before.'

She's brought gifts of flowers, wine and chocolates, all of which I'm sure must have strained her meagre resources, but which go a long way to show her generosity of spirit.

'You shouldn't have,' I say, and mean it. 'Come on in.'

Smiling, I lean forward to greet her with a kiss. She's dressed in work attire, black slacks, and with her hair scraped back into a bun, which is beginning to show signs of falling to pieces. Just as she is.

'I can't tell you how sorry I am about landing you with the box of photos I took from the cupboard,' she says. 'And without even asking your permission. It just seemed like a good idea at the time. And I suppose after all you'd said about – well, about my relationship with my parents – I guess –'

'Sophie,' I squeeze her arm and show her into the front room. 'There's no need to keep apologising. I was surprised, I admit. But I understand your motives. You wanted to help Matt I imagine?'

Sophie looks at me directly for a moment, then lowers her eyes. I'm hoping my interpretation of her motives will help her to open up, to acknowledge to herself, and to me, exactly what it was that prompted her to take this action. Sure enough, she plonks herself down on the chair nearest to Pumpkin and begins to fondle her head and ears.

'I did – I do – want to help you and Matt. I've said that to everyone, right from the start. I felt cross when my sisters kept telling me to let sleeping dogs lie. And cross when – Mum – seemed to want to – I don't know – keep things from you. Especially this particular box. But at the same time –'

The antipathy from her family towards Matt and his research is no surprise. Nor Sophie's resistance to their reaction. Having met them all, now, except for Fiona, I think I've a pretty good idea of what makes them tick. But this doesn't answer what I'm hoping to hear from Sophie. I sit myself down opposite her on the sofa, and silently will her to go on.

'Oh, I don't know, Evie. All the things you pointed out to me when you came for lunch on Sunday. It made me realise how much I've allowed myself to be pushed around. I don't mean that to sound critical. As if I'm condemning my mother. But you made me realise I've been behaving like a little girl. I'm not blaming anyone. It's my fault. There! I've said it.'

I smile, broadly.

'Well done! It wasn't that I was pointing things out to you, Sophie. I was simply trying to help you to see them for yourself. And you've done that. Admitting to liability – no – let me put that a better way. Accepting responsibility for yourself – your thoughts, your behaviour, your response to others. That's a big step and you should be proud of yourself. It takes most people a long time to reach that stage. Some never do.'

Sophie's face softens and her limbs visibly relax. She leans back in the chair.

'So –' I press on, aware I haven't even offered her a drink as yet, but aware, also, that the moment must not be lost, '– how do you see this impacting on your life? What action are you planning to take to rectify matters?'

She sits up again, and leans forward. 'Whatever Mumm… my mother has to say about it, I'm going to stop calling her *Mummy*. Not that I have anything against the term. Lots of people I know still do. But I realise, now, since you showed me, that it's having a detrimental effect on me.'

'Right. Well it's good that you've recognised that. So what are you going to call her?'

'I know she hates 'Mum'. She thinks it lower class. But that's what everyone says now, and she'll just have to get used to it. I don't want to be like Liz and call her Mother. That sounds far too toffee-nosed to me.'

I have to applaud this new-found resolution in Sophie. And as we continue to talk, with a glass of wine in our hands, it's clear that this is not simply a matter of nomenclature. It's to do with helping Sophie to see herself as an adult, answerable to no one, save herself. It isn't until after supper, with which I've gone to town, bent all my own rules of subservience, and made the meat and two veg I used to feel obliged to produce during my marriage to Pete, that the matter of the box comes up again.

'I suppose, if I'm honest,' Sophie admits, with a smile, 'taking the box without permission was an act of rebellion on my part. A sort of kicking Mum's authority in the teeth. Looking back, it seems rather foolish. More childish than exerting my own rules. Immature, really.'

'Well, you've done it. It's what you decide to do now that matters.'

We're sitting in my tiny front room again, with an old record of my mother's playing in the background, Tom Jones' *Green, Green, Grass of Home*.

Sophie flushes slightly.

'That photo I gave you of your parents' wedding, you remember? I found that underneath the box my mother had asked me to bring in. It didn't strike me at the time, but my guess is that she never intended you to see it. I think it must originally have been in the box below – the one I put in your car – and it must have got stuck to the one I was told to bring out. I didn't intend to go against Mum's wishes when I passed it on to you. But I'm glad I did. You're entitled to know about your past.'

There's nothing quite like the satisfaction you feel, as a counsellor, when you witness someone shedding the restraints of their past, and coming out of the shadows into the sunshine of their true persona. Nevertheless, a degree of caution is required. The term *rights or wrongs* comes to mind, but I don't want Sophie to feel I'm passing judgement on her action.

'Whatever the *reason* you had for passing on the photo, I'm very grateful to you. And I'm hoping to have a chance to talk to your mother about it when the opportunity arises. Without letting on where it came from, of course. But what do you want to do with the box you put in my car?'

Sophie glances at her watch.

'I ought to be getting back soon. I've got work to do. I think, if you don't mind, I'd like to go through it on my own. Just to see if there's anything in there you and Matt should know about. And then, somehow, I suppose, I'll have to get it back to the cupboard it came from. Not that Mum ever goes in there. She probably wouldn't even notice it had gone.'

Helping Sophie on with her coat before she loads the box in her car, I feel both relieved and disappointed. I suppose I'd hoped we might have unearthed some stupendous information that evening. At the same time, I don't want to be complicit in anything underhand.

'Is Matt allowed to know about this?' I ask as we say our goodbyes on my front door step.

'I don't see why not, do you? You can tell him if you speak to him before I do. But not a word to my mother, please. Not yet, anyway.'

Chapter Eighteen

A Pregnant Pause

MATT RETURNED FROM his usual twice-weekly game at the badminton club, stripped off and stepped into the shower. Exercise was fundamental to a good writing regime as far as he was concerned, and the sport he played was alternated with a dawn run most mornings. Wasn't it author, Dorothea Brande who, in an appraisal of right-brain writing, had advocated physical activity as conducive to lubricating the creative juices? Whether batting about the badminton court or pounding the pavements of The Embankment, it was certainly his experience. Returning, hot and sweaty each day, it seemed that the words and ideas flowed in his brain as surely as the water streamed over his body from the shower.

That morning, however, his head felt like an arid desert: drought-ridden; devoid of green shoots; a swirling dust storm blown into being by an ill-wind. Alban Goodman, the protagonist of *Murder in Madagascar*, was nowhere to be seen. Instead, Matt had only three thoughts in his head. His daughter's epilepsy. The fact that he now knew, without doubt, that it stemmed from his biological grandmother, Beatrice. And, of course, his discovery of Charlie Rae!

It was, now, nearly ten days since Evie had told him about Phoebe's outburst. She had, said Evie, spoken with contempt about the condition afflicting her sister, as if the stigma of epileptic fits were self-inflicted. As if it, also, dishonoured the entire family.

He'd wept when he'd heard. It was bad enough to know his little princess had a condition that would affect her for the rest of her life. Dominating every decision about what she ate, suffering the bullying at school and the fear of embarrassment whenever she went out, there would be no escape except through the end of a needle. Worse still, though he couldn't think why, was the knowledge that it was his genes that had brought this on.

And where had those genes stemmed from? Following up on the information he'd gleaned from Andrew Bartholomew at the firm of solicitors in Clapham, he'd written to Charlie Rae at a firm of solicitors in Australia. Brief and to the point, he'd introduced himself as a respectable author, linking back to his publishers to give his statement credence and validity. He'd then stated the nature and purpose of his research, revealing his date and place of birth, his mother's name, the fact that he had been adopted, and the name cited on his adoption papers, Dean Rae. Was it possible, he'd concluded, that Mr Rae might know something of his biological family?

He'd taken care not to ask if Mr Rae might be his father, nor to mention Sam's medical condition, fearing this might frighten off any positive response. Neither, despite his earlier intention, had he told Evie of his letter.

For it had struck him, suddenly, during their last phone call, that if his investigation were to lead to his finding Charlie Rae, and if Charlie Rae were to prove to be his biological father, where would that leave his sister? You didn't need much of an imagination to realise that the relationship she'd had with her dad had been pretty toxic. And while there were no guarantees that any future relationship between him and Charlie Rae would be any better, he had no wish to make things more difficult for her. To risk making unfavourable comparisons between her father and his.

Switching off the water and stepping out of the shower to towel himself dry, he reflected on the similarities and differences in their upbringing. Bonnie, his adoptive mom, had always spoken about his having been *chosen*. It had struck him, initially, as an entirely positive concept. It was only recently that it had occurred to him that there was no *choice* on his part in having been put up for adoption. And he could only suppose that his biological mother, Libby, had *chosen* to be rid of him.

So were there advantages or drawbacks in knowing that the man who had fathered you had abandoned you and your mom? Or was it worse to have been born to parents who had been made to marry, as he believed of Evie's mom and dad?

Pulling on his socks and boxer shorts, he then lathered his face prior to shaving, the silent dialogue in his head continuing, uninterrupted.

He found it hard to believe that the probability of a shotgun wedding, in respect of her parents, had never occurred to Evie. The date on her mom's and dad's marriage certificate and wedding photo were clearly out of kilter with the date she had been told. And her own date of birth left no doubt that she'd been conceived out of wedlock. It took only a short step of imagination to surmise that her father had been made to marry her mother. *His* mother! And barely that to realise that this was the reason for his mother being made to sign his adoption papers.

Where was the *choice* in that? For Evie? For himself? For their mother? Who, then, if his hypothesis was correct, had *chosen* this course of action?

Finishing his ablutions and now fully dressed, he stepped out of the bathroom and crossed the hall to the kitchen. Breakfast was his usual buttered bagel followed by fresh fruit. He ate it standing before the window of his study, looking at the denuded plane trees below, while continuing to analyse the situation in which he found himself.

Breakfast over, he made himself a coffee and prepared for work. Seeing the postman cross the road, however, and looking for any excuse for further procrastination, he opened the door to his apartment, loped down the main staircase, and intercepted him in the hall.

''Alf a dozen for you, Mr McEwan. Must be all them female fans writing to yer. 'Ave to let me in on your secret one day soon.'

Matt grinned. 'Nothin' to do with me, sadly. It's all down to Alban Goodman.'

He could see that several of the letters in his hand were from overseas but, not wanting to appear too eager, he refrained from looking at them more closely. Once back in the apartment, however, his real anxiety revealed itself. Taking up the paper knife from his desk, he slit open each envelope in turn, glanced quickly at the contents of each, then – with a shaking hand – withdrew a hand-written letter from one of them.

Dear Dean, he read. Then his vision blurred.

I'm busy titivating, an uncommon feature of my life, because Scott is coming down for the weekend and will be arriving any moment *chez moi*. As always, he'll be staying in Topsham with his invalid aunt, Nancy, and her husband - my colleague, Guy Sampson. He's talked at length with them, and with me, about the offer he's received to become part of the team at Brunel Manor, and has reached a decision. As a result, he'll be moving down to Torbay after Christmas.

'But didn't you have to give a term's notice?' I asked, and was surprised to learn he'd been given special exemption.

'The person I'm taking over from at the conference centre has cancer. They've been muddling along for ages in the hope he'd be coming back, but it's now clear that's not gonna happen. Fortunately, my previous employers were very understanding.'

The question of Scott's move is something we've had under discussion since he first told me about it on our River Thames Cruise. Having been asked my opinion, I've plied him with the sort of questions I might have put to a client. I wouldn't want Scott to have expectations I might not be able to meet. Nor to move down to Torbay in the hope of something more, only for our relationship to fizzle out.

'You said you'd be living in?' I'd asked as we sat in St Katharine Dock after our river cruise. Uncomfortable about raising the possibility that he might be expecting to move in with me, I knew I must clarify the situation. Preparing now for his imminent visit, I recall his response to my question.

'Evie,' he took my hands in his and looked me in the eyes 'I love being with you. But we've both been through the trauma of divorce, and the last thing I'd want would be to put either of us under any sort of pressure. Let's just take it as it comes.'

The relief I felt, and still feel, is unimaginable. Scott has read my mind and sensitively disposed of my fears. There's no expectation from him of meat and two veg every evening. At least not yet. No reason for me to be concerned that my home, and its proximity to Torbay, will be simply a matter of convenience. So no question that he's just using me. With that out of the way, we're free to enjoy our relationship. Wherever it leads us. And whatever it turns out to be in the end.

My titivation and contemplation complete, I survey myself in the mirror. Having received compliments on the violet coloured summer outfit I bought from the charity shop, I've invested in something warmer, but of a similar hue. Hopefully, it too will elicit a favourable response from Scott.

It's the first time he will have sampled my cooking, and I'm feeling both nervous and proud when I usher him into my kitchen-diner and we proceed to partake of the simple fare I've prepared.

'I expect you were hoping for something a little more exotic,' I say, producing a melon starter with a simple roast chicken main course and trifle to finish.

My fears are unfounded, and with praise and obvious pleasure, he tucks into the meal I've set before him.

Conversation, naturally, is focused on the various aspects of Scott's forthcoming posting, and it's not until we're seated on the couch together in my front room, with his arm around me, that he asks me about my recent visit to Sophie's parents' home.

'I felt so sorry for Matt,' I say, my head on his shoulder as I relay the news that our grandmother was epileptic. 'It must be awful for him. Knowing that your daughter's medical condition is down to you.'

'Gee! That must be hard on him,' Scott agrees. 'And what about Sophie?' he asks when we've exhausted the subject.

'Of course! You met her in London when you came to the Cumberland Hotel didn't you.'

'That's right. We bumped into one another at the Reception desk. She overheard me asking for you and introduced herself as your cousin. Gee, she's like her mom. The spittin' image.'

'Like her mum?' Extricating myself from Scott's arm, I sit up and stare at him. 'You didn't meet her mum, did you?'

'Yeah, I did. When I came through to the lounge. She was there with you and Matt.'

The confusion I'm feeling must be showing on my face as Scott attempts to recreate the scene for me.

'Blonde. Good lookin'. A real lady. She didn't stay long. Said she had to get back up to her room, as I recall.'

'That was Liz.' I continue to stare at him.

'Yeah. Liz. That's right.'

'But she's not Sophie's mother. They're sisters.'

'Sisters?' Now it's Scott's turn to look confused. 'You're havin' me on. I'd swear they were mother and daughter. What is it you say? Two peas in a pod? Though –'

'What?' I search Scott's face.

'I dunno. P'raps I'm wrong. But the mom – the sister, Liz – she came across as very self-assured. Whereas Sophie, she seemed a bit of a lost soul, I thought.'

I nod. 'You're not wrong there.'

'Really? So what do you think is goin' on then?'

'I've been trying to talk to her.' I rise from the sofa and cross the room to pour more coffee. 'Encourage her to stand up for herself.'

'She did seem to be at the mercy of her mom – er, her sister – from what I saw.' Scott takes the coffee I hand him, and I seat myself at the opposite end of the couch so I can see him better. 'Bit of a bossy boots, wasn't she.'

I hesitate, keen to have someone with whom to share the thoughts that have been swilling around in my mind for some time, but equally anxious not to indulge in gossip, nor to break the rules of confidentiality. Before I can say anything, Scott speaks up again.

'Sorry. None of my business of course.'

He finishes his coffee, and we move on to a more amenable topic of conversation.

It's not until the following morning, in the office, that I'm able to broach the matter with Guy.

'What would you say,' I ask, feeling my way through the morass of speculation that's been troubling me for the past few weeks, 'if I were to tell you that the young woman whom I believed to be Phoebe Hamilton's daughter could, actually, be her granddaughter?'

As usual, Guy is preoccupied with his early morning coffee-making ritual, while I've taken up my customary place on one of the brown leather chairs.

'This was your client from Kingswear?' he asks, plugging in the espresso machine. 'The one that turned out to be your mother's aunt?'

I nod as he straightens up and pulls on his beard.

'I've learned that nothing should surprise us in this life,' he says. 'But I have to say, if it's the same old lady I saw on the landing the day she visited you –' he leaves the assumption hanging in the air.

Jumping up from my seat, I cross the room to the window and look out at one of my favourite views, across the Cathedral Green.

'Obviously, I can't divulge my concerns to those involved but – I don't know. I just feel a bit apprehensive. If it came to light inadvertently, I could find myself embroiled in something beyond my remit.'

Remaining where I am, I turn to face Guy again. He nods, a serious expression on his face, and seats himself at his desk.

'Go on,' he invites me.

'It's a combination of things. Phoebe's age. She'd have had to be well into her forties when Sophie was born.'

Guy looks dubious. 'I suppose – ' he shrugs. 'It's possible though, isn't it?'

'Possible. But doubtful, I'd say.'

'So what else?'

I sigh. 'There's an incredible likeness between the two sisters, Sophie and Liz. Even Scott picked it up, and he only met the two of them briefly when we were in London. He was convinced Liz was Sophie's mum.'

'Nothing conclusive about that. In fact, perfectly natural, I'd say.'

'It's not only that! Sophie told me about something she overheard her parents discussing a long time ago. Something about Liz having had a difficult labour.'

'Now you're talking.' Guy raises his bushy eyebrows.

'She must have had a child at some point. That's the only conclusion I can come to.'

Guy nods but says nothing.

'I understand it was her father, Phil, who made the remark,' I continue. 'And of course, he was a doctor.'

Guy's silence is pronounced. Then he says, 'What's that got to do with it? Him being a doctor? I'm not sure where you're going with this, Evie.'

Stepping across the room, I plonk myself back on the chair I vacated earlier, in front of the desk.

'Don't you see? If Liz was pregnant, as Sophie indicated, he could have delivered her baby himself.'

Watching Guy's face, I wait for the penny to drop.

'You mean –? You can't mean he might have passed the baby off as his and his wife's?'

I remain silent. A whole raft of questions present themselves. But with the coffee brewed and clients due any moment, there's no time for any of them to be aired.

Sophie sighed. The days following Evie's visit for Sunday lunch had dragged by. She'd so enjoyed the evening meal she'd had at Evie's when she'd collected the box of photographs she'd taken from the cupboard under the stairs at her parents' house, but other than that her life had been nothing but teaching and marking. With the end of term only a couple of weeks away and a nativity play and school reports to be written, she'd had no time to explore the contents of the box. Surveying the unruly class before her, she did her best to maintain discipline.

'Put your phone away Spencer, or I shall have no choice but to confiscate it. No, Ellie, you may not go to the toilet again. You've been once. Your friends will be thinking you're in need of a nappy.'

A titter of laughter rippled through the classroom.

'Now. Where were we? Sam, can you tell the class what an evacuee is. And what you think goes wrong in *Carrie's War*, when Carrie meets Arthur Sandwich at Druid's Bottom?'

More tittering broke out at the mention of Druid's Bottom, and one or two of the boys stood and made an attempt at mooning.

'Sit down, now, or you will find yourselves missing your break,' Sophie said firmly. 'Now, Sam –'

By the time she reached home that evening, she felt exhausted. She couldn't imagine what had attracted her to teaching, other than the fact that Mumm... her mother had thought it a *suitable occupation for a person of her standing.*

Her standing! Anyone would think they were something special.

More determined than ever, as soon as she'd made herself a cup of tea, Sophie pulled the box over to the window of her living room and sat herself at the table. She began pulling things out, a handful at a time, reading the handwritten notes on the back of the black and white photographs where possible; turning the unmarked ones this way and that to see if she could identify the people they depicted.

Some were, very obviously, of her parents, many of them beach scenes from holidays abroad when they were younger; others during the time they'd lived in London. One in particular, was of the two of them dressed in what she imagined were their honeymoon outfits, standing in front of what must have been Rosegreen. Of course! They'd married at St Luke's, her mother had told her, which was only round the corner from Nightingale Lane. She dug deeper into the box and came up with a handful of older photos, faded and yellowing around the edges. Some, she thought, must be of her grandparents. Others were a complete mystery.

Finally, about half way through the contents, she came across two or three sheets of folded, headed notepaper, each handwritten in ink. She opened them up and began to read.

Twenty minutes later, after some arduous decision-making, she rang Matt. He'd taken to ringing her almost daily of late, and she fancied that the two of them were getting on rather well. He seemed to enjoy her stories about school. They laughed a lot. And they discussed literature, films, and plays with a mutual excitement and pleasure.

'Matt,' she said breathlessly, when she got through.

'Sophie! Great to hear you. Everything okay?'

It was typical of him to show concern for her, even in so short a time of knowing one another. How long was it? Barely a third of a year since they'd first met at her parents' home! Yet she felt as if she'd known him forever. Couldn't imagine life without him, in fact.

'Everything's fine,' she assured him. 'Actually, more than fine. Guess what?'

She allowed a few moments of banter, taking great delight in teasing him, and in the enjoyment she heard in his voice. Then she took the three sheets of paper in her hand and looked at the embossed heading again.

'I've got a letter I think you might be interested in. I came across it while looking through among some old photographs.' Deliberately, she withheld the details of how she'd acquired them, not wishing to incite his disapproval.

'Oh?' At the other end of the phone, Matt sounded more than interested.

'It's written on very fancy notepaper which has the address embossed on it. It's one of the hotels Mumm… my mother mentioned when we did the tour of Grandma's properties in London.'

A stunned silence greeted her pronouncement, then Matt said, in tones that spoke to her of excitement and apprehension, 'Who's it from?'

'It's signed by my grandfather. I never knew him, of course. He died years before I was born.'

Silence again. Then Matt asked, 'Who's it to?'

'It's to my mother's eldest brother. She was the youngest of the family, and there was a big difference in age between them.'

'So, presumably, he would have been a young adult when the letter was written?'

'I guess so.'

'Are you going to let me know what it says? Or don't you feel comfortable with that?'

'Of course! I'm going to read it to you. That's why I rang.'

'I don't want you to do anything you don't feel easy about.'

'Matt! I've said right from the start that I believe you have a right to know about your roots. And when I've read it to you, I'm going to go over to Liz to see what she knows of the situation. See if I can find out what prompted the writing of this letter.'

There was no response from Matt other than the sound of an indrawn breath.

'Okay,' she said, 'This is how it starts –'

Chapter Nineteen

A Litter of Letters

TWO LETTERS IN one week! Matt could hardly believe it. Phone to his ear, he paced around the floor of his apartment listening to what Sophie was saying, thinking through the implications. Outside, a steady downfall of rain obscured his view of the plane trees from his window, while promising to wash away the London dirt.

'Have you spoken to Evie about this?' he asked when she finished.

'I thought you might want to tell her,' she replied.

When Sophie eventually rang off, he toyed with the idea of ringing Evie then decided, instead, to jump in the car and drive down. It was nearing the end of the day and he knew that if he booked a room at The Royal Clarence Hotel in Cathedral Yard he could be down there for bedtime. Hopefully, Friday would be Evie's non-contact day. But if not, he could at least meet her for lunch or after work. That would leave him the weekend to see Sophie. And possibly to tackle Liz on his own, if she had drawn a blank with her.

He rang the hotel, made a reservation, threw a few clothes in a holdall, and set off.

The journey down was uneventful, and as soon as he'd had a bite to eat and settled into his room, he texted Sophie: @ *hotel in xter. Hoping 2 c E 2moro. Wd love 2 spend sum time w/u on Sat 2 if pos? xx*

She would no doubt be surprised, he thought as he drifted off to sleep.

First thing in the morning, Matt put in a call to Evie.

'I'm here, at the Clarence,' he said. 'Any chance of meeting up?'

'What on earth are you doing down here?' The astonishment in Evie's voice exploded across the airwaves.

Fortuitously, although she had clients that morning, she told him, her last appointment was at midday. They arranged to meet in the hotel bar for lunch.

Evie was a few minutes late – a difficult session she said. They exchanged a kiss on the cheek, then settled at a side table with a lager for Matt and an Appletizer for Evie.

What's this all about?' she asked when they'd exchanged pleasantries.

'Letters,' he said.

'Letters?'

'Two of them. One from Charlie Rae. The other about Chay Rae.'

'You've had letters from them both? How come?'

'No!' He laughed and sat back on his chair. 'I've only had one. Chay is dead, don't forget. But Sophie found something about him.'

'How exciting!' Evie grinned.

'Very! You remember, I went to see Chay Rae's son-in-law, Andrew Bartholomew, and he told me Charlie worked for the firm for a while. I got the impression he left quite abruptly. Whether there was some sort of confrontation, I don't know.'

Evie nodded.

'It seems he emigrated to Oz. So I did some research. And found a solicitor named Charlie Rae. What's more, he was born in Scotland. In the Highlands, where Chay came from.'

Evie picked up her glass and drank from it. The bar was filling up fast with the approach of lunch hour, and Matt handed her the menu.

'What do you fancy?' he asked.

She chose a toasted ham and cheese sandwich with a side salad, and he a pizza.

'So what happened next?' Evie asked when he'd put the order in.

'I wrote to him, explained who I was etc. And lo and behold, within a fortnight, I had a handwritten letter back.'

Matt could feel his emotions getting the better of him. He tugged at his hair and blinked rapidly. What he'd described hardly seemed possible. But, as before, he was all too aware of the impact this might have on Evie. He reached across the table and took hold of her hand.

'I realise this could be upsetting for you. That's why I haven't said anything before. If you'd rather not hear anymore –' He pleaded with his eyes for her to allow him to continue.

'No. Please. Go on. I want to hear what happened.'

Reassured, Matt let go of Evie's hand and sat back in his chair.

'He addressed me as Dean. Not Matt! He told me he'd met our mom, Libby, when he first came down to work for his Uncle Chay who, of course, was Phoebe's dad's solicitor. Charlie was eighteen. Libby was sixteen. They fell in love. They wanted to marry.'

Matt's voice broke, and this time, Evie reached across the table to comfort him. For a moment, her face swam before him. It was impossible to know what she was thinking. Would she jump to the conclusion he had? That while his dad had loved their mom and wanted to marry her, Evie's parents had been made to marry? There was no logic in it. Why had Charlie and Libby not married? Why had Libby then got pregnant with Evie? Why had she married someone else?

'Matt, that's amazing!'

The waiter came with their food. Matt looked at the pizza he'd ordered, and wished he hadn't. He had no appetite. Evie, however, was about to tuck in to her toastie. He had no option but to follow suit.

'You mentioned a second letter,' Evie said between mouthfuls.

Matt put down his knife and fork.

'Yeah. Sophie came across it among some photos. She rang yesterday evening to tell me.'

Was he mistaken, or was that a look of discomfort he saw on Evie's face?

'And?' Evie wiped her mouth and fingers on her paper napkin, picked up her glass and drank from it.

'And –' he did likewise before continuing, '– she said it was a letter from Aunt Phoebe's dad, written just before he died when she was only a child, and was addressed to her eldest brother.'

'So what did it say?'

'It was quite extraordinary. I haven't seen, it of course. But Sophie read it to me over the phone.'

Matt sat back and looked across the table, fixing his eyes on Evie's.

'What it said was: *under no circumstances is Chay Rae ever to be left alone with Beatrice.* In fact, he wasn't even to be allowed into the building.'

'Goodness!' Evie shook her head.

'Given that Chay was a friend, and the family solicitor,' Matt continued, 'sounds as if it had all come to a sticky end.'

Evie frowned. 'What on earth was going on?'

'Well, that's the point. Sophie said she was going to have a go at her sister, Liz. And if she got nowhere with her, she'd try her mom, or pop.'

Evie looked at her watch.

'Matt, I'm sorry. I'm going to have to go.'

'Would you like a dessert? Or a coffee?'

'Thank you, but no. I'm really sorry. I've got to make a phone call. Family of a deceased client whose funeral is next week. I'd completely forgotten.'

Matt grimaced. 'Don't envy you.'

'I'm fine. Really, thanks. How long are you down?'

Matt stood and helped Evie on with her coat.

'I'm seeing Sophie later.' He hesitated, then thought better of his reticence. 'It was she who wanted me to tell you about the letter she found. Look, why don't the three of us meet up when you finish work. That way, she can let us both know if she's found out anything more from her sister, Liz.'

He arranged a time to pick Evie up, gave her a peck on the cheek and saw her off the premises into the chill air of the Cathedral Green. With an hour or more to kill, he ordered a coffee and went through to the lounge to await its arrival. Standing, looking out of the window at the flying buttresses that held together the walls of the cathedral, he couldn't help thinking that there was a marked lack of any such fortification in this family of his.

What he hadn't told Evie, because he hadn't the heart to rub it in, was that Charlie Rae, his new-found father, was coming over to the UK in a few weeks, in time for Christmas. *'I'll be visiting relatives in Scotland,'* he'd written. *'Any chance we could meet up? That is, unless you'd rather not?'*

Rather not? Not meet the father you've never known? Boy! What a crazy notion. Matt couldn't believe his luck when he'd read that. He'd emailed him, immediately, in the affirmative, stating his delight.

It was only later that it hit him. This might be the man who had fathered him. But it was, also, the guy who appeared to have abandoned him and his mom. And facing that prospect was rather less attractive.

Sophie busied herself plumping up cushions, preparing a tray of coffee mugs and biscuits, and generally tidying up in readiness for Matt's and Evie's arrival. Matt had phoned her earlier and asked if she would mind Evie accompanying him, adding that he and Sophie would have the whole of the following day alone.

'No problem,' she said. 'In fact, I'm glad Evie's coming.'

They arrived early evening, and Matt greeted her with a kiss and a hug which left her heart aflutter and her cheeks burning. Quickly, she turned to Evie, and met with a warm smile which told her, in no uncertain terms, that the blossoming romance between herself and Matt had been duly noted and approved.

'Here,' Evie held out a white plastic carrier bag. 'We bought them down by the harbour as you suggested.'

The three of them had agreed that a supper of fish and chips was in order so as to leave them as much time as possible to talk. Taking the bag from Evie, Sophie proceeded to unwrap each portion of cod and chips and placed them on the plates she'd warmed in the oven. Aware that this was the first time Matt had been to her home, she watched for his reaction as he looked around him.

'Gee, this is so quaint,' he said, his face alight with pleasure.

She smiled. 'Some of the properties around here are 16th and 17th century,' she told him. 'Smith Street Deli, and the Community Bookshop, just down from here, may be even older. I think the church is thirteen hundred and something.'

'Smith Street?' Evie asked. 'That's an odd name for such a historic place.'

'It's where the smithies and shipwrights worked,' Sophie

explained, gratified to have the opportunity to share her knowledge to an appreciative audience. Clearly speechless, Matt shook his head in amazement.

Sophie passed him a plateful of food and another to Evie, then the three of them took their places at the table. Having agreed to leave any discussion about the letter she'd discovered until after their meal, they all tucked in.

'So,' Matt said, when Sophie had served coffee and they were seated more comfortably on either side of the fireplace. 'I was tellin' Evie that you found this letter from –'

'My grandfather. On my mother's side. It was incredible.'

Evie looked across the room at her.

'Most peculiar, from what Matt said. Something about Chay Rae being forbidden to see Beatrice?'

Sophie put her mug down on the hearth.

'I made copies for you both,' she said, 'so you could see it for yourselves. And instead of talking to Liz about it, I decided to raise the matter with my parents.'

'Good for you!'

The look of approval on Evie's face was plain to see, and Sophie felt a positive glow of affirmation. She'd really been trying, since her chat with Evie, to make sure she was her own woman and not her mother's little girl.

'And what did Aunt Phoebe have to say about that?' asked Matt, leaning back on the sofa and putting one foot on his knee.

'She refused to say anything to begin with.'

Sophie recalled her mother's inflexibility, and felt proud of herself for the way in which she'd handled it, refusing to cave in, but refusing, also, to allow herself to become riled. This, she told herself, was no different to a hundred encounters she'd had with recalcitrant pupils at school, over the years. And to her surprise, she'd seen her mother in a completely different light. Gone was the intimidating voice of authority. In her eyes, Mum had become no more than an elderly woman who refused to face up to the fact that other people were entitled to their opinions, and that although it might well have been absent in her day, a new sense of equality now prevailed.

Standing her ground had, eventually, paid off.

'My mother told me the story behind the letter,' she said, looking first at Matt, then at Evie. 'Apparently, Chay Rae acted for my grandparents when they purchased Rosegreen. He'd previously undertaken the conveyancing of other properties for them, and I understand they'd become friends. Chay and my grandfather were both members of the Conservative Club on Balham Hill, for instance. And they saw one another socially. But you probably know a lot of that, already.'

'I'm not sure we *knew* it, as fact,' Matt intervened, 'though I guess I surmised as much. Andrew Bartholomew clearly knows more than he was letting on. He sure was edgy when I mentioned Rosegreen.'

Evie, Sophie noted, was sitting silently, taking it all in.

'I'm not surprised,' Sophie continued. 'My mother said there was some sort of malpractice over the purchase of Rosegreen. Chay Rae, it seems, was trying to get one over on my grandfather, and do him out of ownership of the property.'

'How could he do that?' Evie asked.

Sophie shook her head. 'No idea. My mother said she didn't know, and I believe her. After all, she was only five or six when her father died, so she'd hardly have been of an age to take any of this in first hand. She must have learned about it later – from her brother, perhaps?'

Matt leaned forward, elbows on knees, hands clasped together.

'So that explains why the two of them fell out,' he said, slowly, 'but it doesn't say why he was forbidden to see our grandmother, Beatrice.'

'No!' Sophie stood up. Unsure how Matt and Evie would take it, this was the bit she was dreading. Both were looking at her full of expectancy. She leaned against the fireplace, and tapped her fingers on the mantelpiece.

'My mother actually got quite upset when she told me this. So I hope you two are prepared for the worst?'

Evie nodded, briefly, and Sophie felt the eyes of both firmly fixed on her face, boring into her. She sighed. What she had to say might put Matt off her family, and thence her, forever. It certainly didn't reflect well on any of them.

'You know, of course, that Aunt Bea was epileptic. I don't know a lot about the condition, but I guess it must make you quite vulnerable.'

She stopped, surprised to see a covert exchange of eye contact between Matt and Evie, waiting for an explanation.

'There's something I need to tell you,' Matt said, fidgeting in his seat. 'But later, not now. Please continue.'

Uncomfortably aware of some hidden issue, Sophie shook her head in an effort to clear her mind.

'Where was I? Oh, yes. Chay and your grandmother. Well, according to my mother, the reason he was forbidden to see her was all to do with Rosegreen, and the fact that my grandfather ended up owning it. Seems that Chay – and as I say, this is only my mother's version of events – was determined to find another way of acquiring the property.'

Sophie stopped and plonked herself back in the easy chair she'd vacated. She could see Matt's and Evie's faces crumple with bewilderment and disbelief.

'And how could he go about doing that?' asked Matt.

Evie, it appeared, was one step ahead of him. Eyes still firmly fixed on Sophie, she said, 'He took advantage of our grandmother, didn't he?'

Sophie nodded.

'I'm afraid so. He'd lodged at my grandparents' hotel when he first came down to London to set up his business, and he obviously knew about Beatrice's affliction. Her vulnerability.'

'You mean – he made sexual advances? With a girl of – what age would she have been?'

'My mother thought she'd have been in her late teens. Or possibly just turned twenty.'

'And she would probably have been quite immature and not socially adept, given her condition,' said Evie.

'I'll say!' Matt looked appalled.

'There's worse to come,' said Sophie. 'It seems she became pregnant – which, of course, was what Chay Rae wanted, so my mother said.'

'So he could marry her?' said Matt.

'Exactly! Except that my mother's father wouldn't have it. He was determined that he wasn't having his daughter being a way in for Chay Rae.'

'Goodness me!' Evie shook her head. 'They must have fallen out badly for him to refuse. So what happened?'

Sophie sighed. 'Seems he married Aunt Bea off elsewhere.'

'And packed her off to Scotland in an unhappy marriage.' said Matt.

'From which she kept trying to escape,' Evie finished.

Sophie nodded. There was nothing else to say, as far as she was concerned.

Though neither Matt nor Evie, she noted, had yet asked about the identity of the baby.

From where I'm sitting, I can see Matt's face, and it's clear that he is as shocked as I am.

'So, let me get this straight,' I say ticking each point off on my fingers as I repeat what Sophie has told us.

Matt leans forward.

'Gee. Sounds like the plot of an Agatha Christie crime story. I find it hard to believe.'

'Except that the last point, about her being *married off*, is exactly what Phoebe said when I went for tea.' I look across the room at Sophie. 'You know. The day I came to you for lunch.'

Sophie's mouth drops open.

'Of course!' She smacked the side of her head in a gesture of self-contempt. 'I heard Mum saying something about that when I brought the tea trolley into the lounge. But, stupid me, I didn't put two and two together.'

'Nothin' stupid about what you've achieved, Sophie,' says Matt. 'Frankly, I'm astonished that your mom revealed all this. With all due respect to Aunt Phoebe, you must've worked real hard to prise this out of her.'

I can see Sophie blushing, and can't help wondering if this is

223

because she's unused to being praised, or whether it's because the acclamation is specifically from Matt.

'So!' I continue my point, 'If it's true – sorry Sophie, I'm not meaning to impugn your mother, but it is only one side of the story – that explains a lot.'

'But not everything!' Matt is emphatic.

Silence hangs in the air as we think through the implications of his statement. I must admit, I feel confused.

'Well, I take it that the baby Beatrice was carrying was our mother?' I say to Matt. 'Which means that although she was *married off*, our biological grandfather must be this charlatan, Chay Rae.'

'Not necessarily!' Matt says. 'Beatrice lost that first baby. I've been puttin' together a family tree, based on the research I've done. Seems the baby died when she was only a year or two old. Libby was born soon after.'

'Well that's a relief.' I wriggle to make myself more comfortable on the sofa. 'So at least we're not descendants of Chay Rae. Though I'm not sure that the man our grandmother married sounds any better.'

Sophie nods. 'That's right. And I forgot to say, Mum finally admitted that the reason Aunt Bea spent so much time with her mother was because her marriage was so awful.

'In what way?' I ask, pricking up my ears.

'It seems her husband was already having an affair with one of his employees, and he didn't want an epileptic wife hanging around complaining about things.'

'So all the talk about my grandmother imposing on her mother –' I'm speechless.

'Exactly! Poor thing.' Sophie's face is full of sadness. 'Imagine being married to a man who was openly conducting an affair. She was only trying to get away from a terrible situation. Though I suspect that some of it was his doing, packing her off back to her mother so he didn't have to be bothered with her. I took that up with my mother. Told her what I thought of the whole business. I think she was quite shocked that I'd dared to be so outspoken.'

Sophie exchanges a glance with me, part gratitude, I surmise, and part conspiracy, a plea not to let on to Matt that I've encouraged her to be her own person.

Matt throws one arm along the back of the sofa.

'What I can't understand is why our grandfather agreed to marry Beatrice in the first place? I mean, there she is, epileptic. Pregnant with Chay Rae's child. Why on earth would any man agree to that?' Sophie shrugs and looks at me.

'My guess is that money must have exchanged hands,' I respond.

'You mean our grandfather was paid to marry our grandmother?' Matt looks aghast.

'I can't see any other explanation, can you? Didn't he have a business in Glasgow? A drapery store or something? Suppose – just suppose – that Phoebe's father set him up in that? He might have had shares in the business so he could keep control, as a sleeping partner.'

'Mmm! Something worth researching at Companies House,' Matt concludes. 'Do we know the name of the business?'

'No, but I'll try and find out from my parents,' says Sophie.

Matt rises to his feet. 'Do you mind if I use the bathroom? Then I think we ought to go.'

Sophie points the way up the narrow staircase, and when Matt has disappeared from view, she moves over to sit next to me.

'Evie,' she looks me in the face and I can see tears welling in her eyes. 'I just want to thank you for your help the day you came for lunch.'

I shake my head and raise a hand in denial.

'It was nothing more than a chat between friends.'

'Oh, but it was so much more than that to me. You opened my eyes to something I was only vaguely aware of before. I've spent years feeling guilty. Believing I wasn't good enough. Or doing enough.

'Not that my parents were hard taskmasters. I don't mean to imply that. But there was always this – I don't know – this undercurrent of obligation. As if I owed them something more than is normal. Sorry. I'm not explaining myself very well am I?'

I'm instantly aware of my speculation in respect of Sophie's parentage. If, as I've surmised, it is Liz who is her mother, and not

Phoebe, then there may well have been an air of duty prevailing throughout Sophie's childhood. It's hard to put myself in Phoebe's shoes, but I imagine she might well have felt put-upon if, for some reason, she'd felt compelled to take on Liz's child. And that sense of unwanted responsibility could undoubtedly have been transmitted to Sophie.

'I'm just glad to know I was of help,' I say, now, aware that I can never convey such unsubstantiated thoughts to any of those concerned.

'Oh, you were,' Sophie beams. 'I've been training myself to call my mother *Mum* instead of *Mummy*. It helps to remind me that I'm an adult, not a little girl who's required to be *good*.'

'And how does that go down? Is she happy? Does she understand why?'

Sophie shakes her head. 'She doesn't like it. Not one little bit. To her mind, it's only the lower classes who use the term *Mum*. But I've joked and told her she's simply behind the times. She'd rather I called her *Mother*, as Liz does. But to me, that's too distant and aloof. Because, despite everything, I do still love her.'

Matt's appearance at the top of the stairs draws our discussion to a close.

'Ready to make a move?' he asks, and helps me on with my coat. With warm appreciation, bordering on rather more than mere affection on Matt's part, we bid Sophie farewell and step outside.

It's a short, steep walk from the cottage down to where the car is parked, and despite the overhead lighting illuminating the steps, Matt invites me to slip my arm through his. The evening air drifting up from the river has a winter chill about it. Drawing the collar of my jacket up around my neck with my free hand, I reflect, again, on the unintentional but multifarious issues his search for his biological family has raised. Nevertheless, I can't help thinking how much richer my life has become as a result. Not to mention Sophie's!

Matt held open the car door for Evie, then seated himself behind the steering wheel.

'Well! That was an interesting evening,' he said, setting off down the hill towards the harbour. 'If it's not too much of an understatement.'

'As you remarked, the sort of thing you might expect from an Agatha Christie novel,' Evie replied. 'Or a Mills and Boon's romance, if my eyes don't deceive me?'

He glanced at her sideways, feeling somewhat embarrassed.

'You mean Sophie and me?'

'Who else?'

'Didn't know it was that obvious,' he said, unable to stop himself from grinning. 'But I guess, given the depth of my feelings, I shoulda realised.'

He sensed, rather than saw, Evie smile her approval.

Taking the road that would lead them along the river bank then uphill again and out of town, Matt considered his response, surprising himself with the strength of feeling he bore for Sophie. Was this the real thing? He couldn't remember having felt such devotion for a woman before. At least, not since the early days of his courtship with Sam's mom.

'So! Another positive from what began as a negative reason for your research!' Evie responded. 'I noticed your reluctance to tell Sophie about your daughter's condition. Can't say I blame you. Perhaps it would be better to leave it until it's just the two of you.'

Matt grimaced.

'Wish it wasn't necessary. I mean, I wish it wasn't Sam's condition that had triggered it all.'

Evie put her hand briefly on his arm.

'I understand that. And I sympathise with you, I really do. But it has brought benefits, too, hasn't it. Scott often says to me *all things work together for good for those who love God* – something from the Bible, I think.'

'Sounds like the sort of thing my mom would say,' said Matt.

He changed gear. In the rear view mirror, he could see the lights of Dartmouth twinkling in the darkness. And, above them, etched in the inky blackness, a star-spangled sky, dimmer to the naked eye, but infinitely brighter in reality than the man-made illuminations below.

Much like Evie's take on the current situation, he thought.

Looking back, he could see that despite the human context – the revelation about Sam's epilepsy, the perception he'd had of being cheated because of his adoption, and the duplicity of the Hamilton family – they were only a pale reflection of the good things that now shone in his life. Evie was right.

'Yeah! Spot on. I've gained a sister,' he said as they approached the ancient town of Totnes, the turrets of its 9th century castle clearly visible in the moonlight. 'A real good sister! And I've gained cousins. One rather special, as you've noted. And an aunt, albeit a tetchy one. Plus, it seems, the possibility of a living, breathing dad.'

Evie swivelled in her seat as they sped down the hill and stopped at the lights.

'Charlie Rae? You've met up with him? You didn't say!'

Her voice was full of excitement. Matt turned to look at her.

'Not yet. But he wants us to meet. I didn't mention it cos I didn't wanna upset you.'

'Upset me? Why would you think it would upset me?'

The lights began to change and Matt put the car in gear and moved off.

'I told you he lives down under. In Oz. Not that far from where my Sam lives with her mom, actually. But he's comin' back to Scotland, visitin' family over Christmas. So I'm gonna be meeting him in a couple of weeks. Didn't want you to feel it's all going my way when you have such rotten memories of your own dad.'

'Matt!' Evie placed her hand on his arm, again. 'My past is dead and buried. Yours is alive and well. Don't let the one overshadow the other. Enjoy the limelight!'

Unused to driving on the unlit, narrow country lanes that twisted between the gentle rolling hills of this part of Devonshire, Matt fell silent. Keeping his eyes on the road ahead, he couldn't help but reflect again on his good fortune. As Evie had implied earlier, the purpose and means of his journey had been tortuous and emotionally demanding. It had, however, brought him to a place that had so much to offer.

Arriving, at last, at the main Plymouth to Exeter road, Matt took the slip road and put his foot down hard on the accelerator. To his left, silhouetted against the night sky, lay the sweeping lowlands of Dartmoor. Ahead, lay the open highway. It was, he couldn't help feeling, symbolic of all that beckoned in life. Done with the convoluted dramas of recent days, his ardent wish was that the future would hold only harmony and delight. Softly, so as not to waken Evie who appeared to have dropped off to sleep, he began to hum the old song he'd learned as a child, *I know where I'm goin'. And I know who's goin' with me.*

Chapter Twenty

A Not Quite Crystal Clear Christmas

THE LIGHTS ON the Christmas tree in The Royal Avenue Gardens, near the harbour in Dartmouth, shone bright and clear as Sophie drove home from school on the last day of term. On the back seat of the car lay the gifts the children in her class had given her. Still wrapped, so as not to foster a competitive culture among the givers should they see the contents and make unfavourable comparison, they bore labels addressed to 'Miss Hamilton, the best Miss in the world', 'Miss Hammyton' (made her feel she should puff out her cheeks), and one (the result of a parent's misguided observation?) 'Miss Haveitall'.

Whatever the tag, the thought behind the giving, or the gift itself, Sophie knew herself to be well-loved by her pupils. The feeling was mutual. Her aim was always to build confidence as well as to educate. In fact, to her mind, self-assurance was both the foundation on which education was built and the pinnacle of its success. Without that as the cornerstone of their lives, children, in her experience, became either shrinking violets whose dried-up shrivelled selves were unable to absorb what they were being taught; or so smug and conceited that the teaching of knowledge and understanding failed to pierce their hard and glossy coats of armour.

She parked her car in its usual place and began to unload the contents. Much of her current philosophy, she thought as she staggered, laden, up the steep hill to her cottage, had been confirmed by what she'd learned from Evie. In the months since their first encounter in the summer, they'd become good friends, meeting up for coffee from time to time, and even planning a trip to the theatre together. But it was with her family relationships that Sophie felt she had benefited most from Evie's input.

With difficulty, she unlocked her front door and let herself in, kicking the door shut behind her. Only it didn't shut, because she'd dropped something on the threshold. Depositing the armfuls of gifts on the sofa, she turned to retrieve the obstacle, and was startled to see her sister, Liz, on the doorstep. She must have followed her up the hill, unseen.

'Oh, my goodness! You made me jump.'

'Sorry.' Liz picked up the parcel and handed it to Sophie. 'I hope I'm not intruding.'

With what Sophie noted to be markedly more consideration than usual, she refrained from barging in.

'Of course not. Come on in. I'm just about to make a cup of tea.'

Conversation, over tea and biscuits, proceeded in the usual stilted fashion, but it became increasingly obvious to Sophie that Liz was outside her comfort zone.

'Is everything okay,' she asked. 'Nothing wrong with Gordon, is there?'

Liz shuffled on the sofa, glanced in Sophie's direction, then looked back down at her hands.

'I simply wanted to say how pleased I am to see you getting on with your life.'

Sophie frowned, perplexed. It seemed an odd reason to be making an unannounced call on a sister with whom you rarely had much contact.

'How do you mean?' she asked.

'You just seem so much happier. Free. Unhampered.'

Was Liz referring to her relationship with Matt, Sophie wondered? Had she, like Evie, observed their blossoming romance? But how, when she and Liz saw one another so infrequently? Besides, she'd never shown any interest in previous boyfriends.

'I suppose I am,' Sophie replied, and she could feel the heat in her cheeks. 'Free. And happy. I don't know where our friendship is going, but Matt and I seem to get on very well together.'

Liz looked up, a smile on her face.

'I had noticed,' she said, softly. 'And I'm glad for you. You deserve so much more. But that's not what I'm talking about. It's – how can I describe it? It's about the way you've broken free from the family curse.'

Sophie frowned. 'Family curse?' she repeated.

Liz bowed her head as if for inspiration, then looked up, across the room.

'I knew this was going to be difficult.' She raised her hand. 'Not because of you. It's just – '

Liz's discomfort was plain to see. Sitting silently opposite her sister, Sophie was filled with a sense of compassion. It took Liz a good half hour to explain what she wanted to say, to fill Sophie in with the history of deception and manipulation that had plagued their family, much of which had revolved around Chay Rae, Phoebe's father, and the property they'd owned.

'I'm afraid it had its effect on mother, too,' said Liz. 'And I think that's why she imposed so much restraint on you. It used to make me mad. I felt you'd been cheated of your childhood.'

Sophie felt quite overcome. It was so unlike Liz to open up, let alone to express her feelings.

'You wouldn't know, of course, but –' Liz gulped and blinked hard, '– Gordon and I can't have a family. My fault, not his. I adored you when you were born. And when you were growing up – well, let's just say you were very special to me, but mother – she was so possessive. You were hers, and she wasn't going to let me have a look in.'

'Oh, Liz!' Sophie moved across to where her sister was seated and put an arm around her. There was no way she could admit to having heard her parents discussing the matter of the baby Liz had lost long ago. But so many things now fell into place. The brittle shell with which Liz surrounded herself. The way she distanced herself from people. Her curt mannerisms and shallow interests. They were all there to protect the hurt inside. And no wonder! Because unless she was mistaken, Sophie thought, it was pretty obvious that their mother had done little to alleviate it.

Drawing the curtains across the window later, when Liz had left, Sophie felt a surge of joy. Tenuous though it was, her relationship with Liz seemed to have become so much closer. It might be that Liz would never fully recover from her loss, and that her coping mechanisms were now set in concrete, but without doubt a chink had opened up in her armour. And it was one that Sophie would do her utmost to widen. Love and understanding, she thought, as she placed her pupils' gifts beneath the tiny Christmas tree in the corner of her sitting room, were the best balm she knew of to heal hurts.

The phone rang. Matt spoke to her most days now, and sure enough, it was his voice that greeted her when she lifted the handset from its cradle.

'Just to let you know that Evie and I are going to be meeting with Charlie Rae tomorrow morning,' he said, when he'd asked about her day. 'Is it okay with you if we refer to the letter you found among your mom's stuff? Evie's concerned that we shouldn't do so without your permission.'

Sophie considered the matter. 'The one about Chay Rae? Yes, I think so. It would be interesting to hear what his nephew has to say.'

They continued to talk for a while then rang off. Plonking herself down on the sofa in her sitting room, Sophie reflected on what she'd just done. She hoped, beyond hope, that it would not rebound on her. Not that either Matt or Evie would ever do anything that might incriminate her. Closing her eyes, she pictured the scene when they met up with the man who had known their mother so well. A pang of jealousy assailed her. Fervently, she wished she could be with Matt at this moment.

Matt rose early on the morning of Charlie Rae's impending visit. Once again, Evie was occupying his bedroom, while he slept on the sofa bed in the study. The pleasure this afforded him and, he hoped her, was immense. Increasingly at ease with their newfound relationship as half-brother and sister, he thought their shared sense of humour a highlight, and Evie's occasional off-the-wall take on life hilarious.

'Evie Adams by name, and Adam and Eve by nature,' he joked, and the two of them were convulsed with laughter.

Dressed and ready for breakfast, Matt smiled at the memory. It was Evie's serious side that most appealed, however. Her sensitivity and discernment were incalculable. Despite her emotionally impoverished upbringing – or perhaps because of it, as she would almost certainly have said – he felt she had so much of value to offer. Which, among other things, not least that Charlie Rae and their mother were lovers, was why he'd asked her to be present at the meeting he'd arranged with Charlie that morning.

'He's flying into London from Australia and booking into an hotel prior to goin' up to see his family in Scotland,' Matt had told Evie on the phone. 'And he's agreed to come to my apartment to meet up. I told him I thought it would make it easier, in view of all the research documents we might want to access.'

'That's good of him,' said Evie. 'I'd have thought he'd have preferred somewhere neutral.'

Matt confessed he hadn't thought of that, and had offered Evie's perceptiveness as the reason for his desire to have her present. And to his relief, she'd agreed.

'Ready for this?' he asked her now, as they cleared away the breakfast dishes and retrieved the ring binders into which he'd assembled his research papers.

'Absolutely!' Evie responded, her face alight with pleasure, her curly hair a slightly lighter version of his own, and her whole appearance so like the one he saw in the mirror each morning it defied belief.

'I'm so grateful to you for including me,' Evie continued. 'I know he's your father, not mine, but I'm hoping he'll be able to shed some light on what state of mind our mother was in when she married my dad.'

'Gee, I wish you'd had a better chance at life,' Matt said, squeezing her arm as they set out coffee mugs and a plate of biscuits ready for their visitor's arrival. 'Makes me feel guilty to think of the privileged upbringing I had – emotionally and materially. While all the while, you were floundering in such misery.'

Evie pursed her lips and put her head on one side.

'It wasn't great,' she admitted. 'But I feel just as guilty because, for whatever reason, you were dumped in an orphanage and were deprived of ever knowing your biological mother.'

Matt nodded. 'I guess we were both cheated in one way or another.'

Evie was silent for a moment, then she said, 'Or you could look at it in a more positive light, and say that we both chose to make the best of the lives we were given. You with your mammoth success as a writer. Me, in my humble way, helping others to achieve in life, and thus fulfilling my own potential.'

Matt reached out and pulled Evie into his arms.

'That's what I love about you,' he said. 'Given time, you can almost always put a positive spin on things.'

The outside doorbell rang and, his heart banging against his ribs, Matt broke away from Evie and went to the intercom to ascertain the identity of his visitor.

'Take the elevator to the first floor and I'll be there on the landing,' he said, when Charlie Rae introduced himself in what Matt took to be a broad Highland accent. Hand on the latch, he drew a great gulp of air into his lungs, then flung open the door to his apartment and waited.

The man who emerged from the elevator into the communal hallway seemed vaguely familiar. No more than five foot ten or so, he had the remains of what must, surely, once have been a shock of dark wavy hair, and brown eyes beneath heavy brows. Propping open the door with his foot, Matt extended his hand, aware that, uncharacteristically, he felt incredibly nervous.

'Welcome!'

Charlie Rae approached and grasped Matt's hand.

'Dean,' he said, his Scottish accent unwavering despite the years spent in Australia. 'Och, you look just like your mother!'

'Really?'

'You wouldna remember her, o'course. You were only a bairn when –'

Matt put a hand on his visitor's shoulder to hasten him into the hall of his apartment. He wasn't at all sure he wanted to hear all this stuff about his mother quite so soon after making the acquaintance of his father. A hot drink. A chat about inconsequentials – the weather, perhaps, English style? And then? Then he might be ready. He ushered Charlie – he couldn't think of him as dad or pop or even father – into the main room where the tray of coffee and biscuits awaited them. Evie was not there, but a moment later she appeared from the kitchen with a jug of milk in her hand. Matt made the necessary introductions.

'Evie Adams. My half-sister.'

Charlie scrutinised her for a moment but, to Matt's surprise, said nothing about her being Libby's daughter.

'A grand place you have here,' he said when he'd nodded a greeting to Evie and walked over to the window to look down over Eccleston Square Gardens. 'Must 'ave set you back a tidy penny. There's obviously money in makin' up stories.'

Charlie, thought Matt, was clearly one of those people to whom the niceties of this world were unknown. Even so, he couldn't help but like him. With his easy-going charm, the questions Matt hoped to pose should, surely, be a doddle?

As it happened, it was well over half an hour into the coffee and biscuits and a monologue narrative of the delights of Scotland and the downside of Australia – no pun intended, Charlie explained – before Matt felt able to broach the subject of his adoption.

'I traced Evie, and Aunt Phoebe and her family, last year,' he began. 'But sadly, by the time I got round to meeting them, it was too late to see my mom.'

'Aye. I'd heard she was no longer with us,' said Charlie, setting down his mug on the side table. 'Do you ken how she passed on?'

Matt looked across to Evie who had said very little to date, and who was clearly unwilling to divulge too much detail about Libby's drinking problems.

'She had gastric problems,' she said. It was quite sudden, her death. How long did you know her, Mr Rae?'

'Och, it's Charlie's m'name. We're not standin' on ceremony are we?'

Matt took up Evie's question.

'So how long did you know Libby, Charlie?'

'As I told you in m'letter, I was eighteen, she was going on sixteen

237

when we met. I'd come down to work for my Uncle Chay. She was a bonnie lass, your mother. We had a thing for one another. I s'pose you'd call it love at first sight.'

'And then she got pregnant? With me?'

Embarrassed, Matt stood and gathered up the dirty mugs, stacking them on the tray before returning to his seat alongside Evie, who remained silently taking it all in, on the sofa.

'Aye. She did that.'

'How did her parents take it?'

'They were not well-pleased, it has to be said. But it was your Aunt Phoebe's dad who was the biggest stumbling block.'

'How do you mean? He'd been dead for years.'

The expression on Charlie's face turned to one of disdain.

'I'd have married Libby tomorrow and made an honest woman of her, as Aunt Phoebe bloomin' well knew.'

'So what happened?' Matt glanced across at Evie, willing her not to spill the beans on what they had learned, silently prompting Charlie to tell the story as he saw it.

'Y'dinna ken?' Charlie's voice rose as he glanced from one to the other of them, a look of disbelief on his face. 'I thought you'd done the research. I thought you knew my Uncle Chay put bucket loads of money into the Hamilton business. And that Phoebe's Da diddled him out of his rightful share of Rosegreen. Way back. That he nearly had my uncle struck off as a solicitor. That he preferred to marry off his kith and kin and keep a ransom over their heads rather than risk a rightful share of the property gettin' into the hands of the Rae family. That he put the property in a Trust, and his will stipulated that nothin' was to be inherited by any bastard child.'

Matt recoiled. Whatever was Charlie talking about? This was a totally different story to the one he understood to be the truth. The one Sophie had heard from Phoebe and recounted to them only recently.

'So that's why I was put up for adoption?'

'Aye. But it wasn't what your mam and me wanted. She was pushed into it by the Trustees. That's why she wouldn't sign the papers. That's why you were stuck in the orphanage for so long.'

Matt wanted to ask why Libby and Charlie hadn't simply defied the Trustees and married anyway, but before he could do so, Evie leaned forward on the sofa.

'But Libby got pregnant again – with me – didn't she.'

'Aye, she did!'

'And then she married my father.'

Charlie punched his clenched fist in his other hand.

'Y'dinna ken, do you? I did wonder when I first saw you.'

Evie fell silent, a scarlet flush filling her face and neck and, unless Matt was very much mistaken, tears welling in her eyes.

'What is it Evie's supposed to know?' he asked, suddenly aware that she was ten steps ahead of him. 'What were you wondering when you first saw her?'

Charlie jumped to his feet.

'Only that she's my daughter,' he yelled. 'Only that you're both my bairns, dammit.'

With Twelfth Night approaching, and mindful of all the bad luck superstitions with which I was raised, I've asked my next door neighbour's son, Jason, to help me dismantle the Christmas decorations. I'm not sure why I bothered to put them up, given that I spent Christmas with Matt, in London, following the shock of Charlie Rae's revelation, but there you are. I wasn't to know, was I?

'So how's your friend, Zac?' I ask, steadying the ladder on which my young helper is perched.

Jason removes the drawing pin securing the end of the sparkly streamers that festoon my little sitting room, and passes it to me before replying. Dismounting from the ladder, he tucks his chin in, pushes out his lips and assumes a solemn expression.

'Not a hoppy bunny,' he says, misquoting one of his mum's favourite phrases. 'Sad. Zac's daddy's gone away. An' he's not comin' back.'

'Oh, I'm sorry to hear that,' I reply, moving the step ladder to the far corner of the room ready for Jason's next job. 'What happened?'

'David's daddy is in 'opital. An Zac's daddy is in prison.' Jason nods his head to emphasise each word.

'Oh, my goodness! And what about the mummies?'

Jason shakes his head. 'I fink Zac's mummy is in 'opital, too. Zac's bin stayin' wiv his nanna for Cwissmas.'

'And the baby?'

'Dat's very sad, Auntie Evie. Zac sez the baby's gone to be wiv the little Lord Jesus.'

My mind is running in all directions, but it's clear that Jason needs cheering up. So, once the decorations are safely put away, with his mummy's permission we settle down to watch Star Wars on the TV. Accompanied, of course, by copious amounts of naughty sweet treats.

It's not until Jason has departed for home, and Scott has arrived *chez moi* that I feel able to turn my mind to the complexities of life and love, lust and loss.

'All settled into your new abode?' I ask him, after rejoicing in the warmth of his embrace.

'I guess – not quite up to the homely geniality of your making,' he says, seating himself on the sofa and pulling me down onto his lap.

'Oh, I see! Is that a gentle hint that my services are needed?'

He grins. 'You need no hint to know that your services *d'amour* are always needed. But come on. I want to hear all about what's happened since your meeting with the amorous Charlie Rae.'

I have, of course, already told Scott about the extraordinary revelations of Charlie's visit to Matt's before Christmas, but have barely had time to bring him up to date.

'I still can't quite believe he's my father,' I say, moving from Scott's lap to the sofa, beside him. 'I have to keep pinching myself. And to be honest, I still can't sort myself out as to whether I'm pleased or not.'

'Understandable!' Scott grasps my hand in his.

'I mean, right at the start,' I continue, 'when I first met Matt, he told me that his parents – his adoptive parents, that is – brought him up to believe that he was chosen. They drummed it into him. To make him feel special, I suppose.'

I picture the scene when Matt and I first met and he filled me in with his life-story as a lead-up to telling me that his biological mother was also mine.

'But the thing is, he says he always had this niggling feeling that he had only been chosen by them to fill the gap left by the loss of their own child. And that somehow, he fell short of doing so.'

Scott breathes in deeply.

'But that's Matt for you.'

'How do you mean?'

'He's analytical. Oh, I know he's creative, as an author. But think about what he writes. Crime thrillers. There has to be a certain investigative, diagnostic element to it, doesn't there? The bottom line is, did he feel loved by his adoptive parents?'

'Oh, yes! Without doubt.'

'Well there you are then.'

'But I suppose I feel slightly sorry for him. Being cheated of ever knowing his real mother.'

'Mmm. But no more than either of you were of knowing your father, Charlie Rae. What happened there, I wonder? Why didn't he and your mother marry? They must have felt something for each other to have had two offspring – you and Matt.'

'Funny you should ask,' I rise from the sofa, cross the room, and take a letter from behind the clock on the mantelpiece. 'This arrived last week.'

It's a note from Phoebe Hamilton, no less! Brief and to the point, she simply says that she believes it only right and proper that I should have the enclosed. A letter written in pen long ago, its densely looped script on both sides of three sheets of paper, makes for difficult reading. I've already scoured it several times without truly being able to reconcile what I thought I knew with what now appears to be the truth.

'It's from Charlie to my great-grandmother. Phoebe's mother.'

'I'm surprised she was still around then,' says Scott.

I nod. 'She would have been in her mid–to-late fifties, I think. She was a widow, but she remained very much the matriarch. She was still running one of the hotels, apparently.'

'So what was the purpose of the letter?'

'Basically, it's a love letter. Well, not exactly. More of a begging

241

letter. Charlie's pleading to be allowed to marry my mother because he's madly, passionately in love with her.'

Scott, understandably, looks puzzled.

'So why didn't they marry?'

'You may well ask. It appears that the story we heard from the Hamilton family doesn't quite fit with the Rae's take on things. The Hamiltons say that Chay tried to diddle them out of the purchase of Rosegreen and then got Phoebe's sister, Beatrice, pregnant so he could marry into the family in the hope of acquiring it. Charlie's story is quite the reverse. He says his uncle put money into the business – actually bailed them out at one point when they nearly went under – and that he had a legitimate claim to Rosegreen.'

'Chay Rae was a solicitor, wasn't he? So why go to those lengths to stake his claim? Why on earth would you get someone pregnant in an attempt to assert your rights, when you could quite easily take it to court?'

'Who knows? I suspect that both sides had been behaving irresponsibly, and that Chay might well have been in danger of being struck off. But the point is, that in order to prevent Chay marrying Beatrice, it seems her father married her off to a man from Glasgow. According to Charlie, this man, my grandfather, had stayed at the hotel once or twice, and Bea's father struck a bargain with him. He set him up as a draper, on condition that he took on my grandmother. So she was nicely out of the way when she had what was supposed to be Chay's baby – which she lost – before she then had my mother.'

Scott, understandably, looks dumbfounded.

'Phoebe's brother then did the same thing with my mother, Libby,' I continue. 'He made her put Matt into the orphanage. Then, when she got pregnant with me, he persuaded her that Charlie was no more in love with her than the man on the moon, but was merely trying to do what his uncle had failed to do. Namely, to marry into the family and acquire ownership of some of the property. Libby, it seems, was then duped into marrying the man I believed to have been my father all these years – no doubt, in exchange for some backhander that got him into the prestigious position of Town

Clerk. Plus, of course, this house, my home, which I thought was a wedding gift from my dad.'

Scott, I can see, is speechless.

And suddenly, for no good reason, I find myself recalling the incident with the glass of water when Matt and I first met the Hamilton family. Sophie had been telling us that her birth certificate had been lost and her parents had had to obtain a copy. I'd then shared that the self-same thing had happened to me. Everything now fell into place. In my case it would have been my mother seeking to conceal the discrepancy in dates. In Sophie's, it was possibly more sinister. If, as I believed, she was Liz's child, then under the terms of the Trust she would have been disinherited. But given that this is pure speculation, I am not at liberty to reveal it.

'So,' I continue, with a bright ring in my voice, 'that's my story. And if I'm honest, I suppose I feel we've all been cheated out of nearly forty years of knowing one another. Other people's choices prevailed.'

'I guess that's life,' says Scott. 'I don't mean to diminish your legitimate grievances and distress in any way. But I suppose, as kids, we're all subject one way or another to other people's choices. Our parents, grandparents, teachers, neighbours.'

'Absolutely! It appears that Phoebe's father changed his will when my grandmother was married off, to ensure that no descendant born out of wedlock could inherit the family fortune. And I don't suppose we'll ever have an answer to the riddle of the multiple signatures on Phoebe's mother's will.'

'Or the question of Sophie's parentage,' Scott adds. 'Is she really Phoebe's daughter? Or is she Liz's?'

I shake my head.

'The one thing I have to hang onto is that I was born into this world, and whatever influences the past has had on my life, my experiences, or my personality, I'm a responsible adult and, within certain limitations, I can make my own choices.'

'That's a concept I used to teach at theological college,' says Scott, raising his eyebrows and looking at me seriously. 'The understanding that God chose each one of us before the beginning of time. He's given us all the gift of life. But it's up to us what we do with it. We can accept the gift and use it for good. Or we can throw it back in his face and trash it. He's given us the freedom to choose.'

I find myself forced to look away from Scott. Aware from the start of our relationship that he holds beliefs that are unfamiliar to me, I feel a fraud. What was it Matt said to me: *Evie Adams by name and Adam and Eve by nature.* Yet some of what Scott has just said rings true. I recall my take on Sophie's relationship with her mother as being like that of the higher ferry in Dartmouth. Perhaps we all, at times, have aspects of our lives to which we're tethered? Is this true of me? In which case, I, too, need to break free, to be self-propelled, rather than allowing the events of my past to dictate my thinking and behaviour.

'If that's so,' I say, turning back to look Scott full in the face, 'then I can only hope that most of the time I choose good. At least that choice is open to every one of us, no matter what evil influences others have brought to bear on our lives.'

'Too right!' Scott takes my hand in his again. 'And in view of the fact that I've moved down to be near you – and the way I feel about you – I'm hoping, oh Evie, I'm hoping you might choose me. Because sure as eggs is eggs, I've chosen you.'

He pulls me into his arms. And at that very moment Pumpkin comes into the room. Jumping up onto my lap, she asserts her rights over me in no uncertain terms. Clearly, she has made her choice known.

THE END

Questions For Personal Reflection and Bookclub Discussions

1. Matt's adoptive mother, Bonnie, tells him he's been 'chosen' – a term used frequently for adopted children. Although intended to be affirmative, does this, actually, place an onus on the adopted child to fulfil the hopes and dreams of his parents?

2. Later in life, Matt questions whether some people's choices may mean others are cheated. For example, Evie, was kept by her biological mother but was cheated of a better way of life. In what ways might we feel cheated?

3. Early on in her encounters with Matt, Evie conducts an internal debate on whether she can *face her fears* rather than *fight* them or *take flight*. Is this something you're aware of doing in your own life?

4. At the UK Global Leadership Summit 2015 (a national event) the issues of 'blind spots' were raised. The implication was that we all have areas of our lives which we believe we've dealt with but clearly have not. What blind spots applied to Sophie and her family? Has reading *Chosen?* made you aware of any in your life? If so, what? And are your eyes now open to them?

5. Also mentioned at the GLS, was the matter of 'tethering', which referred to childhood experiences and reactions to these that adversely influence our adult life, similar to those experienced by Sophie. Is this something you have experienced – in your own life, or that of others? If so, how might you deal with them? Cut yourself loose? Move on under your own steam?

6. Given that Sophie appeared oblivious to the reasons for her childishness and sense of obligation, do you feel that Evie was right in likening her to the chained ferry, and pointing out her 'little girl' attitudes towards her parents? Would you welcome this sort of intervention from a friend?

7. Although not mentioned in the book, the Dartmouth ferry actually broke free at one point – and created havoc with other shipping. How may we break free from the restrictive experiences of our lives, without causing mayhem? Is there a pathway to freedom?

8. Evie affirms, at the end of the book, that despite the limitations that may be placed upon us by the choices of others, we are still free to make our own choices in life. How, if at all, does this play out in your life?

9. Scott talks about God having chosen us and given us the freedom to make choices for good or evil. Would you agree with this? Why? Or why not?

10. Would you agree that many of us go through times of feeling useless and without purpose in our lives? How, if at all, has *Chosen?* changed your thinking? (You might also like to read Mel Menzies' earlier book *Time to Shine* to see how Julia, the main character, learns to recognise her own value and fulfil her potential.)

About the Author

With nearly a dozen books behind her, one of which reached number 4 in *The Sunday Times* Bestseller list, Merrilyn Williams has now turned to fiction and writes under her maiden name, Mel Menzies. Her second novel, *Time to Shine* was published in 2015.

Drawing on her personal experience in dealing with divorce, debt, her daughter's drug addiction and subsequent death, she aims to comfort others with the comfort she has received.

www.melmenzies.co.uk

By the Same Author

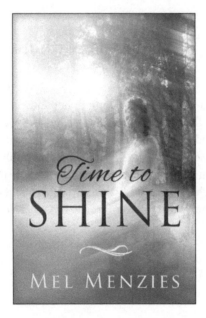

The interweaving tale of counsellor Evie Adams and her client Julia Worth, a well-off 'lady of leisure', unhappily married to Carl.

When Carl suspects Julia of being unfaithful, Julia's relationship becomes emotionally abusive and so her therapy sessions with Evie become an ever-increasing source of strength. Meanwhile, Hilary, a mutual friend of both Carl and Julia, seems to have been involved in a mysterious cover up of a tragic death at Carl's school.

At the same time, Evie has her own issues to deal with. Childless, she discovers that her ex-husband's new partner is pregnant...

Located in Exeter's Cathedral Green, *Time to Shine* is a psychological mystery, which readers of Jodi Picoult and Susan Howatch will no doubt enjoy.